MW00639636

DEATH HAMPTON

Introducing Detective Jericho

Walter Marks

Copyright © 2014 by Walter Marks

All rights reserved.
No part of this book may be used or reproduced in any manner whatsoever
without the written permission of the Author.
Printed in the United States of America.

All characters appearing in this work are fictitious. Any resemblance
to real persons, living or dead, is purely coincidental.

ISBN: 978-0990316107

Top Tier Lit
New York, NY

Also by Walter Marks

Dangerous Behavior

The Battle of Jericho (Coming Soon)

For Joan,
my love, my mate, my helpmate.

"Fear death by water."

- T.S. Eliot "The Wasteland

CHAPTER 1

Midnight. The intruder tried the sliding glass door on the deck of the beach house. It was open.

How accommodating of her, he thought.

He wore dark glasses over a stocking mask. His squashed nose and flattened ears made him look like a being from outer space. His tongue darted across his lips, exposed by a hole in the stocking. He had cut the hole to make breathing easier, and because he liked to use his mouth on them.

He stepped inside. In the bright moonlight shining through an angled bay window, he found his way easily. He could see, up a flight of stairs, a slant of light coming from the door of her bedroom. He took out his automatic pistol. What he liked about the gun was that it forced instant compliance; no screams, no arguments.

As he climbed the stairs he could hear recorded string quartet music through her door — Mozart or Haydn, he could never tell the damn difference.

The top step creaked loudly and he froze, alert to any sound. Satisfied he hadn't lost the element of surprise, he moved forward.

The woman was lying on a pinewood bed, reading *Vanity Fair* by the light of a bedside lamp. Its soft pink bulb made her look like a shining angel — no, more like the Good Fairy, with long blond hair, and an air of sweetness radiating from her lovely face.

Now for the part he loved best. The entrance.

"Don't move and don't make a sound."

She looked up and her mouth fell open.

"I will not shoot you if you do what I say. Disobey me and you're dead. Nod your head if you understand."

The woman's head moved up and down like a bobble head doll. Her eyes widened as he took out two sets of handcuffs.

"My husband will be — "

"I told you to shut up. Your husband flew into the city this afternoon. I saw him get on the plane."

The intruder enjoyed her look of dismay. He could read her mind — *My God. He's planned all this in advance. He's going to do whatever he wants. Then he'll kill me. Maybe — maybe if I just cooperate, he'll let me live. That's my only hope. Try to play along, give in. Survive.*

"All right, Susannah, or perhaps I should say, um, Sweetie, since we'll soon be on intimate terms — "

Jesus, he even knows my name.

"Please put your hands up on either side of the headboard. That's good, Sweetie."

He handcuffed Susannah's wrists to the bed, just below the wooden ball finials. She looked perfect, her arms stretched out like a pitiful supplicant.

He placed his gun on a bureau. From his pocket he pulled out a roll of duct tape, slipped it over his index finger, and twirled it.

"I prefer not to gag you," he said, "because what I'm about to do may provoke groans of pleasure, which I would enjoy hearing. But scream for help and you will suffer in ways you cannot imagine. Clear?"

Susannah nodded.

"Let's dispense with this fiddle music,'" he said, turning off the CD player near her bed.

The intruder took hold of the summer-weight cotton quilt and slowly pulled it off her. She was naked except for her rose-patterned white panties. She had a dancer's body; small breasts, muscled belly, narrow hips, and long, elegant legs suggesting both grace and power.

2

He looked at her with admiration, then hooked his fingers over the top of her panties.

"Raise up," he said. "...Do it!"

Hesitantly she lifted her pelvis so he could maneuver the panties under her buttocks and down over her hips.

He went to the foot of the bed and spread apart Susannah's tense but unresisting thighs.

Bending over, he stuck out his tongue and formed it into a delicate point.

She shuddered and moaned in disgust.

Then he began.

CHAPTER 2

Burton Lloyd Cascadden whipped his fiberglass fishing rod, sending the red/yellow Gotcha jig out two hundred feet, splashing into the roiling surf. The powerful rip current seized the lure, and the rod bent as if a fifty-pound striper had taken the hook. He let the monofilament play out till it slackened, then he reeled it in with short jerks, hoping some predator fish would mistake the jig for a crippled herring. He'd been at it for two futile hours.

Burt was a big man, with a muscular build and a large belly which was hard to the touch, indicating dangerous visceral fat. But because it was hard, Burt considered it manly. His eyes, hidden by sunglasses, were bloodshot. He had a blunt nose and full lips, which would've been called bee-stung, were he a woman.

Burt wore a black baseball hat, a black Polo shirt, and spandex swimming briefs, which bulged at the crotch. He was proud of his package, but that pride was tempered by his dirty little secret; his equipment was dysfunctional. He'd tried the little blue pills, but all he got was splitting headaches and bluish vision. The only way Burt could achieve tumescence was by playing his Games.

But recently even the Games weren't working. Last night, he'd come up with a new, more intense one — "The Intruder". He was sure it would do the trick. Everything started out fine. His heart pounding with excitement as he acted out the scenario — pulling on the stocking mask, breaking into the house, surprising his victim and watching her face as she confronted her deepest fear — violation by a depraved sex fiend.

But then it happened — he got the feeling that Susannah was acting. Just acting. And all his Games depended on her creating a reality for him. She was supposed to moan with pleasure. But last night — she seemed to be moaning out of annoyance. That totally killed his hard-on.

Burt had gotten really pissed off, but it was late and he was too tired to start yelling and screaming. So he un-cuffed her and went to his own bedroom, hoping to get some sleep. But angst over his sexual failure and a problematic business deal kept his mind racing, and he tossed and turned till dawn.

When Burt got up he knew one thing: Susannah was turning into what all women eventually became — a hostile bitch.

He was starting to feel unstable again. He recognized the signs. A shrink once suggested the hallucinogens he'd done in his twenties, when he'd run off to India, had produced a chronic chemical imbalance in his brain. But Burt knew the real cause of his distress. From now on his wife was going to have to shape up. Or else.

Susannah Cascadden was in the kitchen making coffee. Images of last night blazed in her mind; Burt in his stocking mask, his mouth on her, his gross body, her revulsion and shame at participating in this new humiliating fantasy.

In a rage she pushed down hard on the plunger of the French press. It resisted, then shot to the bottom of the carafe, spritzing coffee and grounds all over the granite countertop.

She groaned and slapped both hands over her eyes, as if to deny the existence of the sloppy mess. Then she grabbed a kitchen sponge and started cleaning it up, wishing it were that easy to clean up the mess she'd made of her life.

One year ago Susannah was at a real low point. She'd just passed her twenty-seventh birthday and her life's goal seemed out of reach. Twenty-seven is young to consider yourself a failure — unless you want to be a dancer.

6

Dancing had been Susannah's childhood dream. She took ballet, tap, and jazz classes in Metairie, the New Orleans suburb where she was raised, but she discovered her true calling when she attended Tulane University. The head of the dance department was an acolyte of Martha Graham, and the first time Susannah experienced the Graham Technique — the rugged floor work, the fierce pelvic movements, the method of breathing and impulse control called Contraction and Release — she was hooked.

After Tulane, Susannah went to New York determined to become a dancer. She took classes at the Graham school for a couple of years, while waiting tables at night. She hoped to get into the company, but they were hiring fewer dancers because of cutbacks in federal arts funding. One night, after a particularly demanding class, Takiko, the teacher and keeper of the Graham flame, took Susannah out for a drink and gave her the devastating news: "Sorry, Susannah. You're just not strong enough to make the company."

Then Burt Cascadden came into her life.

He sat at a table in the restaurant, with a silver haired gentleman.

Burt did some cornball flirting with her, saying that someone that pretty *had* to be an actress. Susannah said she was a dancer, then told a whopper by claiming she'd been in the Martha Graham Company till a knee injury forced her to retire. She was immediately ashamed of lying — it was very unlike her — but she had felt the need to build herself up, her life being so crummy at the moment.

After her shift, Susannah got an urgent voicemail message from her mother Ethel. Her father, a boorish, chain smoking car salesman, was in the hospital with stage IV lung cancer, metastasized to his lymph nodes. He needed costly experimental therapy that his insurance wouldn't cover. In a voice choked with emotion, her mom begged for help.

Susannah had $3,000 in savings. She promised she'd wire it right away. Susannah disliked her father but wanted to be there for her mom.

"Is Edgar chipping in?" Susannah asked.

"You know your brother's a tightwad. And with four kids he's got a perfect cop-out."

Susannah sighed and promised she'd work overtime and send more money soon.

A few nights later, Burt Cascadden returned to the restaurant alone. He said he had tickets for the Paul Taylor Dance Company. They were doing *Arden Court*, which he felt was Taylor's most significant work.

Susannah didn't usually date customers, but she was lonely and depressed and the guy obviously had a real knowledge of dance, so she agreed.

After the performance Burt took her to Devi, a trendy Bangladeshi restaurant in Flatiron. Speaking to the waiter in Hindi, he ordered a selection of kormas, biryanis and tandooris.

He explained to Susannah that after college, the death of his boyhood idol John Lennon inspired him to go to India for spiritual enlightenment. He'd spent three years in Benares studying yoga chakras at the feet of Swami Nittiya Vivekanda, and learned to practice *Pranayama* (keeping bodily forces under control), *Dharana* (concentration of mind and will), and *Samadhi* (self-hypnosis leading to a state of ecstasy). He also learned to perform certain acts of devotion, such as sticking pins through his cheeks and lying on a bed of nails.

Susannah was duly impressed. "Did you ever levitate?"

"No," he replied smiling. "It takes thirty years to master *Laghina*. But in India I found lots of other ways to get high."

They both laughed, and he told Susannah he was still a Hindu in the spiritual sense, but he was long past his hippie-dippy phase and was now into the karma of capitalism.

"But I'm monopolizing the conversation," he said. "Tell me about yourself."

She described coming to the Big Apple in hopes of making it as a dancer. When she got to the part about the Martha Graham Company, she felt comfortable enough to admit she'd lied to feel better about herself. He smiled, touched her hand, and said that he had told a few whoppers in his life, for the same reason.

Later he took her home in a cab. On the way, she asked what he did for a living, and he said she'd get a package the next day containing

8

the answer. He gave her a peck on the cheek as he dropped her off at her apartment.

In the morning the package arrived by messenger. It contained a game of *Monopoly* with a note saying, "Check the rule book." In it she saw a section highlighted in neon yellow:

The object of the game is to become the wealthiest player, through buying, renting and selling property.

When Burt had first proposed marriage, Susannah was hesitant. But all he wanted, he explained, was companionship. His first wife had died of heart disease several years before and grief had robbed him of all sexual desire. At his age, he said with a rueful smile, sex wasn't that much of a much anyway. In return for her company, Burt would give her the security she'd never had, a lavish lifestyle, and he would make sure her ailing father had the best of care.

Susannah knew she didn't love him. But they got along well, she trusted him, and she could depend on him. No, it wasn't love, but maybe it could develop into that. Things like that did happen...

A year later, as she sat sipping coffee on the teakwood deck of her Gwathmey-Siegal designed beach house in Montauk, Susannah Dahlgren Cascadden was painfully aware of what she had become: property.

CHAPTER 3

Siren whooping, red and white roof lights flashing, the squad car raced along Pantigo Road, passing nervous motorists who hit the brakes and tried looking casual to avoid a speeding ticket.

Detective Neil Jericho slowed at the East Hampton traffic light, then swung right onto Newtown Lane and headed toward the high school. He was responding to a 911 report of a rare occurrence in this peaceful town — a knife attack, phoned in at 9:35 a.m. from the high school gym. Chief Manos had assigned Jericho to the case because of his prior NYPD experience with violent crime.

Jericho could feel the adrenaline kicking in, his brain on red alert. *Jesus*, he thought, *I've really missed this feeling.*

Up ahead was a road sign warning "Slow — School Zone — Speed limit 20." Jericho turned onto a long gravel driveway leading to the high school football field.

The crunching sound of tires over pebbles grated on his nerves. He gripped the steering wheel hard and his testicles tightened against his crotch. It was a sensation he knew well, a signal that he was ready for anything.

His hand moved unconsciously to his service revolver. The gun was optional for EHTPD detectives — in fact the Chief suggested his men not wear them on routine calls, because the town board preferred a non-threatening look. But after years of homicide duty in the city, Jericho never felt comfortable unless he was strapped.

11

Jericho parked outside the athletic equipment building. A burly, balding man in a sweat suit with a whistle around his neck was waiting for him. Jericho flashed his badge and ID. The guy ushered him in to the scene of the attack.

Someone had slashed three tackling dummies.

Knife attack, he thought. *Shit. Obviously Chief Manos is yanking my chain.*

The green dummy had the nickname Big Block, printed on its front. The red dummy was The Hulk, and the blue one was Backer. All three were stand-up dummies, with weights in their bottoms so they'd always remain upright. They had been viciously stabbed, their vinyl-coated nylon covers rent by multiple knife wounds exposing their white poly-filled innards.

"And look what they did to the blocking sled pads," the man said.

It was more of the same. They were brutally slashed, the stuffing hanging out and strewn on the floor.

Jericho took out his spiral notebook and questioned the witness. Virgil Conforti was head football coach of East Hampton High. Virgil said he'd discovered the crime when he arrived that morning. Upon entering the equipment building he saw that its single window, which had been locked, was smashed and open.

"The perp must have broken in during the night," he said.

"Who do you think this *perp* was?" Jericho asked.

"I couldn't tell ya who," Virgil replied. "But I'm damn sure it was someone from Southampton High. We play them in a few weeks and they're scared we're gonna whup their butts."

Jericho checked out the crime scene and noticed right away that the dummies and sled pads had plastic patches and adhesive tape on them, indicating they hadn't been in such great shape even before the slashings. He went outside and saw two footprints on the ground under the broken window. Looking closely he could make out the words "GET SOME!" and the brand name *Saucony* in the sole patterns made by the shoe.

12

He looked at the open window. It was double-hung and both the top and bottom windowpanes had been smashed. He brought out his Canon PowerShot camera and took some pictures.

Jericho went back into the building where Conforti sat waiting. The coach was wearing street shoes.

"No sneakers?" Jericho said.

"Beg pardon?"

"Loafers are not exactly usual attire for football practice."

"What do you mean?"

"I saw footprints outside the window — made by *Saucony* running shoes. You do own *Sauconys*, right?"

Virgil's eyes glazed over.

"We can easily find out," Jericho said. "I could ask your wife..."

"Okay. I do have a pair.. But those footprints aren't mine."

"My guess is, this morning you noticed your sneakers were muddy and figured maybe you left footprints, so it'd be better not to come in wearing them."

"That's not true."

"Look, Coach," Jericho went on. "I know you broke that window. You did it after you cut up your dummies. Your mistake was you shouldn't have opened the window from inside. 'Cause afterwards, when you went outside and smashed the glass, you broke not only the upper pane but the lower one as well, which was right behind it, you see, because you'd just raised it up. Now, if that window had been locked, you'd've only needed to break the top pane to get to the latch. You following me?"

Jericho was having fun. He knew the guy couldn't really follow his words, but he sure as hell knew Jericho had busted him.

"The only thing we need to find now," Jericho went on, "is the tool you used to break in through the window. Golly, this is sounding like CSI East Hampton."

Coach Conforti tried a smile but it turned into a grimace.

"Now let's see —" Jericho said, looking around. He noticed a rack with about twenty baseball bats. He walked over to them.

"I'm sure one of these bats will have some glass shards or splinters in it. Are you gonna make me examine each one? Why not make it easier on both of us and show me which bat you used?"

The coach's face was covered with sweat. His mouth moved a few times before he got any words out.

"Please, please, Officer," he said. "Gimme a break, huh? I... I got a family. Two kids..."

"Why'd you do it, Virgil?"

In a shaky voice, the coach explained. Fundamentals, he said, are the key to winning football games. You can't teach fundamentals without proper equipment, and his gear was ready for the junk heap. He'd requested new stuff, but the East Hampton Town Board turned him down, citing budgetary constraints.

Then it turned out the high school's soccer team, tennis team, even the goddamn girl's fencing team had gotten brand new equipment.

"They're always dumpin' on football," Conforti complained, "'cause these two wimpy ladies on the Board disapprove of contact sports. That's bullshit. Football is the all-American game."

"Then I came up with this plan," he said. "I figured the insurance company would pay for replacing the dummies and sled pads, and at least my guys would have a fighting chance. All I wanted to do was level the playing field."

Jericho listened sympathetically. He had played tight end for Central High in Maspeth, Queens (at age seventeen he already had the size and speed: 6-2, 230, 4.8) so he understood the passion of a football coach.

After hearing Virgil's pleas, Jericho didn't have the heart to bust the poor bastard. But he couldn't let him get off scot-free.

"I understand your motive, Coach," he said sternly, "but you broke the law. We can't have that, can we?"

"I... guess not."

"How much did you think the insurance company would pay?"

14

"I dunno. I guess the replacement value of whatever got busted."

"Which is?"

"Well... let's see. Three dummies—say four hundred bucks. A four man blocking sled—about a thousand."

"Okay, let's say fifteen hundred, including the window."

Virgil nodded.

"Tell ya what," Jericho said. "I'll let you off on one condition. You make a contribution of five hundred dollars to my favorite charity."

Jericho smiled at the coach, who saw he was being solicited for a bribe.

"And that would be..." Virgil said knowingly.

"Doctors Without Borders," Jericho said. "They're MDs who'll go anywhere in the world to help poor people who need care. They won the Nobel Peace Prize a few years back."

"Oh. Oh, sure."

"Send them a check for five hundred. They're located in Manhattan, look them up online. When the canceled check comes back, bring it to me at the station house. I'm Detective Jericho, like in the Battle. Got it?"

Coach Conforti nodded gratefully. "Yes. Detective Jericho. Geez, I don't know how to thank you."

"You better not mess up. I see that check next month or you'll be dropping the soap at Riker's."

"You have my word."

"From now on, Coach," he said as he walked to the door, "Better stick to blocking and tackling. Breaking and entering just ain't your thing."

15

CHAPTER 4

Susannah was reading the New York Times on the deck when she heard Burt's feet clumping up the wooden stairway. He appeared, carrying his Polo shirt and fishing gear. He took off his baseball cap, revealing his coal-black, obviously dyed, black hair. He did the coloring job himself with Just For Men gel, out of paranoid vanity, he didn't even trust a hair stylist to keep his secret.

"Fishing was dreadful," he complained. "Damn rip tide is so strong even the stripers can't swim through it. Guy at the tackle shop told me the current is moving at five feet per second when the rip is —"

A chirping version of Beethoven's *Für Elise* emanated from his tackle box. He took out his Blackberry.

"Yeah, Quinn," he growled to his lawyer.

"Jesus, that fucking Landmarks Commission," Burt shouted. "Look, I can't come in today, I've got a meeting out here at the North Fork Bank. Yeah, refinancing. But I'll fly in tomorrow. Meet you at the FS bar at five and we'll figure it out. Right."

Burt punched the End button on his phone and plopped down in a hammock suspended on a zinc-coated steel frame. He sat there, rocking to and fro.

"We have to talk," he said firmly.

She didn't respond.

"About last night."

She said nothing.

"Susannah, I'm afraid you're failing badly in your wifely duties. We had an understanding—"

The pent-up anger burst out of her. "Yes, we had an understanding: that I'd give you companionship. You never said anything about your ridiculous sexual games."

"We're not having that discussion again. Sexual role playing is common in modern day marriages."

"Look, I didn't mind your little playful fantasies at first. I wanted to please you. But that rape thing last night was going way too far."

"You agreed to it."

"Reluctantly. And I shouldn't have," she said forcefully. "But from now on, Burt, know this: I will no longer take part in your fantasy sex life."

"Like hell you won't," Burt shouted. "I take care of your needs, and you must take care of mine."

"That doesn't mean I have to be a slave to your every whim."

"I don't like your tone, Sweetie."

"And I don't like being degraded by your sick—"

Burt stood up and whacked her across the face. Back handed, hard.

He'd never hit her before.

She stared at her husband. Her fusion of terror, rage, and hatred stunned Susannah. He became once again the Intruder from the night before, a cruel brute against whom she had no defense, only the hope of survival through passivity.

"Now be a good girl and get me a cup of coffee," he said. "I didn't sleep well last night—thanks to you—and I've got to be alert at my meeting with the bank today."

Burt stretched out in the hammock and closed his eyes. His large body, now cradled in the nylon hammock cords, swung slowly back and forth. Susannah watched as his hirsute chest and plump belly rose and fell. She let her gaze wander to the bulge of his hateful genitals, then up to his thinning, dyed shoe polish black hair.

"While you're up, Sweetie" he said without opening his eyes, "toast me a Pop-Tart."

She gave him a look of fury, turned and went into the house. As the door slammed behind her, it was suddenly clear what she had to do.

CHAPTER 5

The rebuilt 1967 silver Piper Super Cub flashed in the sunlight as it flew eastward at 500 feet over the Montauk town beach at Kirk's Landing. The single-engine aircraft strained against the banner it was towing, advertising *"Kowabunga Disko — Party! Party! Party! North Sea Road, Southampton."* The pilot, Jessie Russell, looked down at the few sunbathers on the beach at the Briney Breezes motel. It was after Labor Day, and the summer crowds were gone.

Jessie's face was dark and weathered, his hooked nose and prominent cheekbones indicating he was Native American. He was, in fact, a Shinnecock Indian, raised on the poverty-stricken 800-acre reservation near Southampton.

Around Jessie's neck hung a Nikon F3 camera with a high-powered telephoto lens.

"Nothin', zilch, nada," he muttered to himself as he flew over the jagged sandstone cliffs at Ditch Plains. The strand below was a favorite of nude sun worshippers, because it was more private than the town beach. At locations like this Jessie could indulge his hobby—art photography. When he first got into it, he showed the guys at the hangar a print he'd developed in his home darkroom. It was his first muff shot. They all drooled and leered over the photo of the naked lady spread-eagled on a blanket, but then they began calling him Voy-*eer*, Peeping Tom, and Fuckin' Perv, so he decided in the future he'd better keep his hobby to himself. Sure, beaver shots were okay for Hef and Larry Flynt, but if somebody blew the whistle on his sorry red ass, he'd lose his pilot's job for sure.

Just ahead was Montauk Point. Atop its rocky hill Jessie had a great view of the chocolate-brown and white lighthouse, jutting up 110 feet into the air. Its dome-shaped top, with a circular platform beneath it, once prompted Jessie's pal Norm Blechner to say it looked like a phallic symbol. Jessie said it looked more like a pecker.

Jessie switched on his radio and called to the ground station in the hangar at East Hampton Airport, his home base. When he reported his position he did not say MONtauk. He said MonTAUK, accenting the second syllable, the way the people in the Montauk (MonTAUKet) tribe pronounced it. Not that Jessie gave a rat's ass about Native American culture. It was just how he learned to say it as a kid.

"Beaches are pretty empty, Norm," he said into the headset mic, "But there's busloads of tourists at the lighthouse. I figure weekends'll be good, and if the weather holds, I'll be towin' banner till mid-October." In the off-season Jessie worked part-time as a handy man at the Sea Crest motel, which, as he put it, sucked.

He flicked off the radio, banked right, and swung out over the Atlantic. A wind shear caught the banner and Jessie reflexively eased the yoke back, pitching the little Piper toward the sky. He could feel the pressure on the yoke as the banner sank down, then rose again, flapping in the fluctuating air currents.

About two miles offshore was a flotilla of sport fishing and party boats, with anglers casting their lines into the foamy water, churned by bluefish in a feeding frenzy. The humans were hauling in the bluefish, as the knife-toothed blues were devouring schools of menhaden; above them, the gulls joined in the food chain, gliding and diving, picking up bits of rent herring flesh.

Farther out, Jessie could see the shark charters trailing foul smelling bunker chum in their wakes, trolling for makos, grays, hulking threshers, and even bigger monsters of the deep. Jessie felt a shiver of fear as he pictured the polyurethane model of the 3,427-pound great white hanging from a hook at the Montauk Viking Fleet dock, which shark hunter Frank Mundus had caught with rod and reel. Jessie was phobic about sharks, and the possibility of someday having to ditch in

22

these waters terrified him. That's why he'd never go up in questionable weather. Never.

He was approaching False Point, so named because before the lighthouse was built sailors approaching from Block Island Sound often mistook it for the larger promontory. Jessie reduced power and descended to 250 feet. Then, after trimming the plane for level flight so his hands would be free, he popped open the cockpit's side window. He wanted to get a closer look at an isolated beach house that had become an obsession with him this past summer.

It was because of Blondie. There was this blond babe who sometimes sunned herself on the deck. She was built like a brick shithouse, and he was dying to get a muff shot, or at least a tit shot. But so far, no luck. He'd seen her laying out in her birthday suit several times, usually around noon, but always on her stomach. Sure, he could have gotten her ass but that wasn't his thing; it was tits or muff or nothing. Still, it was just a matter of time. One day he'd fly by and there she'd be, buck naked on her back, with her bare boobs and shaved pubes, and bingo! he'd have his pic.

He removed the lens cap from his 600mm telephoto and peered through the viewfinder. The long lens extended out into the air stream, directing a welcome blast of fresh air into Jessie's face. Blondie was nowhere to be found.

He did see Rich Fuck, the guy Jessie figured was Blondie's husband. He was sunning his fat-ass body in a hammock. Sometimes he'd seen Rich Fuck surfcasting nearby. With a fancy beach house, a Lamborghini and Bimmer in the driveway, and a babe like that, he had to be worth mega millions.

One of these days, Jessie swore to himself, he'd get that muff shot of Rich Fuck's wife, and then maybe he could blackmail the guy, threaten to send Blondie's picture to Hef or TMZ or Larry Flynt (if there was a little pink in the shot). Wouldn't that be somethin'?

Jessie'd had that fantasy a lot during the summer. Once he even drove past the beach house to see if there was a name on the mailbox. There was no name, only the initials BLC.

CHAPTER 6

Susannah felt emotionally paralyzed as she drove to Gosden Dock Fish Market. She was certainly in no mood to cook that night, so she got some take-out fish and chips. All afternoon she'd relived Burt's violent behavior. The slap to her face hadn't left much of a mark, and she only felt the pain when she touched it. But she kept touching it, as a reminder of how bad her situation had become.

At dinner, Burt was rattling on about his business problems. Susannah knew about his plan to build a luxury apartment building in the Bay Ridge section of the Brooklyn waterfront. She also knew it was opposed by a group of artists who lived in nearby lofts and feared the scheme would lead to gentrification and rent hikes.

When she first heard about it, she voiced sympathy for the artists, but Burt bristled, so she shut up.

Now he was telling her about the six abandoned row houses he'd acquired to complete the land parcel.

"Those dip-shit artists have petitioned the Landmarks Commission to grant the row houses landmark status. Today they got some judge to issue a restraining order till the matter can be adjudicated. You believe that crap?"

Susannah answered with a non sequitur: "I want to talk about what happened this afternoon."

"I'm discussing my business. I could lose everything. This concerns you as much as— "

"What concerns me most is that you hit me."

Her eyes showed a resolve he'd never seen before. She raised her voice. "That's totally unacceptable."

Burt hesitated before he responded.

"All right," he said. "It won't happen again,"

"You're damn right it won't."

"I promise you. It won't happen again," he repeated reassuringly. Then his voice turned harsh with menace. "As long as you do as you're told."

My God, she thought, *he's gone off the deep end.*

"This isn't working," she said.

"Beg pardon?"

She looked at him steadily.

"I'm leaving you, Burt."

"Don't be silly.

"I can't live like this any more."

"Don't be silly."

"There's nothing you can— "

He cut her off. "I would definitely advise against it."

"I'm not asking for your advice."

"You won't get a penny."

"I can always wait tables."

"Your father. He'll die without my money."

"He's on life support. It'll happen soon anyway."

Burt moistened his lips and massaged his eyes.

"Let me put it this way," he said in measured tones. "It would be a mistake for you to leave, because—I'm sure it will bring you bad luck. You know what happened to my *first* wife."

"She died of heart disease."

"Well, yes, in the sense that her heart did stop. But it was actually a karmic thing. As Swami Vivekanda taught: when a bird is alive, it eats ants. When the bird is dead, the ants eat the bird. In other words — what goes around comes around. Carol tried to leave me and her death was the cyclical consequence of her behavior."

"Oh, come on."

"No. No. No. No," Burt said. "Misfortune strikes people when they act dishonorably. Don't you see? There is a penalty that must be paid. And you can't avoid paying it. Am I making myself clear?"

Fear grabbed at Susannah.

"Tell me you see the wisdom of my advice," Burt went on.

She didn't answer.

"Ah. I know what you're thinking," he said. "You'll leave first chance you get. Go someplace. Just disappear. But it won't work, Sweetie. You will be found. You can never escape your karma."

She looked at him in disbelief.

"Anyway," he went on, "Do you really want to spend the rest of your life on the run, fleeing the inevitable?"

He paused and took a sip of wine.

"Besides," he said casually, "if you leave, you'll have to be gravely concerned about your mother, dear Ethel — because then she'll have to pay for your transgressions. Sins of the daughter, so to speak."

He got up.

"Clearly the best course of action for you is to stay here, turn over a new leaf and be, simply put, a good wife."

Susannah looked at him, stunned.

"I've got a lot of work to do tonight," he said. "I'm going to my study now, and then early to bed."

He crossed to the door and stopped.

"Oh, and I'll need you to drive me to the airport tomorrow at nine — the Lambo's transmission is acting up again."

"I have to work tomorrow," she said. Her voice sounded strange, robotic.

27

"You don't have to be at your class till noon. If we leave at 8:00 you'll make it back in plenty of time."

He turned and left the room.

Susannah's spirits sagged. She'd always considered herself an independent woman. Now she faced a life of servitude, totally dependent on the whims of a man who was a monster. There seemed to be no way out.

CHAPTER 7

The next morning Jessie Russell arrived early at East Hampton airport. When he'd landed the previous afternoon, he didn't like how his wheels swerved on the tarmac. So now he had to put the Piper up on a jack to change the brake pads. Figuring he'd lube the wheel bearings too, he pulled the wheels. After a half hour's work, his clothing and face were smeared with black grease. Like a crime scene, the airplane was covered with his fingerprints.

Jessie looked up and saw six passengers crossing to the Cessna Caravan amphibian plane parked near the terminal gate. It was the usual group of well-heeled Hamptonites opting for the thirty-five minute $545 flight to Manhattan, rather than the usual three-hour car, bus, or train trip.

Jessie watched the passengers with a mix of envy and loathing. Then he spotted a familiar figure walking and talking on a cell phone. It took a moment to figure out who he was.

Well, I'll be damned, he said to himself. If it ain't Rich Fuck. Didn't recognize him without his bathing suit. But where's Blondie? No Blondie.

Jesus, he's a smug-looking bastard. And he's yammering on that dumb-ass smart phone, talking some bullshit business just to show how important he is.

Jessie saw the flight attendant stop Burt. He knew she was telling him to turn off his cell phone before boarding the plane because the signal could interfere with the airline's radio transmission.

"You officious bitch," Burt shouted. "I'm not inside the plane yet."

He argued for a while, then stuffed the phone into his pocket. He boarded the commuter plane, and a few moments later Jessie saw him seated at one of the windows, yammering again on his Blackberry.

What a jerk, thought Jessie.

Jessie knew the pilot would put a stop to it, but Christ, that kind of crap pissed him off. He rubbed his face, adding another black smudge to his darkening visage.

Scowling, he made a vow to himself: *One way or another I'm gonna get that beaver shot of Blondie. Can't wait to see the expression on Rich Fuck's face when I present him with a glossy print of his wife's pussy. Then I'll show him a Hustler centerfold and ask him how he'd like to see his wife there, all pretty and pink for the world to see. That should make Mr. BLC pay — big time.*

The Cessna rumbled down the runway, then roared up into the sky. It banked right over Wainscott Woods and the noise flushed a white-tailed deer and her fawn out of the forest. They bounded across a clearing, then disappeared into the trees again, bewildered by the growing human encroachment on their natural habitat. The plane flew toward Sag Harbor, then took a western turn heading to New York City. The pilot was following his clear-weather flight plan over the north shore of Long Island at an altitude of 1,500 feet.

Burt Cascadden looked out the window at the pine barrens and the patchwork of green, amber, and umber farm fields along the Montauk highway, which connected the Hamptons, Hampton Bays, and Quogue. When the plane passed over Riverhead, he could see the Long Island Expressway, free of traffic now but soon to be clogged with cars inching past the endless road repair sites, giving credence to the LIE's reputation as the world's longest parking lot.

Quinn Healey's phone call the day before had Burt really worried. At this afternoon's meeting, his lawyer was going to remind him of his financial problems: Citibank had reduced his credit line, and Prospectis Ventures had bailed, citing doubts about Burt's solvency. He'd committed most of his assets for the property and air rights. If he didn't tear down the row houses and begin construction right away, the deal would collapse.

30

Burt tried reassuring himself. I'm a brilliant man, for God's sake — Yale, Phi Beta Kappa, Magna cum laude, my brain a marvel of cognitive power. So why is everything falling apart?

That unstable feeling seized him again — the vertigo, the sense of dread. The drone of the plane's engine sounded like the low snarl of a beast, and he could feel his eardrums vibrating in his skull.

Burt closed his eyes. He thought of Swami Vivekanda's words. *The power of the mind should be concentrated and turned back upon itself, and as the darkest places reveal their secrets before the penetrating rays of the sun, so will this concentrated mind penetrate its own innermost secrets.*

His concentrated mind focused on his wife, heard her erection-killing moan of annoyance, saw the fierce defiance in her eyes as she threatened to leave him. *Hostile bitch!*

After all I've done for her. She has clothes, a BMW, two beautiful homes, credit cards galore, care for her sick father. And how does she repay me? With sullen ingratitude.

It had been the same with his first wife, Carol. In the beginning she was docile and loving — then she turned into a bitch. But with Susannah it was worse. Her negativity was poisoning his life. His real estate deal was on a fast track when they got married. Then, as their relationship deteriorated, the deal turned sour, too.

Coincidence? he asked himself. *I don't think so.*

Oh, I've got her cowed now. She'll obey me because of my threats to both her life and her mother's. But there will always be the resentment, the barely disguised disdain, the hostility. And the Games? The Games will sure as hell never work anymore. From now on, my life with Susannah will be intolerable.

Divorce? No. The bitch'll hire some Raoul Felder type and take me to the cleaners.

Penetrating rays of truth illuminated his mind in a moment of exquisite clarity.

Threatening her life is not enough. Just like Carol, Susannah has to be eliminated. Now.

The pilot throttled down to begin his descent and the engine noise dropped to a lower decibel level. To Burt it sounded like an easing of his anxiety. The aircraft banked left and he looked down to see City Island with its boat slips and harbor view seafood restaurants. The plane passed over the grim fortress of Riker's Island Penitentiary and descended. The prison-like Manhattan Psychiatric Hospital, a warehouse for the criminally insane, whizzed by at Burt's eye level.

The amphibian Cessna flew south over the East River, buzzing the Queensboro bridge, past the UN Building, then splashed down on its pontoons a few hundred feet from the Twenty-third Street marina.

As the aircraft taxied through the water, Burt took out his cell phone. The moment he was ashore, he was going to call the man who had solved his Carol problem, an Algerian killer-for-hire, known to his clients by a single name, a macabre French pun — *Mort*.

CHAPTER 8

Detective Jericho was at the East End Arts Center, a converted Montauk garage, watching a dance class through a large Plexiglas window. He was the lone dad among a group of mothers, each enthralled by her offspring's terpsichorean talent. As a favor to his ex-wife, Jericho was picking up their daughter Katie.

It had been two years since he left the NYPD. He'd been a highly regarded detective with the Twenty-third Precinct homicide squad, in the crime ridden *El Barrio*. Jericho made every effort to be a decent husband and, when Katie was born, a good father too, but his ability to love disintegrated with daily exposure to shootings, stabbings, rape victims, suicides, drug pushers, child molesters, and what cops call "public service homicides" — one crack dealer killing another. His marriage foundered as his wife realized that for Jericho, "How was your day?" had become an unanswerable question. He sought escape in booze, working the "4 to 4 shift" – 4 p.m. to midnight on duty, midnight to 4 p.m. boozing in a bar with his buddies – and patronizing the occasional street hooker.

Then he started experiencing nightmares and flashbacks of one horrific confrontation he'd had in an East Harlem crack house.

His life was on a downward spiral. His wife left him, his work was slipshod, and he became increasingly dependent on alcohol and tranquilizers.

Jericho tried to hang in there but eventually he couldn't hack it. At age thirty-six, burned out, he quit the force and moved from the city.

He chose Montauk because his ex-wife and five-year-old daughter had moved there. Sarah had remarried, this time to a nice, well-adjusted house contractor, who — even Jericho had to concede — was an okay guy. Sarah allowed Jericho to see Katie whenever he wanted, as long as he called first, so things were working out pretty well.

He applied for a job with the East Hampton Township Police Department because he needed work and being a cop was all he knew. He was required to start at the bottom, taking the twenty-six week training course at the Suffolk County Police Academy in Brentwood, but it was worth it, because the important thing was to be near Katie.

And without the aid of counseling or AA, by an act of sheer will, he quit drinking — cold turkey.

His main duties as an EHTPD patrolman were cruising in a patrol car: handling misdemeanor crimes, traffic violations, neighborhood disputes, noise complaints. And being part of The Thin Blue Line around the celebrity-studded house parties of Donna Karan, P. Diddy, Steven Spielberg, et al.

Recently, after Detective Lieutenant Dominick Manos had been appointed Police Chief, he offered Jericho a promotion to detective. Jericho was reluctant to wear a gold shield again, but then he figured local detective work was fairly stress-free, plus he could use the money, so he took the job.

"Okay, kids," Susannah said, "For our last exercise, you're gonna be cowboys and cowgirls. So you'll have to ride horses."

Her students were sitting on the floor of the dance studio; a group of small children — seven little girls wearing leotards, and three boys (eschewing such sissiness) in shorts and T-shirts.

"I didn't bring any horses to the studio today," she explained, "because — well, they'd just take up too much darn room."

She got a giggle with that one.

"So you'll have to ride make believe horses. Okay, pardners? Time to saddle up."

34

She took a bow-legged position, her butt sticking out, her hands on imaginary reins. The kids got up and eagerly imitated her stance. A few started bumping up and down.

"No. No. Hold on," Susannah said smiling. "Wait for the music."

She punched Play on her CD boom box. The Western strains of the Hoe-down section of Aaron Copland's *Rodeo* filled the room.

The music kicked the kids into high gear. Beneath them, their steeds were walking, trotting, cantering, and galloping, as each child bounced, flounced, and jounced in their saddles, responding to Copland's spirited polyrhythms.

"That's great, Bruce," Susannah shouted. "Nice goin', Ashley."

One little girl decided she was riding a bucking bronco and began rocking back and forth, waving one hand in the air and shouting *"Yahoo!"* at the top of her lungs.

"'Atta girl. Ride 'im, Katie-did."

Katie-did, that's cute, Jericho thought. This was his first visit to the dance class, and though it was a treat to see Katie perform, he couldn't help watching the teacher.

Susannah was barefoot, wearing white tights and a denim work shirt tied at the waist. Jericho admired her lean figure and lovely-even-without-makeup face, but what really got him was the way she carried herself; the confidence of her movements, head held high, shoulders relaxed, her entire body always in balance. As she crossed in front of a window, the afternoon sunlight struck her blond hair and turned it into spun gold. Then it flashed on the gold of her wedding ring.

Damn. He turned his attention back to his cowgirl daughter.

When the piece ended, Susannah shut off the boom-box and said good-bye to the kids. They all came over to hug her and she basked in their unabashed affection. She heard Katie shout, "Daddy! Daddy!" and watched her dash out the classroom door, arms outstretched. *A father,* Susannah thought. *That's nice.*

A moment later, standing there alone, she felt a stab of fear. She recalled Burt's menacing words, warning her not to leave.

"There is a penalty that must be paid," he'd said. "And you can't avoid paying it. Am I making myself clear?"

On her way out Susannah stopped by the studio office to pick up her paycheck. She'd met the owner, Gretchen Silverman-Lewis in April at a Wainscott antiques shop, when she was refurnishing the beach house. They'd chatted about the merits of a Shaker hutch, which Susannah ended up buying, then adjourned to The Golden Pear on Newtown Lane, where they became friends over currant scones and cappuccino. Gretchen was a director who'd worked mainly in regional theater for about fifteen years, before marrying Arnold Lewis, a Bridgehampton attorney. They bought an old garage and converted it into a community theater, cabaret, and drama school.

The two women found they had a lot in common, and a few weeks later Gretchen invited Susannah to set up a dance program for kids.

In the office, Gretchen commented that her friend looked worried.

"I'm fine," Susannah said. "Just a bit tired."

"C'mon, honey. I've known you long enough to know the difference between worried and tired."

"So now you're an expert on my feelings?" Susannah said edgily.

"No, no, no," Gretchen said. "I didn't mean to pry. I'm just concerned."

"I'm sorry, Susannah said. "I guess I'm a little freaked out these days."

"I understand. Just know that I'm here if you need me."

"I appreciate that."

Susannah was tempted to tell her about Burt's death threat, but she knew Gretchen would advise her to notify the police, and she'd seen enough movies to know the cops would do nothing unless she had proof of Burt's threat to kill her. *Even then*, she thought sardonically, *they'd probably tell me to wait till after I'm dead.*

Driving home, Susannah realized — seeing it clearly for the first time — that she'd married a man who was dangerously unstable, whose

36

behavior was irrational and uncontrolled. He'd gained power over her by devoting all his obsessive psychic energy to manipulating her.

And she had allowed it.

She went over her two choices — stay with Burt, or leave. Staying would mean becoming a virtual slave, participating in God knows what humiliating sexual games, losing what was left of her dignity and sense of self. Leaving? He had closed off that option by threatening her life, and even worse, threatening her mother.

But wait. It was in fuzzy metaphorical terms — karmic punishment. Was it a real death threat?

Maybe he's bluffing, she thought. *Just trying to scare me into staying with him. But am I prepared to call his bluff? What if he goes after my mom? No, I can't take that chance.*

By the time Susannah got home she felt hopeless and powerless. She went to the kitchen to find some solace in food. In the freezer, she saw an Entenmann's chocolate cake.

While she defrosted it, she sat at the kitchen table and read the calorie count on the box. When the microwave dinged, she brought the cake to the table. Screw it, she said to herself, and proceeded to eat the whole thing. Without pleasure.

Then a question surfaced, which would always be too painful to answer: *How could I have married this man?*

CHAPTER 9

It was 10:15 p.m. and the hired killer was late. Burt was sitting on a bench outside the Central Park Chess & Checkers House, which Mort liked to call his "office." The facility consisted of a one-story building, currently closed, and an outdoor area surrounding it. There were about twenty concrete playing tables, with purple and tan checkerboards imbedded in them; the sixty-four squares were made of colored pebbles. On either side of the tables were wood-slatted park benches. Above, sheltering the site, was an arbor with some scruffy vines entwining themselves half-heartedly around its crossbeams.

Burt was nervous. The place was deserted, dimly lit by a few street lamps. It was up on a hill, and Burt could see the East Park Drive below, closed to evening traffic. It was empty, except for an occasional intrepid jogger running past.

The hitman always met his clients here, and only after dark. Mort, who was given to puns and literary allusions, described the location in the *grave* words of Andrew Marvell as "a fine and private place." Burt hadn't been nervous on their previous meetings, but that was because Mort had arrived first, and there was certainly no reason to feel unsafe in the company of a world-class assassin.

From where he sat, Burt could see the iconic General Motors building on Fifth Avenue, renovated in 2003 by realtor Harry Macklowe and later sold at a huge profit to Boston Properties, a Hong Kong businesswoman, and a Brazilian banker. He remembered the twenty or so miserable years he'd spent working for Macklowe, learning the business while Macklowe promoted his two arrogant sons to positions of power. Patiently, Burt had waited for his wealthy, tight-fisted widowed mother to croak, till at last she complied and Burt's inheritance enabled him to go off on his own. He'd sunk everything into Bayview, his waterfront housing tower overlooking the Verrazano Bridge. But his earlier meeting with his lawyer had exacerbated his anxiety. He was hanging by a thread!

Burt's jumpiness caused him to start worrying about Susannah. What if his wife had flown the coop, panicked by his threats? Dammit. He was going to hire Mort to whack her in Montauk. If the hitman had to go chasing her all over the country, it was going to get complicated, and way too expensive.

He decided to give Susannah a call. He'd apologize, chill her out. Then she wouldn't think about leaving, and she'd be an easy target for Mort.

He dialed their landline, which he knew rang at her bedside. She answered on the second ring.

"Hi, Sweetie, it's me.

"What is it, Burt?"

"I'm calling to apologize. I know my behavior has been appalling recently. I... I don't know what came over me. I've been under a lot of strain because of business, but I don't want to make excuses."

"Then don't."

"On the plane today, I kept thinking about you, about how much you mean to me. And how empty my life would be without you."

"Burt, you think some cornball sweet talk can make things right? You think an apology can make up for your threats, your bullying, your violent behavior?"

"I know my words can't make things right," Burt said. "But my actions can. I promise, from now on things will be different. Whatever you need me to do, I'll do. Sweetie, I love you. You mean everything to me."

A rough hand gripping his shoulder jolted Burt with fear. He turned in a panic and looked up to see Mort's stone-faced visage staring down on him. The assassin dug his fingers harder into Burt's shoulder, as if to say "I could hurt you if I wanted to."

"Sweetie," Burt said nervously into the phone, "I... I've gotta go into a meeting. I'll stay in town tonight. Got an appointment with the dentist in the morning. Will you pick me up at the airport at eleven? That'll be the start of our new life together. Okay? Remember — I love you."

Burt exhaled and put down the phone as Mort took a seat on the bench across from him.

The Algerian killer was in his late thirties, tall, dark, and graceful of movement. He was dressed, as always, in impeccable Savile Row style: narrow-waisted navy tropical worsted suit, pale white silk shirt, and a crimson polka-dot cravat.

Susannah was about to hang up her phone when she heard a strange foreign voice, and realized that Burt had forgotten to end the call.

"Terribly sorry to be late. The traffic was absolutely horrendous." The voice she heard had a Middle Eastern accent with clipped touches of Oxford English. The voice continued.

"There was some Negro hippity-hoppity concert at Radio City, and Sixth Avenue was jammed." Through the phone, Susannah heard some tapping noises. She had no idea what was going on, but if Burt was trying to keep this meeting from her, there was no way in hell she was going to hang up.

"So, you wish to engage my professional services again?"

"Yes. My wife." Susannah's blood was like ice.

"Another wife? Goodness. You're certainly unlucky in love. But then, not so unlucky as she."

Susannah winced as she heard Burt chuckle.

"Let's see now," the foreign voice went on, "As I recall, your first wife met an untimely death Her name was...Carol? "

"You have a good memory, Mort.

Mort? He sure doesn't sound like a Mort.

"Your move again," Mort said. There was a silence on the line. Again Susannah didn't understand.

"Where is wife No.2?"

"My beach house. You know it."

"Right. Any preference as to method?"

"Your call."

Method? I don't believe this! He's letting Burt choose how I should die. Like it was an item on a menu.

"I would suggest death by drowning," Mort said. "I imagine your wife — what's this one's name?"

"Susannah."

"Susannah. Hmm." After a moment he sang in a melodious voice. "Oh Susannah, won't you die for me."

Both men laughed. Susannah was stunned. This couldn't be happening!

"I would imagine she walks by the sea from time to time," Mort said. "Simple enough to bop her with a sap, hold her under the surf until she expires, then let the ocean carry her away."

Burt: "There's a strong rip current. And if she drifts out far enough, sharks may get her. She might never be found."

"So much the better. When would you like this done?"

"Right away."

"I have an opening this weekend."

An opening? she thought. *Jesus!*

"I suggest you leave town on a business trip. The accidental death of yet another wife will surely seem suspicious. You need a solid alibi."

"I'll go to Miami."

"Wherever. Now about remuneration. My fee is sixty thousand."

A silence on the line.

Then Burt's voice: "But — last time it was fifty."

"Mr. Cascadden. You know it's rude ever to question the fee of a professional."

My God, Susannah thought. *They're actually negotiating how much it will cost to kill me!*

"And like everything else in this economy," Mort said ruefully, "the price of wet work has gone up."

"Of course,"

"Payment in cash, as usual."

"I — I'll have to get it in East Hampton. I've got a stash in a safety deposit box."

"Good," Mort said. "Get it tomorrow. Bring it to me here at seven the following evening. Then catch a plane for Miami and stay through the weekend. When you come home on Monday, you'll be horrified to find that your beloved wife has disappeared."

"Perfect."

"Bring me a recent photo of her, and, oh yes, a pair of her sunglasses. I'll leave them on the beach, which will suggest she went swimming and drowned."

"No problem."

No problem? Susannah thought. *You bastard.*

Burt's voice again: "All right, Mort. See you Wednesday at seven."

Susannah placed the phone back on its base. She was in shock, unbelieving, overwhelmed with fright.

She sat there trembling, trying to grasp the reality of her situation. Then it hit her —

I have two nights to figure out a way to save my life.

CHAPTER 10

Hidden behind bushes on a sandy hill abutting the Cascadden beach house, Jessie Russell had a clear view of the living room, part of the kitchen, and Blondie's bedroom. It was nighttime, and he'd been lying there for the past few hours, peering through his camera's telephoto lens and taking occasional breaks to smoke, work on a six-pack of Bud Light, and snack on some Ring Dings. This is what a police stake-out must be like, he thought. Hour after hour of total boredom, bearable only because in the next mother-grabbin' moment you might hit pay dirt.

So far it was nothin', zilch, nada. Blondie had changed from shorts and T-shirt into a robe, but the closet door blocked his view. He'd seen her eat, read a magazine, and now she was lying on the bed, watching TV. Boring. But Jessie had all the time in the world. And high hopes. He put out his cigarette in the sand and opened a Drake's Ring Ding.

Jessie was watching Blondie as she answered the bedroom phone, talked for a while, and then just listened. It was hard to tell but she seemed upset. Then she hung up, rose from her bed and moved toward the bathroom. She tantalizingly took off her robe as she walked. But she was in the john before Jessie could get a shot.

She stayed in there a long time. Long enough, he hoped, he prayed, for her to take a bath or a shower. Because then there was a chance that she'd go into the bedroom, dry herself off, then drop her towel —

He listened for the sound of water running, but the wind made too much noise. Patience. Patience. His mother had always told him patience was a virtue. Fuckin' A.

He started fantasizing about Susannah taking a shower. He could see her tan naked skin glistening as the water streamed down it, her soapy hands moving to her titties, making little circles around the nipples till they poked out like pink pencil erasers. Then the hands sliding down to her flat belly, washing but also teasing herself a little, working slowly down to that bald muff.

Oh, God, she's soaping it, working up a lather and sliding her middle finger through the soap-bubbly triangle, right into her —

Jessie had a major woodie now. He raised his hips to ease the pressure on his swollen prick. He looked through the viewfinder of his Nikon. There was a crashing sound. He sat up and twisted, looking in the direction of the noise. He was terrified.

In the darkness he saw two small glowing disks of silver. It took him a moment to realize they were the eyes of a deer, reflecting the bright moonlight. In that same instant the browsing creature bounded away into the night.

It took Jessie a minute or so to calm down. By the time he was breathing normally, his erection had wilted. He stretched out on the ground again and focused the camera on Susannah's bedroom window. But now there was nothing to see; she'd lowered the Levelor blind.

"I fuckin' blew it," Jessie said out loud. Then he began packing up, putting his camera, leftover Ring Dings, and beer into a nylon duffle bag. By the time he was ready to leave, he'd given himself a good talking to: Patience. Patience. This is the right M.O. Much higher percentage than trying to snap a picture from an airplane.

Getting this shot had now taken over his life. As he walked away he found himself singing: "Sooner or later — I'm gonna getcha, getcha, getcha, getcha, getcha ..."

Then he got an idea. He would call in sick tomorrow and take the day off.

Plan B.

CHAPTER 11

Susannah sat waiting anxiously for Burt on the veranda at East Hampton Airport. Her head ached, her eyes felt grainy from lack of sleep. Ever since Burt's phone call, her mind had been in overdrive, exploring every conceivable way to avoid being murdered. And the frightening truth was — she had no answer.

Her brain kept replaying the possibilities, in a desperate, never-ending loop.

Run away? Not an option. He'll kill Mom.

Go to the police? I've been over and over that. I have no evidence that Burt put out a contract on me. The police would tell me there was nothing they could do without proof of threat or previous violence.

Court order of protection? Same problem, and anyway it would be useless in this situation. And there was no time.

Hire my own private bodyguard for protection? Even if I could find one, I'm up against a $60,000 hitman here. He's clearly an expert — he'd find a way to get the job done.

Burt has a licensed handgun. Could I use it to protect myself? Same problem, only worse. Besides, I'm not a killer. To take the life of another human being? It's just not in me. But what if it were self-defense? Kill or be killed?...

She spotted the commuter plane, then watched as it landed, taxied to the terminal, and discharged its passengers. Burt was the last one off.

Susannah forced a smile and greeted her husband. He hugged her and kissed her on the cheek.

"Sweetie," he said. "Just knowing you were waiting for me here made my flight a joy. And I promise you—from now on, things are going to be very different between us."

He embraced her and they strolled through the terminal. Susannah was sick with fear but she played along.

"By the way," Susannah said, "How was your dental appointment?"

"Okay. Dr. Kern says my teeth are fine, but my gums gotta come out."

He gave such a genuine laugh that she felt of flicker of hope — *maybe he's changed his mind.*

As they were getting into the car, Burt turned to her,

"I need to swing by the bank to get some cash. I'm going down to Miami tomorrow night for a real estate convention and I hate traveling without cash in my pocket. A greased palm here and there gets you the best of everything."

The words "cash" and "Miami" quashed any hope Susannah had that Burt had reconsidered. It was certain—he was going to have her killed.

"While I'm at the bank," Burt said. "Why don't you run into Cashmere Hampton and buy yourself something for Fall. Maybe a full-length coat."

Yes, she thought, *and you can return it next week because of your wife's untimely demise.*

As Burt walked away, the loop in Susannah's mind started again — *What can I do? Run away? No. Go to the police? No. Protect myself? No. Oh, God...*

When they got home, Burt said he felt like doing a little surfcasting while Susannah made lunch. "Serve it on the good china," he said. "And pull out a bottle of the Meursault. You can chill it as soon as I get back, remember—exactly eight minutes in ice water."

"Okay," she said pleasantly. "Maybe you can catch a fish for dinner. Come back in an hour."

Burt changed into his bathing suit and Polo shirt, grabbed his rod and tackle box, and headed down to the beach.

Susannah watched him from the deck, as he ambled along the water's edge toward his favorite fishing spot about three hundred yards away. It was a gorgeous sunny day, mild and breezy. The tide was high and the surf was up. The ocean was ultramarine blue with foamy white-caps dappling its surface all the way to the horizon.

Susannah could see her husband wading out into the deeper water. *Please...please,* she thought. *Keep on going, Burt. Maybe you'll go out too far and the rip tide'll get you.*

Burt smiled as he waded into the sea. He felt the powerful tug of the undertow on his legs. *Soon,* he thought, *Susannah's corpse would be swept out to sea, drifting in the currents until it became fish food somewhere in the briny deep.* Susannah had fallen for his apologetic number big time and was set up perfectly for Mort's hit. In a few days, he'd be free of his wife's negative influence on his Purusharthas (especially Moksha, Kama, and Artha), and his instability attacks would be history.

And soon a judge's ruling would clear the way for the rise of his seventy-story Bridgeview, the first skyscraper that could be seen from ships entering New York harbor — a monument to the brilliant imagination of Burton Lloyd Cascadden, Master Builder.

Susannah went to her bedroom and pulled on a swimsuit bottom while standing in front of a full-length mirror. She scrutinized her body, something she'd done habitually since she began training as a dancer. Women outside the dance world were always envious of her. "I'd kill for a body like yours!" was a frequent comment. But they didn't understand that while her body was great by normal standards, dancers were always comparing their bodies with other dancers and invariably feeling inferior one way or another. Susannah wished her buttocks were rounder, her hipbones less prominent, and her arms — God, she hated her arms — if only they were two inches longer.

Susannah thought of Martha Graham's principles, the ideals that had been drummed into her by her teachers: centered body, centered mind. Build your strength to prepare you for the daring leap.

Yes, she thought. *Somehow I have to find the strength. The strength to save my life.*

Then she remembered Takiko's assessment of her: "Sorry, Susannah. You're just not strong enough to make the company."

She stared again at her body in the mirror. She looked strong, even powerful, but in her mind she heard those humiliating words again — *You're not strong enough, not strong enough. You're just not strong enough.*

Burt was casting with his favorite lure, the green-feathered jamboree. As the plug plunged into the pounding surf, he imagined a big striper taking it and then waging a twenty-minute struggle before he reeled in the big lunker. Tonight, his devoted wife would steam it in ginger and garlic and they would dine by candlelight — a meal that would be for them as a couple — The Last Supper.

Susannah put on her swimsuit top and a men's denim work shirt over it. She felt dazed, detached, as if she were sleepwalking.

She went to the wine rack and pulled out the wine Burt wanted— the big, buttery, hazelnut-nuanced '96 Genevieve Meursault. She filled a silver ice bucket with ice and put the bottle next to it. She selected two crystal wine goblets, then set about preparing a lunch of *pâté de foie gras,* along with cold steamed asparagus and a sourdough boule.

When she finished, Susannah walked out onto the deck. Her eye caught the large bronze statue of the flute-playing avatar Krishna, which Burt had placed there to watch over their home. Lord Krishna seemed to be giving Susannah a pitying look.

She dragged an aluminum chair close to the railing, where she had a view of the beach. In the distance, she could see her husband surfcasting.

She recalled Burt explaining Krishna's doctrine—it is not wrong to take action in the world, but rather it is often appropriate to do so, given the situations we encounter in life.

When Burt quit fishing and started packing up his gear, Susannah went to the kitchen, plunged the wine bottle into the ice cooler and brought it out on the deck. She set the table with silverware, linen napkins, and two china plates with the *pâté* and asparagus on them. The bread was in a straw basket.

She heard Burt clumping up the stairs to the deck. He appeared with his rod and tackle box. Without fish.

"No luck, huh?" Susannah said.

"Had one strike, but the fish snapped the line and took off with one of my best lures. He must've been a monster."

"How big, you think?"

"Maybe forty pounds. I have thirty-pound-test line on the reel, and it didn't hold him. Wait a minute." He bent down, opened his tackle box, and reached inside. He held up a roll of monofilament. "I got some seventy-five-pound-test at the tackle shop last week. I'll put it on after lunch."

Susannah led Burt to the table and sat him down. She uncorked the Meursault, poured it, and handed him the glass of white Burgundy. "Chilled for eight minutes exactly," she said, looking at her watch.

Burt raised the goblet and offered a toast.

"To a new us," he said.

She picked up her glass.

"Yes, Sweetie," Burt whispered, "From now on our life together will be a thing of beauty. I promise you that."

His benign smile only accentuated his evil intent.

They clinked, drank.

"Mmm," he said. "Love the Meursault."

"It's wonderful."

He took another swallow. "Reminds me of Aix-en-Provence. I should take you there some time."

Burt broke off a piece of bread, ate it, then washed it down with another swig of Burgundy. "Did I ever tell you about the first time I tasted Meursault?"

"I don't think so."

"It was when I was at Yale. I saw a bottle of it in a New Haven wine store, and it was right when we were studying the French novel *L'Etranger* — *The Stranger*, by Camus. Do you know it?"

"No."

"It's about this guy who kills a man on a beach, for no apparent reason. When I first read it, I thought the book made no sense. The main character's name is Meursault, and when I saw his name on the label I bought the wine, went back to the dorm and re-read the book while sipping the Burgundy. By the end I was pretty zonkered, but I realized this Meursault character was a real antihero, *un vrai existentialiste.*

Meursault believed that human life had no meaning in the grand spectrum of the universe. He was unencumbered by conventional emotions like guilt, remorse, hope, fear, the need for acceptance. And he was too honest to fake it. In fact, at the end of the book, he's convicted and executed, not so much because he killed a man, but because when the prosecutor asked him if he cried at his mother's funeral, Meursault answered, *'Non, Monsieur.'*"

Susannah refilled his glass.

After lunch Burt yawned. "Boy, that wine really got to me." He'd consumed about three quarters of the bottle and his slurred speech showed the alcohol's effect. "Think I'll take a little snooze," he said.

He got up and moved unsteadily to the hammock. He stumbled over an inflatable swim-raft that was propped against the wall. Then he flopped down into the hammock.

His bulky body was cradled in the nylon webbing, swaying slightly back and forth. He closed his eyes.

Susannah recalled the last time she'd seen him like that, arrogantly ordering her to toast him a Pop-Tart. She felt a surge of rage and hatred.

She turned, crossed to the table, and put the dirty dishes on a serving tray. After carrying them into the kitchen, she came out and picked up the wine bottle. It was almost empty, so she swigged the last of it as she headed back into the house.

When she passed the hammock, Burt reached out and goosed her. Susannah screamed in shock, not only from the violation, but from the slice of pain on her inner thigh, caused by Burt's sharp fingernails.

She turned and saw his body bouncing up and down in the hammock as he laughed uproariously.

She screamed at him. "You bastard!"

"Aw, c'mon, Sweetie," Burt said in a boozy voice. "You're my slut and you love it." He rose from the hammock and lurched towards her.

"You know you like it rough!"

His large body loomed over her, his hands reaching for her.

Without thinking she brought the empty wine bottle crashing down on his head. There was a loud crack and his laughter ended.

Susannah looked down at Burt. He had fallen backwards, his torso twisted against the hammock, his legs resting on the deck. Blood was oozing from his scalp, matting his dyed black hair.

She was still gripping the wine bottle. It hadn't shattered, but there was a fissure near the bottom of the thick glass.

She stood there, stunned. Her mind went blank. Then the knowledge of what she'd done swept over her. She heard herself sobbing, and mumbled words resounded in her head.

Oh, my God. Oh, my God, Oh, my God. I didn't mean to do this. I just reacted. It was...a reflex.

She saw Burt was out cold but still breathing.

At least I haven't killed him.

53

Her first impulse was to call 911, but she quickly realized that was exactly the wrong thing to do. Then, in a "blink" moment, a plan formed rapidly in her mind. She would act out of strength. Centered body, centered mind.

She looked out at the beach. It was deserted. At high tide there was never anyone around. To the north was an inlet that created swampy wetlands which were virtually impassible. The only beach walkers would have to come from Montauk Point, about two miles to the south. But at high tide the waves crashed violently over a natural rock-pile barrier, keeping visitors away.

She looked over at Burt. He was still unconscious. She took hold of Burt's legs and yanked them back up into the hammock. The hammock sagged under his heavy weight and swayed back and forth.

Moving quickly, she went to Burt's tackle box. She opened it and picked up the spool of seventy-five-pound-test fishing line.

She stripped off about sixteen feet, opened Burt's Fisherman's Friend knife and cut the line. She closed the knife, put it in her work shirt pocket, and buttoned the flap.

She went to the far end of the hammock and tied the middle of the fishing line tightly to the wooden dowel that spread the hammock out. Two eight-foot-long strands of fishing line dangled near Burt's feet.

Susannah began weaving the monofilament in and out of the hammock's nylon cord webbing, as if lacing up a sneaker. From time to time she pulled hard, closing the reinforced edges of the hammock together over Burt's body.

Burt snorted and his shoulders jerked. Susannah dropped the monofilament and grabbed the wine bottle. She held it poised over his skull and watched him. He didn't move; his breathing was again even.

She resumed lacing up the fishing lines, in and out, over and under the webbing, working her way up his body.

When she reached the top of the hammock, she yanked both lines hard, drawing the outer edges of the hammock together and sealing Burt's hefty body in the webbed enclosure. She looped the lines around the end ropes of the hammock a few times, pulled them tight, then fastened them to the spreader bar with triple knots.

54

She paused to view her work. Burt's eyelids fluttered and he looked around blearily.

"Huh? What the — what's going on?"

He was disoriented. His eyes struggled to focus. "Sweetie? I don't understand."

He moved his head and felt a sharp pain.

"Ow. My head. What—?"

He became aware that he was enclosed in the hammock and started pushing and kicking at the nylon mesh.

"What have you done to me?" he shouted.

She didn't answer him.

He blinked his eyes and tried to get his bearings. "Come on," he said. "This isn't funny."

"It's not a game, Burt."

"My head hurts."

She didn't respond.

"I don't understand."

"Burt, you forgot to turn off your cell last night. I overheard your conversation with that Mort person."

"Who?"

"You know who."

"No."

"I'm talking about your hitman—Mort."

"Oh, Mort," he said. "No. No. No. No. He's a film producer, I was pitching an idea..."

"Oh, please."

"It's true.

"Stop it."

"Listen," he said after a pause, "what you heard last night was a pitch. A movie pitch. It's a Hollywood thing. See, when somebody does a pitch, they act out all the parts — "

"You expect me to believe..."

"Susannah, lack of trust is a core problem in our marriage. We have to learn to trust each other, or..."

"Enough, Burt. Enough." The force of her words silenced him. Susannah was in a zone, her mind unswerving, driven by a singularity of purpose.

"So now what?" Burt asked timorously.

Susannah didn't reply, but Burt saw the fierce menace in her eyes. Fear caused a powerful adrenalin rush in his body. He shouted at her with frantic energy

"You think this thing can hold me? Don't be ridiculous."

He grabbed the webbing of the hammock and pulled with all his strength, but he was unable to tear it apart. He began kicking violently. The nylon wouldn't give. He tried to force his hands through the mesh. He failed.

"Susannah. Why are you doing this? "

"Not only did you put out a contract on me," she said calmly, "but I know you had your first wife killed the same way."

"That's not true. Carol's death was an accident. She — "

"You, Burt, are an evil man. You're manipulative, egocentric, and if you don't mind me saying so — you're also a demented son of a bitch."

Susannah unhooked the hammock from its steel frame and lowered Burt's feet to the teakwood deck.

"Okay, okay. I admit it." he said. "I *was* going to, y'know, hire that guy. But today, while I was down there fishing, I thought about it. And I changed my mind. I started thinking how sweet you are, and how beautiful, and how lucky I am to have you, and I realized I can't live without you. So I decided to call the whole thing off. You've got to believe me."

"Some people say the death penalty is not a deterrent," Susannah said, "But in this case it definitely *is*."

She lifted the other end of the hammock off the hook and lowered Burt's head to the deck.

56

"My God, you're gonna kill me? Susannah, please. You can't do this. I was gonna call the whole thing off!"

She took hold of the wooden spreader above Burt's head and dragged him toward the stairway. He began struggling desperately.

"You better quit that," she warned him, "You'll hurt yourself when we go down the stairs."

"Okay. Okay," Burt replied. His feet thumped on each step.

Susannah hauled him out onto the beach. She stopped, wiping the perspiration off her brow. *God, he's heavy.*

"Can't we talk about this?" Burt said.

As he spoke, she made a decision not to say another word. She would just ignore whatever Burt said. She would focus on self-preservation: Kill or be killed, kill or be killed —

Susannah picked up the spreader bar and dragged Burt across the beach. His weight made it difficult. He frantically tried to dig his heels and his fingers into the sand.

"For Chrissakes, Susannah," he whined.

She kept pulling him towards the ocean.

"Help!" Burt shouted. "Help! Somebody! Please! Help me!"

He felt the wet sand under his back and completely panicked. He screamed at the top of his lungs, while his body wriggled and thrashed like a tuna caught in a trawler's net.

As the first waves rolled gently over him, Susannah set down the hammock, grabbed several of the hammock cords, and flipped Burt's writhing body over so that he was lying on his belly. He tried to right himself, but she put her left leg onto the back of his neck, keeping him face down.

She began to haul the hammock into the ocean, pulling with her other leg and tugging with both arms. She reached a spot in front of a sand bar, where there was a three-foot-deep depression filled with water. The ocean breakers were crashing some fifteen yards beyond them.

Burt was alternately yelling for help and pleading with Susannah. His hysterical voice, the whistling wind, and the pounding surf created a nightmarish cacophony. Susannah dropped the hammock, placed both hands on the back of his head, and pushed down hard until his face was underwater. His voice was stilled.

His resistance grew weaker and weaker, and she knew it would all soon be over.

Suddenly a giant wave swept over them and wrenched Burt's body from her grasp. Susannah's mouth and nostrils filled with brine and she went under. She felt herself being carried up and backward, thrown violently onto the hard-packed wet sand. Gagging and choking, she pulled herself up to her knees. She saw Burt a few yards ahead of her, wrapped in the hammock netting, awkwardly maneuvering his big, thick body toward dry land. She got to her feet, ran forward, and grabbed him around the waist. She pulled him back and up, causing him to be dragged to his feet in the shallow water. Now she was wrestling him standing up, trying to control this large, flailing, mummy-like creature, who was suddenly possessed with hysterical strength.

Burt fought gamely, but she managed to kick his feet out from under him, and he collapsed face down against her, like a sack of potatoes.

He had nothing left. She pulled him back into the water. He was dead weight now, and her arms began to ache from the effort. She dragged him over some razor-sharp mollusk shells and they cut into Burt's naked belly. He let out a moan, and a stream of blood stained the water around them.

Then Burt did a peculiar thing. In a calm, almost musical voice he began to speak in a strange language: *"Na jayate mriyate va ka kadacin nayam bhuta bhavita va na bhuya/ajo nitya sasvato 'yam purano na hanyate hanyamane sarire ..."*

Burt was quoting in Sanskrit from The Book of the Bhagavad Gita: "It is never born nor does it die; Nor once that it is will it ever not be; Unborn, unending, eternal, and ancient, It is not killed when the body is killed ..."

Susannah forced Burt's face into the ocean, letting her weight bear down while she held him tight between her legs. She could feel his body's upward thrashings grow increasingly ineffectual until at last they ceased. The sea currents swept in and out, swirling around them.

58

Susannah looked out at the breakers—no interfering wave was coming this time. She kept holding Burt down, to make certain he couldn't survive.

At last she released him, and the body in the hammock floated to the surface. She grabbed the nylon death trap and, towing it behind her, she waded into shore. There she heaved the ponderous bulk up onto the beach and looked at Burt.

He had the perfect stillness of death. No movement of chest or abdomen, no spasm of muscle, no twitch of nerve.

She pulled pieces of slimy brown kelp out of the nylon webbing in order to get a clear view of Burt's face. It was a shock. Instead of a serene death visage, she saw a face contorted in mortal agony. His eyes were clamped shut, his mouth was agape, frozen in a grimace, with his lips pulled down at the corners like a Greek tragedy mask. He appeared to have swallowed his tongue.

Susannah had to turn away. After a few moments she regained her composure. She reached her finger through the hammock cords and placed it on Burt's neck artery. She could feel no pulse.

She hauled him back into the water, out past the sandbar, almost to the crashing breakers. She felt the undertow pulling at her legs. She braced herself against its relentless drag, reached into her shirt pocket and took out Burt's fishing knife. She cut the monofilament in several places and yanked it out. The hammock opened like an unlaced shoe, and Burt's body floated loose.

Susannah pushed Burt's body deep under the water, down to where she could feel the intense suction of the undertow. She released the body, and abruptly it was gone.

She watched for several minutes to see if it would resurface. She looked out at the high waves that were cresting and breaking, thinking the body might reappear in the surf. It did not.

She stood there panting, as she visualized her husband's corpse being sucked away by the irresistible rip current of the Atlantic Ocean.

Susannah waded back to shore, carrying the broken hammock. When she reached the beach, she turned and looked out at the vast, sunlit expanse of ocean before her. She pictured the murderous madman she'd married, now sinking down to his final resting place in depths of the eternal sea. She spoke in a quiet voice.

"Strong enough."

CHAPTER 12

When Susannah opened the door, she saw a tall, well built, sandy-haired man dressed in a double-knit golf shirt and shapeless pants, with a gun on one side of his belt and a cell phone on the other. He had a surprised expression on his face, as if he knew her. But the look quickly changed to one that was all business.

"Mrs. Susannah Cascadden?" Jericho said. "East Hampton Town Police responding to your 911 call."

He spoke politely but there was a tough edge to his voice. He flipped open a wallet, showing a photo ID and a gold badge.

"Come on in," she said.

Susannah led him into the living room. *Have we met before?* she wondered. *I doubt it. I'd have remembered a guy who looks this good.*

She sat down on the couch, and he took a seat in a bentwood rocker.

"I'm Detective Jericho — like in the Battle."

Detective?, she thought. *Why did they send a detective? I expected just some ordinary patrolman.*

"You reported your husband missing," he said, taking out a notepad.

"Yes. I'm very worried."

"What are the circumstances?"

Susannah took a deep breath. *I have to project just the right degree of concern, not desperate yet, hopeful that Burt would turn up.*

"Maybe I shouldn't be so worried," she said, "But I can't help it. Burt went fishing down on the beach. Surfcasting, about one o'clock this afternoon. When he wasn't back by three, I phoned to tell him to come back because sometimes he stays out in the sun too long and ends up red as a lobster."

"Phoned him? On the beach?"

"He always keeps his cell in his tackle box."

Jericho nodded.

"Anyway," she went on, "He didn't answer, so I went out on the deck and didn't see him fishing at his usual spot. From up here you can see the whole beach and I couldn't see him anywhere. So I went down to where he usually fishes, and found his shirt on the sand, along with his fishing stuff, and his baseball cap with his sunglasses in it. Oh, and a towel. It looked like he'd decided to go for a swim. But I didn't see him anywhere in the water. That's when I got worried. There's a bad rip current this time of year, and I thought — "

She broke off, as if unable to articulate her fears. No tears, though. Only a momentary closing of the eyes.

"Maybe your husband just went for a walk."

"I don't think so," she said. "He hated the glare of the sun, so I doubt he'd go off without his sunglasses, and his baseball cap."

The detective scribbled on his notepad.

"The BMW and the Lamborghini out front," he said. "Those are your only cars?

"Yes."

"Any bicycles? Scooters?"

"No."

"I'll need a description of your husband," he said. "His full name?"

"Burton Lloyd Cascadden." Jesus, this is surreal, she thought.

"Age?"

"Uh — fifty-seven.

"Physical description?"

"About six feet. Weight, I dunno, maybe two thirty. He was on the heavy side."

"Facial characteristics?"

"Um, full lips, black hair, dyed black and thinning." She paused. "He has beautiful eyes, brown and very — expressive." She wanted to sound like she loved him.

"What was he wearing? Shorts, swimsuit?"

"Swimsuit. Blue Speedo briefs. Hugo Boss polo shirt. Black."

Jericho finished writing, then stood up and put the pad in his back pocket.

"Okay. Why don't you take me down to where he was fishing."

"Sure."

"Oh, and get me a large plastic trash bag from your kitchen if you have one."

Susannah led the detective out to the deck, then went to the kitchen. When she returned he was surveying the white-capped ocean and the curving stretch of beach. He turned and looked at the exterior of the house, then at the deck itself. He seemed to be scrutinizing each detail—the statue of Krishna, the swim-raft, the wrought-iron table, the deck chairs—his eyes recording everything like a video surveillance camera.

Damn, Susannah thought. *Where is police indifference when you need it? I'm sure glad I moved the empty hammock frame to the garage. He certainly would've noticed.*

"Where was your husband fishing?"

"Down there," Susannah responded, pointing at the beach to her right.

"Let's take a look."

They descended the stairs and Susannah suggested they walk along the water's edge, where the receding tide left hard packed sand for better footing.

"Did you leave all your husband's stuff just as you found it?"

"Yes."

"Good."

When they got to where Burt had been fishing, the detective saw the evidence that Susannah had carefully planted. There was the beach towel, with a rock on top of it so it wouldn't blow away. The Fiberglas rod was set into an aluminum tube inserted in the sand. She'd worn dishwashing gloves to make sure her fingerprints weren't on anything.

"Did your husband do a lot of fishing?"

"Pretty much. It was his hobby — his way of relaxing."

Jericho put on a pair of plastic gloves himself, knelt down, and examined the glasses in the baseball hat.

"Oliver Peoples. Prescription?"

"No."

He picked up the polo shirt Susannah had placed over Burt's tackle box. He opened the lid and saw the cell phone with a missed call from *Home* sitting on a tray with his lures. He stood up and looked around.

"No shoes?"

"No."

"Isn't the sand kinda hot?"

"Not in September. July and early August, when it's like in the eighties, nineties. But not now."

Susannah was feeling edgy. *Why is this guy asking so many questions?*

"Was he wearing a watch?"

She shook her head no. "It's a Patek-Phillipe, not waterproof. Burt would never take it to the beach."

Jericho nodded.

"Tell me something, detective," she said with a quiver in her voice, "You think — what do you think happened? I mean, it sure looks like he went swimming, doesn't it?"

64

"I wouldn't jump to any conclusions, Mrs. Cascadden," he said. "Let's go back to the house. We can take your husband's stuff with us. Just let me get some pictures." He pulled his phone out of his pocket and took several shots of the scene. Then he photographed each item of evidence close up.

"All done," he said. "I'll take that plastic bag now."

She handed him the bag and he put Burt's stuff into it, except the fishing gear, which he carried in his other hand.

As they walked back to the house, Jericho explained that physical evidence can be misleading. "There well may be a simple explanation to all this," he said. "The thing for you to do now is call all his friends and associates. What business is your husband in?"

"Real estate. He's a developer."

"Out here?'

"No. In the city."

"Call everyone," Jericho said, "especially locally, and ask if they've seen or heard from him."

"They'll get worried."

"Can't be helped. And don't make up something like he's late for cocktails. Tell them he's missing."

"Oh, gosh."

"That's the best way," he said. "It'll be dark in an hour. If you prefer, you can hold off till then, and maybe he'll show. It's up to you. I'd call now."

"Then, then you think something happened to him?"

"I didn't say that."

The detective stopped on the deck and looked out at the sea. The sun had begun to set and the bright blue sky was fading slowly to mauve. "Beautiful view you've got here."

"Yes. We love it."

"Did your husband have any cash or credit cards with him when he was fishing?"

"I doubt it."

"Where would he keep his cash and wallet?"

"His pants and jacket, I guess."

"Mind if we take a look?"

"Sure."

As Susannah led him to the bedroom, he explained he wanted to rule out robbery in case there turned out to be evidence of foul play.

When he entered the bedroom, Jericho was aware that it was the husband's room. There was no indication that a woman slept there. *Separate bedrooms*, he thought. *Possible marital problems?*

He spotted Burt's watch on the nightstand. *Patek Phillipe.*

Susannah picked up Burt's pants, which were neatly folded on a chair. She reached into a pocket, and took out his gold money clip. It contained a twenty, two fives, and a single. She showed the money to the detective.

The detective nodded. "Have you noticed anything missing from the house — cash, jewelry, art, anything of value?"

"No."

"Where are his credit cards?"

"They'd be in his billfold," she answered, "In his jacket pocket. But I'm sure they're there. Why would he take credit cards when he went fishing?"

"People are unpredictable."

She went to the closet where Burt had hung his poplin jacket, and reached into the inside pocket. She felt something and was about to draw it out when she realized it wasn't a leather wallet, it was paper, some kind of — envelope. It was bulging — it had to be the bank envelope containing the $60,000 for Mort. For a few seconds she froze; if the detective saw it he would ask questions. He was asking too many already. She moved her body to make sure he couldn't see the jacket.

"Can't find it?" he queried.

She took a deep breath and felt around in the other side pocket until she felt his billfold. She pulled it out and handed it to the detective. He opened it.

"American Express, Visa, Mobil, MasterCard," he said. "Anything missing?"

"Not that I know of."

He gave the wallet back to Susannah.

"Well, I've gotta get going," he said. "Make those calls, and if you can't determine your husband's whereabouts by, let's say, nine tonight, phone the East Hampton station and they'll page me. I'll set our missing person protocol in motion tomorrow morning at first light. That's an all-out search."

"God, I hope that won't be necessary."

"Well, we'll do what we have to do."

Susannah nodded bravely.

They walked to the door. "Thank you so much, Detective Jericho."

He smiled and his expression took on an unexpected warmth. "No problem," he said gently.

He opened the door, then turned back to her, Columbo style.

"Oh. I'm curious about something," he said. "There seemed to be some sort of track in the sand, leading from your house to the water's edge. As if something had been dragged down to the ocean."

"Huh? I can't imagine ..."

Oh my God, she thought. *It's all over. I didn't think of that.* Her mind raced, searching frantically for an explanation.

"Oh. Oh, yes," she said. "I guess that was from my swim raft. I dragged it down there this afternoon."

"That's the raft I saw out on your deck?"

"Yes."

"So you went swimming?"

"Well, rafting. I like to ride it on the incoming waves like a surfer. But when I got out a ways, I felt this strong current dragging me out to sea — the rip tide, grabbing hold of me, and I panicked. I started paddling frantically. Then I remembered you're supposed to float parallel

67

to the shore until you're out of the rip. I did that and then I made it back to the beach. It was so scary. That's why I'm so worried about Burt."

"Try not to worry, Mrs. Cascadden," Jericho said. "These things usually have a way of sorting themselves out."

He smiled again and left. Susannah closed the door, leaned against it, and sighed in relief.

She went into the living room, sat down and put her face in her hands. Susannah had been raised in a non-religious home, and she believed in God without defining exactly what that meant. She hadn't read the Bible, but she knew one of its precepts was indisputable — "Thou shalt not kill."

God forgive me, she thought. *I've killed a man. It was kill or be killed. Still...I've killed a man!*

Driving back to the precinct house, Jericho reviewed the facts in the case. The one question mark was the track in the sand. Mrs. Cascadden had explained it satisfactorily, but she was a bit too detailed in her account. From his experience Jericho knew that when people give too much information, it often means they're lying. Often, but not always. In this case, her response was certainly credible and there was no reason to think she wasn't telling the truth.

His mind made a jump cut to Mrs. Cascadden's lovely face—her prom queen looks. Then he visualized her dancer's body, as she taught the kids. Today she'd greeted him wearing sweatpants and an oversized T-shirt, but he could see hints of the woman beneath. He started fantasizing that her husband had indeed drowned, leaving his beautiful wife alone and devastated—alone so he could ride to her rescue in his white, blue, and red Ford Crown Victoria patrol car, offering her comfort, understanding, and love.

Oh, brother, he said to himself. *Obviously I've been womanless way too long. Probably Mr. Cascadden will show up at suppertime, saying he went for a long walk, without his sunglasses and baseball cap because—because he wanted to get a suntan on the bags under his eyes. Who the hell knows?*

Come on, man. Start acting like a gold-shield detective, not some horny rookie who can't keep his mind on his work.

As Jericho pulled onto the Montauk Highway, he reminded himself of what he'd told Mrs. Cascadden: *These things usually have a way of sorting themselves out.*

CHAPTER 13

At 9 p.m. Susannah called the police station and told them her husband still hadn't shown up. They promised to inform Detective Jericho.

Then she spent a very strange night. She had killed a man, yet when she tried to assess her emotional state she drew a blank; all she felt was a vague sense of relief, and an awareness that she must keep her wits about her, concentrate on the task at hand.

When Susannah made the phone calls Detective Jericho had suggested, she realized how few friends she and Burt had. When they were in New York, she attended a number of social events with her husband—art openings, charity fund-raisers, an occasional dinner party—but they never seemed to make any real connections with other couples. And after she moved out to Montauk in April, she was mainly involved with decorating the house and teaching dance classes. Burt had arranged her life in such a way that she was quite isolated. Aside from Gretchen Silverman-Lewis, her only social activity was her weekly trip into the city for a class at the Broadway Dance Center, and lunch with her former New York roommates, Blanche and Maurezio.

So she had very few phone calls to make. She alerted Burt's lawyer, who was clearly alarmed and said he'd phone Burt's business associates. She rang Gretchen who offered to come over, but Susannah said she was fine, at least for the moment.

She made a few perfunctory calls to the Getty station, the IGA market, and the East Hampton Commuter Airline office. Then she phoned Maurezio and Blanche in the city, to further establish she was really worried about Burt's disappearance.

One area of concern was the money in Burt's jacket pocket. Susannah couldn't leave it there, because if there was a police investigation they might discover it. Detective Jericho was clearly a cop who overlooked nothing and he'd definitely view $60,000 in cash with suspicion.

There can be no loose ends, she thought. *Also, who knows what's going to happen in my life? The cash might come in handy down the line.*

She took the envelope with the money and went to Burt's office. She opened his bottom desk drawer and put the envelope in the back, behind some files. There, if the police found it, she'd claim it belonged to her husband and she knew nothing about it.

The other issue was Burt's automatic pistol, which he kept in his nightstand. She opened the drawer and looked at the gun. The weapon might raise questions in Detective Jericho's mind, but on the other hand Burt had a pistol permit ("Some people don't like me," he used to say). Susannah decided to leave the gun where it was.

There was so much to think about, so many decisions to make, bases to cover—one misstep could be disastrous. She'd already messed up with the track in the sand.

I wish to hell Detective Jericho wasn't on this case, she thought. *He's too damn good.*

Susannah was awakened at dawn by the *stut-stut-stut-stut* of a helicopter's rotor blades beating in the sky above her. She went out on the deck and saw the Coast Guard chopper flying low over the beach, heading toward the marshy inlet north of the house. Out in the ocean she could see an orange and black outboard patrol boat slowly cruising near the shoreline.

She heard a car engine and turned to see a police Jeep kicking up sand as it traversed the dunes. Then it rode out onto the beach and began a slow reconnoiter of the area.

She went back inside the house, threw some water on her face, and heated a cup of coffee in the microwave.

The phone rang and it was Detective Jericho.

"Any word from your husband?"

"No."

"Then you'll need to fill out a missing person report. Can you come down to the precinct house this morning?"

"Okay. Montauk?"

"East Hampton. 159 Pantigo Road."

"Detective," Susannah said. "I'm getting really scared." For once she was telling the truth.

"I understand, Mrs. Cascadden," Jericho said. "This must be a very difficult time for you. Rest assured I'll do everything in my power to help you."

"Thank you," she said. But she wasn't sure if his help would save her or destroy her.

The East Hampton precinct house is a modest one-story red brick building set behind the town hall and next to the courthouse. It is surrounded by a group of Eighteenth Century wood frame houses that were moved there by the East Hampton Village Preservation Society to create a sense of what the town once looked like. The entrance to the police station is landscaped on either side with oval shaped privet hedges; it looks more like a real estate office than a police station.

Inside, the walls are painted matte atrium-white, unlike the color scheme at Jericho's former station house in East Harlem, which featured several layers of barf green and turd brown. There is no smell of urine or disinfectant, and the lighting is mostly incandescent, not fluorescent. There are no cries of "Muthafuckah!" and "I'nt do nothin', a'ight!"

Jericho was in his office, speaking on the phone to Coast Guard Lieutenant Tommy Gibbons, a pal he knew from the East Hampton Bulldog Gym, where he occasionally worked out.

"The patrol boat's out trollin' for floaters," the Coast Guard officer said. "But so far all they've seen is flotsam, jetsam, and used condoms. Air-Sea chopper's been doin' orbits, five miles in both directions from the house. We'll keep on patrolin', but if we find anything, chances are it's a Loved One."

"Okay. Thanks, Tommy."

"Unless of course, the dude just took off."

"Doubt it," Jericho said. "We've got cars and men out looking for him, and we're checking the marinas. But he was wearing only swimming briefs, no shirt or shoes. He apparently had no money or credit cards with him. So how far can he get?"

"Right. Well, I'll ring you if there's any news. Take care."

"Thanks, Tom."

Jericho hung up, knowing Lieutenant Gibbons was correct. What they'd probably be looking for now was a dead body. Two summers before, a few months after he joined the force, a woman had drowned off Sagg Main Beach and her body had washed up three days later, a mile from where she'd gone swimming. She was horribly disfigured—having been slammed by waves against rocks, nibbled at by crabs and fish—and bloated by the natural decomposition process of being submerged so long.

Jericho grimaced when he recalled going to the beach with Detective Dominick Manos that day. The sight of the corpse had caused Jericho to become dizzy, and he'd almost blacked out before he managed to turn away and pull himself together. Without anyone noticing, Jericho knew it was a mild version of the flashbacks he used to get back in East Harlem. Still, he felt it wasn't serious, especially since it hadn't happened again in over a year.

His intercom buzzed and the desk clerk said there was a Mrs. Cascadden to see him.

Susannah entered wearing a man's button-down white shirt over jeans. She wore no lipstick, her hair was mussed and she had on owlish sunglasses. She looked as if she hadn't slept all night. *Wow.* Jericho thought. *Even when she's a mess, she looks terrific.*

Susannah took a quick look around Jericho's cramped, cluttered office. One wall was lined with blue statute books, and a computer dominated the cluttered desk. She saw a silver frame that looked like it contained a photograph, but it was facing away from her. The office had one window, with a view of a red-leafed maple tree.

"I wanted to ask you," she said as she sat down, "how come this is being handled from East Hampton?"

"What do you mean?"

"Well, I would've thought the Montauk Police— "

"Montauk is a precinct of East Hampton township. A missing person case requires a detective, and they don't have any detectives out there."

"Oh, I see. Well, I'm sure glad you're— "

"You'll have to fill this out," he said, handing her a form. "Here's a pen. Press hard, there's carbons."

Susannah took off her sunglasses and began writing on the legal size report, backed by a carbon and a green sheet. The Suffolk County Missing/Unidentified Person Report was an exercise in minutia. It asked for military time and date of report, date last seen, character of case (disabled, involuntary, disaster victim, custodial interference, endangered) and so on.

"Endangered?" she asked the detective.

"What?"

"Character of case."

"Oh. Yeah, that's fine."

She read the list of Race Codes: 1-White, 2-Black,

3-Amer.Indian/Alaskan Native, 4-Asian/Pacific Islander,

5-Hispanic White, 6-Hispanic Black, 7-Other. She checked No. 1 and moved on. For Build she was asked to choose between Thin, Muscular, Medium and Heavy/Stocky. Burt would have preferred muscular or medium, but she chose Heavy/Stocky. Scars, Marks, Tattoos? None. Deformities? She thought of listing Burt's genitals, but checked None. Blood type? No idea. Circumcision? On and on it went.

When she finished, she handed the form to Jericho.

"This phone number," the detective said. "Area code '917' means it's your cell, right?"

"Yes, I have a line land but it's best to reach me on my cell."

Jericho nodded and turned the form over. "You've gotta sign the certification on the back," he said. "The green sheet."

She turned the report over. She reminded herself that she was the very upset wife of a beloved missing husband.

Tears. Tears would be appropriate here. She recalled the exercises she'd been taught in her college acting class. Sense memory. Think of something in your past that will evoke the emotion you wish to convey.

Drinks with Takiko. "Sorry, Susannah. You're just not strong enough to make the company."

The tears came welling up, then flowed down her cheeks. She signed the form, pulled herself together, and looked up at Jericho.

"I'm sorry, Mrs. Cascadden," he said. "Look, here's my card. You can call me if you need me for any reason."

"What happens now?"

"Well, we'll continue the investigation. But basically all you can do is wait."

"Wait?"

"Yes," the detective said. "In cases like this, sometimes a body will turn up. Other times— " He broke off and shrugged.

She put on a brave face and sniffled.

CHAPTER 14

Jessie Russell lived in a dilapidated bungalow, on the grounds of the Montauk Sportsman's Dock Marina. He rented it from the Grogan family, who also owned the Liar's Saloon, a fishermen's hangout next door overlooking the marina.

Jessie had converted his bathroom into a makeshift darkroom. He'd covered the windows, rigged up a safe light, and built a counter and shelves over the tub. When he took a shower, which wasn't that often, he used the one in the marina. The toilet he kept as a toilet.

He did his developing and printing after dark, because in the daytime there was always some light leakage from outside. He had no interest in that newfangled digital photography. Part of the thrill of doing your own darkroom work was seeing that image materialize like magic out of a pan of developer.

The day before, Jessie had put his Plan B into action. Afterwards he'd needed to work in his darkroom but he was out of stop bath. He was pissed, but there was nothing he could do.

He waited till the next morning, then picked some up at the East Hampton Camera Shop.

After work he drove home from the airport, and went straight to his darkroom.

He filled the developing tank. In the eerie red light he loaded his film onto the plastic reel, then placed the reel in the tank. He screwed on the lid and started the timer.

He agitated the tank at regular intervals, rapping it sharply against the edge of the bathtub, and shaking it up and down in smooth, gentle motions.

When the timer went off, he drained the developer and filled the tank with his fresh-bought stop bath. After shaking it for thirty seconds, he poured out the stop bath and added the fixer. He agitated it some more.

Five minutes later, he opened the tank and set it under the tub's faucet and let the running water wash through it. This was the aggravating part, because he was dying to see his negatives but he had to wait another thirty minutes to make sure there was no trace of fixer on the film. Otherwise the film was liable to deteriorate rapidly.

Jessie went out in front of his bungalow, lit a Camel, and sat down on a rickety lawn chair. It was a balmy night, and he amused himself by blowing cigarette smoke at fireflies. The fireflies were clearly not amused.

From where Jessie sat, he could see the bow of a sleek-looking sport fishing yacht, christened "Tuna Helper". *Sweet*, he said to himself. *A fifty-foot Chris Craft 500 Constellation. Oh, yeah, that would do me just fine.*

He thought about the film and felt the excitement building in him, like when he was a kid on Christmas morning—waiting in bed till his mom's alarm clock went off so he could go to the living room and open his presents.

Finally he heard the timer ring and he rushed back to his darkroom. He removed the film from the wash water and wiped it off carefully with a damp photo chamois.

He held the strip of negatives up to the light and congratulated himself. His Plan B had worked.

Having failed to get a shot of Blondie at night, the next morning Jessie called in sick, went back to her house around noon and hid in the dunes with his camera. He figured that if she sunbathed it would be around midday.

What he got was much more than a muff shot, and he didn't need to print out a contact sheet to be sure of what he'd captured with his telephoto lens. There, in the blacks and grays of the negatives, were the images, clear as day: Blondie and Rich Fuck having lunch on the deck; Blondie slugging him with the wine bottle; the husband collapsing into the hammock; the wife tying him up, dragging him down to the beach, pulling him into the surf, and—drowning the crap out of him.

Smile pretty for the camera, Blondie!

CHAPTER 15

In the morning, Jericho went to the Police Chief's office to brief him on the Cascadden disappearance.

Jericho and Chief Manos had a good relationship. When Manos was a detective lieutenant, they'd spent a lot of time together. The older man had a gray crew cut and a touch of rosacea around the nose. He reminded Jericho of his father: cold nature, warm heart.

Manos was an experienced and dedicated cop, and functioned well on the local level. But, in Jericho's view, as Chief of Police he was living proof of the Peter Principle—he had risen exactly to the level of his incompetence. Manos loved to bust Jericho's chops from time to time, but Jericho didn't mind. He knew it was the Chief's way of overcompensating for being underqualified.

"So we're looking at an accidental drowning?" Manos said.

"Yes. But there *is* another possibility."

"What's that?"

"Well, first thing this morning I called the New York City Real Estate Board," Jericho said. "They said the word around town is Cascadden was in deep financial shit. All his money was in one project in Brooklyn, and it was falling apart. So it's possible he committed suicide. Or—he faked his death and disappeared to duck his creditors."

Manos nodded.

"Or," Jericho said, "there could have been illegalities. Maybe the whole project was a scam, and he split to avoid prosecution."

"Any forensic info?" the Chief asked.

"Only one set of prints on his stuff. Gotta assume they're his."

"Blood?"

"No blood."

"How's the wife taking it?"

"She seems shocked and upset," Jericho replied.

"Nothing suspicious?"

"Listen, as a detective, I tend to be suspicious of everybody." Jericho stood up. "Well, I better get back to work."

"There *is* another possible scenario," Manos said.

"What's that?"

"Cascadden faked his death because he was having a midlife crisis. He decided 'Fuck it', jumped on a plane and left the country—maybe flew off to Bora Bora with his bimbo secretary."

"Could be," Jericho said.

"But wait," Manos said. "If he did that he'd have to go through US Customs at the airport. We should check with them..."

"If he wanted to disappear, he'd probably hire a private jet."

"That's expensive. I thought you said he had financial problems."

"Yes," Jericho said. "But guys like that always have tons of cash stashed away."

Manos sighed. "So — what's your best guess on this case?"

"Well," Jericho said thoughtfully, "My guess is what we've got here is a 3-D."

"Huh?"

"Oh. That's what we called a dead body when I worked in East Harlem."

"But why 3-D?

"Definitely Done Dancing."

CHAPTER 16

That afternoon Susannah was riding the Hampton Jitney bound for the city. She'd made an appointment with Burt's lawyer to discuss the legal ramifications of Burt's disappearance.

She felt very jumpy. She had to play a role with Detective Jericho. Now she had to do it again. How convincing could she be with a slick attorney like Quinn Healey?

Remembering Jericho, she thought it might seem suspicious if she'd left Montauk without letting him know. She took out his card, called him, and got his voice-mail. "This is Susannah Cascadden," she said. "I'm going into the city to see our family lawyer. I dunno, maybe he can help. If you have any news, please call me. Thanks."

The bus bumped along the elevated section of the Long Island Expressway, approaching the Midtown Tunnel. Off to her right Susannah could see the vast acreage of Mt. Zion and New Calvary cemeteries.

She looked at the countless gravestones, row upon row, each signifying the existence of one life, lived with its unique combination of pleasure, pain, fulfillment, and disappointment; then buried and forgotten.

She remembered her last lunch with Burt — how he'd savored the taste of the wine she served him, the Meursault, which had become the very instrument of his death.

How ironic, she thought, *that he'd told me about the novel* The Stranger *and its central character, also named Meursault — a man who*

believed that human life has no meaning in the total spectrum of the
universe. If Meursault was right, I'm just a minuscule speck of dust in an
infinite cosmos, whose troubles don't really matter. So why sweat it?

But that was philosophy, not reality. Her reality was coping with Burt's death and her own life — which was a matter of life and death.

The bus shifted gears and rode downhill toward the East River, its air brakes emitting flatulent hisses as it approached the EZ-Pass tollbooth. The vehicle stopped, then when the orange steel arm swung up, it eased forward into the gloomy Queens Midtown Tunnel.

Susannah got off at Forty-second and Lex, and walked to Quinn Healey's office at Forty-fourth off Madison. She had the disoriented feeling she always got coming in from the laid-back beach town of Montauk. Although she considered New York her home, she felt as if she was in a foreign city, walking by unfamiliar buildings and street signs, passing strange people who avoided eye contact as if it would be fatal.

The law office of H. Quinn Healey, Esq. PC, was in a building just down the block from Brooks Brothers. Healey's office appeared to be an extension of that store; leather club chairs, leather stuffed elephants, plaid couches, forest-green walls, duck decoys, and lithographs of sailing vessels.

Healey himself seemed part of the décor: silver hair, WASPy face, lockjawed speech. His fawn-colored, natural shoulder three-piece suit seemed color-coordinated with the tan law books that lined the wall behind his desk.

"Good to see you, Susannah."

She smiled.

"Any news?" he asked.

"No."

"Do you think it's possible Burt just ran off somewhere?"

"Don't know why he would."

"Neither do I," the lawyer said. "Do they hold out any hope that he's alive?"

"The detective said there was always a chance, but I shouldn't count on it. I'm afraid— " She broke off.

86

Healey pursed his lips and opened a legal folder. He glanced at it, then looked up grimly.

"We've got a problematic situation," he said. He detailed Burt's involvement in the complex and costly BridgeView deal. Burt's disappearance had generated a series of events which would lead to default. Within a week Healey was going to be forced to file for Chapter 11.

"Is that personal bankruptcy, or is it Burt's company?"

"It's the company," Healey said. "But unfortunately Burt put up his own personal holdings as collateral. You'll be losing the town house, the Indian art collection, plus the securities at Morgan Stanley. "

"How am I supposed to live?"

"Well, you've got a Visa card with a $20,000 line of credit, which should hold you for a while. The good news is Burt didn't put up the beach house. It carries a mortgage, but it's got to be worth eight million, so you should clear at least, oh, three, four million, depending on market conditions. Problem is—you'll have to petition the court to get permission to sell, because it's not yours till Burt's declared legally deceased. That could take as long as seven years if... if there's no evidence of his demise."

"This is all too much for me," Susannah said. It was part acting and part real.

Healey reached across his desk and patted her hand.

"Don't worry, Sweetie. I know it's a lot to handle. But we'll deal with it, one step at a time."

Sweetie? she thought. *Burt's pet name for me. What does that mean?*

"Am I — I mean, in his will, am I the sole beneficiary?"

"I believe so."

"Could I see a copy of his will?"

"Of course," he answered. "But not today, I'm afraid. The will is stored in a bunch of file boxes we recently moved to a document warehouse in Jersey City. We just plain ran out of storage space here.

It'll take a couple of days to access it, but I'll put my girl on it right away."

His girl! Susannah had never liked Healey—he was sexist, and way too smooth. Now she didn't trust him either.

Susannah stood up, shook his hand, and told him she'd stay in touch. *Why doesn't he know the details of the will? He seems to know everything else about Burt's affairs. And now he claims the will is in Jersey City? Sweetie? Something's not right here.*

As she rode down in the elevator, Susannah thought: *I better get my own lawyer.*

As she sat on the bus, riding up Madison Avenue to the town house, money was on Susannah's mind.

Thank God I've got the sixty thousand. With that and my credit card I can get by for a while. I'd hoped Burt's body would never be found; now I wish it would wash up on shore—and soon. Otherwise I'm in for a long wait and legal wrangling till the will's probated. Well, at least I can send the four thousand a month for Dad's care. It would be nice if the doctor's are right and he lasts through Christmas. Mom would like it if we could have one last family holiday. But then again, if he dies by Thanksgiving, I wouldn't have to—My God, I'm getting awfully casual about death. Is that because I've taken a life?

Susannah got off the bus at Sixty-eighth Street and walked east. The town house was a narrow limestone building on a tree-lined street between Madison and Park Avenues. It was a four story Victorian Italianate structure traversed by two ornamental stringcourses, with round-headed windows and a wide stoop leading up to an entrance flanked by flat pilasters.

The interior design was totally inappropriate. Burt had gotten the brainstorm of "going industrial"; he'd stripped the walls down to the bare bricks, exposing iron gas and water pipes, then installed stamped metal stairways suspended by steel cables, and room dividers of sandblasted glass. The modern office furnishings were anachronistically accented by Indian sculpture mainly from the *Kushan* and *Gupta* periods.

The entire house had been Feng Shui'd two years ago by a Chinese master who assured Burt that harmonizing his environment would eliminate all hostility and aggression from his life. But when Susannah moved in she felt something was still out of whack—why else would the guppies in the obligatory Feng Shui fish tank keep going belly up?

The building's central air-conditioning was off, and the house was hot and musty. Susannah punched the main A/C control button in the entrance hall. She'd thought about staying overnight, but as she climbed the stairs to the second floor she realized it was an awful idea. There were too many upsetting reminders of Burt. And she had an odd sense that his spirit was lurking in the house, maybe in Burt's Hindu shrine up in the attic. A night alone in that house would be too creepy.

She went to her bedroom and took a rolling travel duffle out of the closet. She packed her jewelry box — with her earrings, bracelets, and diamond necklace. She added some favorite shoes and clothes, her dance books, and a small, smiling *Khmer* head she'd bought with her own money at Sotheby's. These were the few things she either needed or cared about; if the house was later foreclosed and padlocked, at least she'd have them.

Susannah went into Burt's office and looked for a copy of his will. She went through his desk and file cabinet but found nothing.

She booted up Burt's computer and found files containing business letters, tax returns and contracts, medical reports, a list of "Favorite Diets of the Stars" downloaded from a website —but no will.

She noticed Burt's address book on the desk. It was open to the "B" page.

Her eye caught a peculiar entry: *Ubaf Sing*. In the address section below it: *A-be-deghi*. There was no phone number.

She was puzzled. *Why is it on the "B" page and the listing starts with "U"? This makes no sense. Is it Arabic, or maybe Hindi? Sanskrit? What's this gibberish doing in an address book? Could it be some kind of code?*

Susannah shrugged. On a whim, she also packed the address book in her suitcase. Suddenly she felt an intense need to get out of the house.

She checked her watch. If she hurried, she could walk to the Jitney stop at Fifty-ninth and Lex and catch the 3:40, with time to stop at

Hale & Hearty for soup and pick up *The New Yorker* to read on the trip. She left quickly and locked the door behind her. As she descended the limestone steps, she felt a sense of relief.

Ubaf Sing. A-be-deghi. Those cryptic words stuck in her brain all the way back to Montauk.

CHAPTER 17

Jericho and Katie were walking along the ocean's edge at low tide. It was an overcast afternoon, the sky a chalky gray, and there was barely a breeze.

"Look, Daddy. What's that seagull got in his mouth?"

"Well, I'll be darned," Jericho said. "It's a bagel."

They watched the slate-gray-and-ivory gull drop the bagel on the sand and peck at it vigorously. Sharp as the bird's beak was, it couldn't pierce the hard, slick crust of the bagel. The gull picked it up again, worried it in his beak, then flew off. He landed about fifty feet down the beach and once more pecked futilely—he knew the damn thing was food but he couldn't figure out how the hell to eat it. Two more gulls arrived on the scene, followed by a raucous fish crow emitting its high nasal *ca-hah*. The interlopers tried to cop the bagel owner's meal, but he fought them off with a great flapping of wings. The gull grabbed the bagel again in his beak and flew off, heading inland over the dunes with the crow in hot pursuit.

"Where do you think he's going?" Katie asked.

"Probably to get some cream cheese."

Jericho watched his five-year-old daughter's face grow thoughtful for a moment and then blossom into a grin. A musical giggle followed. "Oh, Daddy!"

Jericho smiled at Katie's response to his rather complex joke. He picked her up and hugged her with unrestrained joy. Katie didn't know the reason for Jericho's impulsive action, but she sure liked the hug.

He set her down and they continued their walk.

"So," he asked, "how are you getting along with Irwin these days?"

"Fine," the little girl answered. "He's real nice. He drives me to play school every morning before he goes to work, and sometimes he even makes me oatmeal for breakfast. It's dee-licious. He makes it from scratch, he doesn't nuke it, he actually cooks it in a pot. Irwin says the secret is to stir from left to right, not right to left. Did you know that?"

"No, I didn't," Jericho replied cheerfully, his heart aching with jealousy.

"Daddy," Katie said hesitantly, "would you mind if I called Irwin 'Daddy' too?"

That was a tough one. "Well, I guess — "

"I don't mean to his face. Mommy told me I'm supposed to call him Irwin, and that's okay. But I mean, in school, when I talk about him and Mommy, I feel funny saying my Mommy and *Irwin*. The kids always say 'Who's Irwin?' and then I think I should say, 'My mommy's husband,' or 'My stepfather,' but that sounds weird, like he's, y'know, my 'wicked stepfather'? So, if I could just say daddy, I mean, just in school— "

Jericho took a deep breath. It was always there, waiting to blindside him— the guilt, the self-reproach. He had created this situation; all he could do now was make the best of it.

"You can call him anything you like," he said. "You and I know who your real daddy is, right?"

"Right."

They walked on in silence. Suddenly Katie ran ahead. When Jericho caught up with her, he saw what had captured her attention. A blue crab had been washed up on shore and was flipped over on its carapace. Its snow-white abdomen was etched with the outline of what looked like the dome of the U.S. Capitol building. Its blue-tinged claws were tipped with bright vermilion, which the guy at Duryea's fish market called "nail polish," indicating the creature was a she-crab. Her claws flailed frantically as she attempted to turn herself over.

A woman's voice reverberated inside Jericho's head: "*Por favor ... por favor.*" It became a whimper—high-pitched, magnified many times over, then it turned into a long pitiful keen. He saw the crab's scrabbling limbs clawing helplessly, then transmogrifying into multiple swirling images that inflamed his mind—limbs reaching out, grasping at nothing, seeking purchase in thin air. He felt the blackout coming, the darkness seeping into his brain like a malevolent ink stain.

One step too many. One step too many...

"Daddy. Daddy. What's the matter?"

Katie's voice burst through the impending blackness, calling Jericho back. He fought to shut out the images of desperate, spastic clawing and the high-pitched wail. He managed to force his eyes open, letting in the gray daylight.

"It's nothing, honey," Jericho said. "Daddy just got a speck in his eye. It's all right now. It's out."

"I got scared."

Jericho was scared, too. It was the first flashback he'd had since he viewed the drowned, disfigured woman at Sagg Main Beach. "Nothing to be scared about," he said. "C'mere."

He gathered his daughter to him, smelling the Johnson's baby shampoo in her hair—a scent he remembered from when she was an infant. He held Katie tightly and she clung to him, open, vulnerable, loving. And he prayed nothing would ever come between them, especially the bad things from his past that he'd moved out to Long Island to forget.

CHAPTER 18

The morning fog was beginning to lift at East Hampton Airport. Jessie Russell was hoping for rain, but the National Weather Service had predicted a perfect beach day.

He walked across the tarmac to his airplane, tied down in its parking spot next to the maintenance hangar. There was nobody around, except for Bernie, the flight instructor, who was fueling his dual-control Beechcraft in preparation for a day of teaching nitwits how not to stall during takeoff.

Jessie approached the Super Cub, his hand in the pocket of his blue overalls. When he got to the plane, he walked around it as if doing a morning preflight. He grabbed the rudder with one hand and pulled it to check the hinges. He pulled a box cutter out of his pocket. After a furtive look around, he slashed a six-inch gash in the rudder's fabric skin.

"Ow."

The blade had nicked his thumb as he held the rudder. He checked his wound.

"Aah, it's nothin'. Just a scratch."

He blotted the cut on the bib of his overalls, put the box cutter back in his pocket, and continued around the plane.

Then he went to the office and phoned his boss.

"Mr. Grunfield, I'm sorry but I got bad news. Some birdbrain musta been taxiing on the ramp last night and nicked the rudder of the Cub pretty good. Sliced the skin about six, eight inches."

The expected string of profanities blasted out of Stanley Grunfield's mouth.

"It ain't *my* fault, boss," Jessie interjected. "Look, I'm sorry, but there ain't no way she can fly. The wind'll get in there and tear the rest of the skin right off the rudder."

"Well, patch the sucker," Grunfield shouted.

"That's a tricky job. It should be done by an A&P mechanic."

"*A&P?*" he said incredulously.

"Airframe and powerplant," Jessie explained. He wanted to add 'you ignorant asshole', but didn't. "Kaminicki's licensed. He'll be in soon and I'll put him right on it."

"Will you be able to go up this afternoon?"

"Negative, boss. The patch gotta be sewn on, then a couple layers of butyrate dope have to dry. Can't be ready till tomorrow."

"Jesus Christ, this is a *weekend.*"

"Look, these things happen." Jessie said. "And if you don't mind me sayin', I think you should pay me for the day anyway. It's not my f— "

Grunfield told him to shut the fuck up or he'd shit-can him on the spot. Jessie almost challenged him to do it, but he didn't want to burn his bridges. After all, he'd gotten what he wanted— another day off. Plan B, part 2.

At Gurney's Inn and Health Spa, Susannah was showering after a two-hour treatment called Six Degrees of Relaxation: Thalasso mud therapy, reflexology, scalp massage, skin exfoliation, aromatic herbal rejuvenation, and hot lava stone rub. Gretchen Silverman-Lewis had treated Susannah to the session, saying her friend deserved some relief from the stress she'd been under.

The treatment had soothed away some of Susannah's tension, but the anxiety remained, tugging at her like an annoying child.

She wrapped herself in a towel and went down to the women's Jacuzzi for a soak with Gretchen, who was meeting her there after a facial.

96

When Susannah arrived at the whirlpool area, Gretchen was there alone, immersed in the steaming, bubbling water. She wore a green flowered bathing cap, and her voluminous breasts could be seen rising and falling gently in the foamy currents.

Susannah took off her towel.

"Girlfriend," Gretchen said, admiring her trim body. "You just made me a candidate for total-body liposuction."

Susannah eased herself down into the tub. The steam rose up around her. "Gretchen, thank you so much," she said. "You were right, I needed a little pampering."

"You deserve it."

"How was your facial?" Susannah asked.

"Good."

"Your skin is glowing. In fact, you look radiant."

Gretchen grinned. "That's 'cause I'm sitting on my favorite jet. I call him Throbbin' Robin."

They both laughed.

"So," Gretchen said, "nothing new about Burt, huh?"

"No."

"Y'know, I think you're handling it very well," she said. "I mean, as well as anyone could."

"It's not easy."

"I understand," Gretchen said with compassion. "I have no idea how I'd be if Arnold were suddenly ... not with me.

"You can't know, till it happens."

"Is there anything I can do to help?"

"Actually, there is one thing," Susannah answered. "I met with Burt's lawyer yesterday, and, I dunno, I don't really trust him. I was wondering, do you think Arnold could give me some legal assistance?"

"I'm sure he'd be glad to. I'll speak to him tonight."

"That would be great."

"This lawyer," Gretchen said, "why don't you trust him?"

"Just a feeling," Susannah answered. "I asked him a question about Burt's will and he was sort of evasive."

"You think he's not on the up and up?"

"Exactly. I'm so lucky to have a friend like you."

"Suze. You'll get through this," Gretchen said. "Oh, I wanted to ask you — do you mind if I take some pictures of the kids at your next class? Some of the parents asked me to."

"No problem."

Gretchen heaved herself out of the water. "I better get going. I'm meeting with the Montauk town council. Trying to pry a few bucks out of 'em for our community theater."

"Good luck," Susannah said. "I think I'll percolate here a little longer.

"Slide over a few feet. Throbbin' Robin'll ease your troubled mind."

"I don't think so, Gretch. But thanks. Thanks for everything."

As her friend left, Susannah realized she was now living in an alternate reality, in which sincerity and deceit were conjoined. Her life had become a performance. First she was the frightened wife of a missing husband. Now she was playing a more subtle role—a woman hoping her husband was alive, yet doubting she'd ever see him again. And next? The grieving widow. After that? Who knows?

Suddenly, without thinking, she slid herself down and submerged her head in the heated, churning water. Eyes tightly shut, she heard the pounding of the whirlpool motor and felt the swirling, eddying bubbles rising up and over her, the hot wetness, the pressure, the bursting in her lungs.

This is what Burt must've felt, she thought. *Just before his life was drowned out. Now it's my turn. One deep inhale, my lungs will fill with water, and it'll be over.*

But the life wish took over and she pushed up to the surface, gasping.

98

No, she said to herself. *God has another punishment in mind for me. My penalty for taking a human life is that I'll have to lie, and lie, and lie, and lie. I will never have another honest moment for as long as I live.*

When Susannah went home she checked her e-mail. There was an order confirmation from Amazon.com, six pieces of spam, and an e-mail from her New York friend, Maurizio:

Suze — Good news. I finally got into a company, Deerlake Dance. It's small but they do great work. Google them. XXX OOO M.

Online, she read: *Through their daring, athletic movement and integration of ballet and modern vocabularies, DeerLake dancers take audiences on a choreographic exploration of the infinite possibilities of movement and multimedia.*

Susannah felt a pang of regret for leaving the city and giving up any chance of doing what she loved. Teaching dance was fine, but still...

On an impulse she typed *Burton Cascadden* into Google. Up came a link to the East Hampton *Star* with a news story from five years back. The headline read: MONTAUK WOMAN KILLED IN FALL. The article reported that *"Carol Cascadden, age twenty-five, wife of realtor Burton Lloyd Cascadden of 67 East Dune Way, had fallen from the Ditch Plains cliffs onto the rocky beach below. Her husband said she often jogged on a path along the cliffs, because she loved the view. Police noted that the edge of the sandstone cliff had crumbled above where she fell, and surmised she had ventured too close to the edge and plummeted to her death. Investigators ruled her death an accident."*

Jesus, she thought, *that hitman—what's his name? Mort—is a real pro.* Susannah pictured the terrible fate that awaited her, had she not taken action.

Maybe God won't be so harsh with me on this. I mean, if ever a homicide was justifiable, this sure as hell was.

She was about to log off when she got an idea. Maybe Google could tell her the meaning of the perplexing entry she'd found in Burt's address book. She typed in the words *"Ubaf Sing A-be-deghi"* and waited. A screen popped up saying: *"Your search – Ubaf Sing A-be-deghi did not match any documents. Suggestion: Try fewer keywords."*

She tried "*Ubaf*" alone. Instantly she was sent to a site which read: "*UBAF — Union De Banques Arabes Et Francaises Offices - Suntec Tower 2, 9 Temasek Boulevard, Singapore 038986*"

The bank advertised itself as "*The Perfect Environment for Cultured Private Banking*".

Whoa, she said to herself. *An off-shore bank account in Singapore. That would be just like Burt. Wonder how much money he'd socked away? And what does "A-be-deghi" mean? Is it somebody's name? Something in a foreign language? What language do they speak in Singapore?*

Wikipedia told her: English, Chinese, Malaysian, and Tamil.

What the hell is Tamil?

She went to Online Translation — Tamil to English, Malaysian to English.

She entered *A-be-deghi* in each language, but got nothing.

Chinese to English required logographic characters rather that alphabetic script, so she couldn't check that out.

The Internet was finished helping her.

CHAPTER 19

At seven AM every weekday morning, about fifty undocumented Latino workers congregate at Industrial Road near East Hampton airport, hoping to find jobs as day laborers. For years they had assembled daily at the East Hampton railroad station, till the town board, responding to complaints from residents that these scruffy *peons* were an eyesore, ordered the police to chase them off.

As citizens they would have protested, citing their Constitutional right to free assembly. But as illegal aliens, they avoided the police at all costs, even failing to report crimes against them. Fear of deportation dominated their lives.

So they'd found a less conspicuous place. Lined up in front of a junkyard fence, they were now waiting like mendicants, hoping a Spanish-speaking contractor would choose some of them to board his truck and spend the day working on a construction site. The housing bubble having long burst, this morning only six of them were needed.

Mort drove up in a rented Buick, got out and approached the men. He wore jeans and a safari jacket and had a back pack and binoculars slung over his shoulder.

"Yo necesito un hombre!", Mort shouted.

Immediately he was surrounded by desperate day workers, offering their services with pleas, hopeful grins, and tearful stories; every entreaty punctuated with the word *"trabajo!"*

Mort eyed the workers, then focused on a tall, solidly built young man, with black hair tied in a scraggly ponytail.

"Como se llama usted?"

"Jesús Castillo Cardoz..."

"Jesus!", Mort interrupted, saying to himself — *I fucking love it!*

"Soy un observador de aves," Mort said. *"Necesito un asisente para el dia, para levar mi equipe. Se paga cincuente dolares."*

"Soy su hombre!" said Jesús, thrilled to be getting fifty bucks for a day of carrying this bird-watcher's camera equipment.

"El equipo es muy pesado."

"Soy muy fuerte," Jesús boasted, flexing his arms.

Mort took off his backpack and handed it to his eager porter. He slung it on his back with ease.

"Vamos!" Mort said, leading the man to his car. Jesús gave a thumbs-up sign to his envious *compadres*, as he got into the Buick.

Camp Hero, just west of the Montauk lighthouse, is a decommissioned and abandoned military base that is now a state park. It was set up during WWII to counter the threat of invasion from Nazi submarines and possible air strikes.

Later, it reputedly played a role in a government conspiracy involving the Montauk Project and the Philadelphia Experiment—which included efforts to render an enemy warship invisible, electronic waves that could cause psychotic symptoms in anyone they struck, and teleportation: the transfer of matter from one point to another without traversing the physical space between them. Hikers who explore the site during the summer are inevitably struck by the creepy, otherworldly atmosphere of the place.

Mort parked on Camp Hero Road. The park was now closed for the season, so it was unguarded and easy to access.

He took out a State Park map. It had a trail delineated on it by a yellow Magic Marker, which his client had instructed him to follow.

Jesús, now carrying Mort's backpack, followed him along Battery 112 Trail, through dense woods, crossing over streams with busted wooden bridges and torn-down, rusty chicken-wire fences. After a twenty-minute hike, they came to two old gun embankments, which housed immense cannons, now blocked with concrete. Looming before them was the iconic radar dish tower, which can be seen from miles out in the coastal waters.

They followed a trail further into the woods. Jesús stopped when he saw a posted sign reading "Danger", and a word he did not understand

"*Peligro!*" he exclaimed.

"*Si, ten cuidado,*" Mort said calmly. "*Se dice hay arenas movedizas aqui. Quédese en el camino.*"

Jesús nodded. He had no intention of venturing off the path and sinking into quicksand.

Suddenly Mort grabbed his binoculars and peered up at the trees.

"Look. A Cooper's hawk!"

"*Como?*"

Mort pointed upwards. "*Un halcón muy raro!*"

He handed the binoculars to Jesús who excitedly scanned the trees above him.

Jesús heard a muffled explosion, but his brain was dead before it could process the information. One moment he was alive, the next moment he simply was not.

Mort had blasted a hole in the base of his skull with a silencer-equipped 50 caliber Glock. The bullet pierced the cerebellum and lodged in the medulla oblongata, causing what medical examiners call "severe brain insult." Jesús fell face down in the dirt.

Mort ripped the backpack off his victim and pulled out a plastic tarp. He rolled Jesús onto the tarp and then took out a cloth napkin and unwrapped a surgeon's scalpel. This wasn't his usual modus operandi, but the client had requested it and paid handsomely.

He took out a painter's smock and put it on.

Mort tested the scalpel's sharpness with his fingertip, then snapped on pair of latex gloves and bent down to start his gruesome task.

When he was done, he wrapped the remains and the knife in the tarp and dragged it off the trail to the nearby quicksand bog. He rolled the bundle of corpse, napkin, and cutlery into the mud and watched it sink slowly into the slimy depths.

As Jesús disappeared, Mort made the sign of the cross and quietly crooned Johann Sebastian Bach's poignant cantata: *"Jesu, joy of man's desiring."*

CHAPTER 20

Out on the sundeck Susannah was pushing her bikini-clad body through Martha Graham's classic floor exercises.

On her Ipod she'd downloaded four slow sections of Aaron Copland's "Appalachian Spring". She was playing the music on her wireless speakers, working unhurriedly, experiencing her whole body while breathing slowly and deeply. This workout had always been Susannah's way of relieving stress and enhancing self-awareness.

She was almost finished, kneeling on the mat, eyes closed. The music was in the finale section, marked "*Moderato (like a prayer)*". Exhaling, she performed the contraction, her pelvis back and her spine curving in. Then she inhaled into the release, her pelvis thrusting forward and her spine lengthening skyward.

The strings played in the low register, signaling the end of the piece. The music was mournful yet peaceful, as if portraying death as a natural occurrence, more to be reverenced than feared.

Susannah allowed her body to sink back on the mat as she extended her legs, face up to the afternoon sun. She felt the warmth soothing her skin, and through her closed eyelids she saw the intense orange glow of sunlight. Shapeless floaters swam in her field of vision as the last notes of a silvery flute faded away.

Suddenly the bright orange was eclipsed and she heard the sound of handclaps. Susannah opened her eyes to see a male figure looming above her. She sat up, instinctively grabbing a towel to cover herself.

"Damn good show, Blondie," Jessie said laughing. Susannah saw his dark face, his hooked nose, and his brown overalls. She jumped to her feet, clutching the towel to her.

"What do you want?"

"Hey, honey. Don't panic. I ain't here to hurt ya."

"I'm warning you. Get off my deck or I'll call the police."

"I told you," the man said. "I ain't gonna hurt ya. I'm a member of the Native American Charity Committee — Shinnecock Tribe. I'm just here askin' for a small contribution."

"I don't have any cash in the house. Give me an address and I'll send you a check."

"Yeah, yeah, I get that all the time. Y'know, you people oughta take responsibility. After all, not so long ago all this here land belonged to the Shinnecock Indian Nation. Now ya got us jammed up in a crummy reservation in Southampton, while you're livin' high on the hog. I'm just lookin' for a little justice."

"I'm asking you nicely to leave," Susannah said as calmly as she could. "My husband will be home soon and— "

"I don't believe that," he said, laughing. "Y'know, I get the feelin' you're afraid of me. Are you afraid of me, huh? Look at me. Do I look scary?"

"All right," she said. "I'll go inside, see what I've got in my purse. You wait out here."

"Oh, no," Jessie said. "I know what you're gonna do. You'll go inside and lock the door. Then you'll call 911 and tell 'em there's an Indian outside harassing you.

No. No. I'll end up in the slammer just for tryin' to help my people."

"Well, I'm certainly not going inside with you."

"Honey, if I wanted to hurt you I could just as easily do it out here. There's nobody around. Guess you bought this house for the privacy, and you sure as hell got it."

Jessie watched the fear twisting Susannah's face. She backed away from him.

"Hold up, lady," he said, adopting a more genial tone. "We seem to've got off on the wrong foot here. Just lemme show you some pictures. You take a look at 'em and if they don't make you want to make a contribution, I'll be on my way. Deal?"

"Okay. Fine."

Jessie unsnapped the bib pocket of his overalls and took out a piece of glossy photographic paper. He looked at it for a moment, shaking his head sadly.

"These pictures are gonna break your heart," he said as he handed her the photos.

She looked at the contact sheet, twenty-four photographs showing, frame by frame, Susannah's killing of Burt. For a moment she stared at the pictures in shock. Then a wave of dizziness swept over her. She reeled backward, till she felt the bronze Krishna statue and grabbed onto it for support.

"Where—where did you get these?"

"Took 'em myself," Jessie said proudly. "It's my hobby—art photography. Developed and printed 'em in my home darkroom. Pretty good resolution and depth of field, don't ya think?"

"What do you want?"

"Like I told ya. A contribution."

Susannah studied him, her mind working. *How can I deal with this man? Is there a way out?*

"How much do you want?"

"Well, Blondie, I figure the rich fuck you married was worth millions, but I ain't greedy, so I'll settle for two hundred and fifty thousand."

"I can't get my hands on that kind of money."

"Then the police get their hands on these pictures."

Immediately Susannah saw the trap. There'd never be an end to it. Even if she bought the negatives, the blackmailer could always save other prints.

God, what can I do? Time. That's it. Gotta stall him till I can figure something out.

"Everything's in my husband's name," she said. "I won't have access to his money until his will is probated."

"Not my problem. I'm sure you can raise it, borrow it, whatever."

Susannah thought of the $60,000 in Burt's desk. She could pay him something now and promise more to come. But she was afraid to go into the house with him there. What if he followed, forced his way in? It was too dangerous.

"All right, listen," she said, looking at her watch. "I've got $10,000 in a bank safe deposit box. I'll go get it now, before the bank closes. Why don't you come back at four and I'll give you the cash."

"I want quarter of a million."

"Okay. But that'll take some time. This'll be a down payment."

Jessie thought it over. Ten grand was a nice taste to start with. He had himself a cash cow—he'd be milkin' her for years. No sense pushing it. Besides, he didn't want her to get too pissed off, because the truth was—he liked her.

"Okay, honey," he said in a reasonable tone. "I accept your offer."

"Good. See you at four then. Meanwhile, I'll start figuring how I can get more. And we'll work out a payment schedule."

"All right," he said smiling. Then his expression darkened. "Listen, you're not gonna try any funny business, are you?"

"You've got the pictures. What can I do?"

"That's right. And the negatives are in a place where the cops'll find 'em if you try to pull somethin'."

He grinned, turned, and walked a few steps toward the stairs to the beach. Then he stopped and came back.

"Tell you what. Why don't you give me a little on account?"

"On account?"

108

He took a step toward her. "On accounta right now I'm real horny."

He reached out a hand and touched Susannah's cheek. Reflexively her right arm shot up and swatted his hand away. He smiled and reached out again. Once more her arm swung out, rejecting him.

Jessie's other hand rocked her with a backhanded slap. Pain flared into her eye socket and along her jawbone. She backed away, rage boiling inside her.

He was on her, with his foul tobacco breath, his mouth on her tightly closed lips, his tongue flicking in and out like a lizard's, trying to force entry,

Susannah struggled to push him away but he held her vise-like, pinning her arms to her sides. He backed her up against the concrete wall of the house. She felt the coarse fabric of his overalls on her bare thighs, the bib buttons scraping her chest, the bulge of his arrogant hard-on grinding into her.

His fingers hooked her bikini top and tugged. She felt the horror of forced nakedness as the lizard-like tongue lapped at her bare breasts; then the mouth took a nipple, suctioning with cruel force.

Susannah wrenched her hands free and raked her nails down her attacker's cheeks. He yanked his face away, yowling in pain. Then he drove a fist hard into her belly. He stepped back as she doubled over, clutching her gut.

He got behind Susannah and seized her under the armpits.

Susannah could feel herself being dragged along the teak deck, then the padded thickness of the mat sliding under her back. She looked up and saw the rapist fumbling with the metal buttons on his fly.

"Wait a minute," she said, trying to catch her breath.

He stopped and looked at her.

"Look," she said. "I don't want to fight you any more. There's an old saying: 'If rape is inevitable, you might as well enjoy it.'"

She gave him a seductive, inviting smile. "So if we're gonna do it, at least let's do it right. Take off your overalls so I don't have those damn buttons digging into me."

"Okay, Blondie," he said, kicking off his shoes. "Any way you want it."

He unhooked the straps on the bib, then started on the side buttons at his waist.

He dropped his overalls, stepped out of them, then took off his white undershirt. Grinning, he slid down his jockey briefs and she saw his jutting erection spring up, swaying slightly as he moved.

"Some folks call us the Skinnycocks," he said, "but you can see ain't no truth to it."

She faked a smile. With his black socks on, he looked like an actor in an old time porn flick.

"Why doncha slip off them panties, darlin'?" he said. "Show me the gateway to heaven."

"Why doncha slip 'em off for me?"

He straddled Susannah and bent over to grab her bikini bottom. With lightning suddenness she brought her knees to her chest, then kicked forward with her powerful dancer's legs.

Jessie lurched backward, and in the same moment Susannah jumped up and ran to the sliding glass door of the deck. She heard a loud clanging sound as she entered the house. She slid the door closed and locked the latch.

She peered back through the glass door. Her assailant looked very odd, — naked and upright in a contorted position, leaning back in the arms of the bronze Krishna statue. His head was tilted at a freakish angle. Blood streamed down his cheeks from where she'd scratched him.

Susannah expected him to push off the statue, rush at her, and yank at the door handle. But he didn't move. His penis had shrunk and was now cringing within its nest of black groin hair. He wouldn't be using it any more. The rapist had cracked his skull on Lord Krishna. He was dead.

My God, I've just killed another man, Susannah thought. *What have I become?*

She felt tears coming, but stifled them with an effort of will.

Don't lose it, girl, she told herself. *This is no time for panic or self-pity. There's too much at stake.*

There's no sense calling the police—not if that pig had left incriminating negatives where the cops could find them.

She had to get rid of the body.

She'd do what she did with Burt drag him down to the ocean and let the riptide take him.

Jesus, she thought, shaking her head. *I'm getting to be an old hand at this.*

Susannah picked up her attacker's overalls and looked through the pockets. There was a wallet containing a driver's license, a pilot's license, and an East Hampton Airport ID card: *Jessie Russell, Grogan's Cabins, Unit 3, 631 West Lake Drive, Montauk, L.I.* There was a key ring with car keys and what looked like house keys. Also half a pack of Camels, a matchbook with "Liar's Saloon" printed on its cover, and twelve bucks.

As she lowered the corpse to the deck, she saw the deep, bloody gash in his skull where it had smashed into the statue. Jessie's fresh, red blood had dripped down, staining the bronze avatar and the teakwood beneath him.

She would have to remember to hose down the deck and the statue thoroughly. *Do not,* she told herself sternly, *forget like you did with the track in the sand.*

There were scratch marks on his cheeks, which might look suspicious if his body were found, but they could easily be attributed to rocks, crabs, or whatever.

On his wrist was a Timex. It was waterproof, so she didn't remove it — if he went swimming he would probably keep it on.

She realized she'd have to put the man's underpants back on. If later the body washed up on shore, it would have to look like an accidental drowning; skinny-dipping was not common in these parts. Besides, she didn't want to look at his thing.

She laid him out on his back and picked up his briefs. They were inside out and there was a brown stain in the crotch.

"Shit," she said, aware of the double meaning. Then, averting her eyes, she pulled the underwear up around his waist. She removed his socks and put them next to his shoes.

After making sure the beach was empty, she dragged the body down the stairs to the dunes. His head slammed violently into each step as she descended, giving her a strange sense of satisfaction, as if it were additional punishment for that vicious bastard. She started pulling him toward the ocean. As she did, she noticed she was again leaving a tell tail track in the sand. And in that track were spatters of his blood.

She started out dragging Jessie by his feet, her back to the sea. But that forced her to look at him, so she turned around to face the ocean, and pulled him behind her.

Jessie was heavy. His dead weight was lighter than Burt's, but she'd been punched hard in the abdomen and the pain sapped her strength.

Often she had to stop and rest. And each time she looked up and down the beach, praying no beach walker would come strolling by.

Finally she got Jessie's body into the surf, which was relatively calm this afternoon. She waded into the water till she could feel the tug of the undertow. She let go of the body and it was soon caught in the rip current and sucked away.

Susannah walked back onto the beach, peeling slithery gray-green kelp off her hands and arms. She kicked sand over the blood-spotted track made by the dead body as she returned to the house. There she turned on the deck hose and sprayed it forcefully on the statue of Lord Krishna.

She watched as the water diluted the blood on the bronze avatar and drained onto the deck. For a moment Krishna's eyes seemed to be dripping tears, though his lips still showed his classic benign smile. Suddenly, Susannah could no longer hold back her own tears, and she just let go. She sat down, hands covering her face, and wept uncontrollably. She cried until there were no tears left.

Crying solved nothing, but it was cathartic enough so that she could face with clarity what she had to do next.

CHAPTER 21

Jericho was at his desk, typing up his notes on the Cascadden case.

Toward the end of his NYPD days he'd become remiss at doing his paper work during investigations. He'd been written up several times for not having adequate documentation. The result was that some of his arrests ended in non-convictions. He was deeply ashamed about that.

Now he was diligent about writing everything down. And the process actually helped clarify his thinking.

He was at a section captioned "Cascadden Disappearance — Possibilities":

Cascadden was surf-fishing, ventured too far out in the ocean, got caught in the rip current and drowned. Accidental death.

Cascadden faked his death to avoid exposure of shady business dealings, or debts he didn't wish to pay. Or he ran off with another woman.

Cascadden was murdered. Possible but not probable at this point in the investigation. No suspects except maybe his wife, which doesn't seem likely. Motive? There may have been problems in the marriage, so his wife could have a motive, but so far nothing points to that. Better: Cascadden's business dealings undoubtedly resulted in making many enemies, people who'd be angry at him. That should be explored...

Jericho's phone rang. The desk sergeant said there was a Mr. Conforti to see him.

"Who?"

"Conforti. Says he's the football coach out at the high school."

"Oh, yeah. All right, send him in."

Coach Conforti appeared a few moments later. He had a canceled check in his hand.

"Hiya, Detective Jericho. Here it is, like I promised. Five hundred bucks made out to Doctor's Without Borders."

"That's good, Coach. How's the season going?"

"We lost our opener to Christ the King."

"Guess they have friends in high places."

The coach missed the joke completely. "But I'm sure we're gonna whup Southampton."

"Don't forget to set your tight end as a slot receiver and hit him over the middle." Jericho said. "It's the easiest first down in football and it's the most overlooked."

The coach looked impressed, as if Jericho were Vince Lombardi.

"Now, you'll have to excuse me," Jericho said. "I've got a ton of work."

"Okay. Listen, do you know Officer Karlin?"

Teddy Karlin, Jericho thought. *There are a lot of numbskulls on the force, but Karlin is definitely in the highest percentile."*

"Yes, I know him."

"Is he around?"

"He has the day shift," Jericho said. "So he'd be out on patrol."

"Too bad. I wanted to thank him in person."

"For what?"

"Somebody stole a Jeep Wrangler," the coach said. "It belonged to one of my players—Randy Cohen. Karlin found it. It was abandoned in the town lot. Y'know, off Edgemere Avenue?"

"Where was it stolen?"

114

"Montauk. North Beach. Randy and his pal were spear-fishing in the afternoon. When they came out of the water, the car was gone, along with their clothes, wallets, and money. Figure somebody was walkin' on the beach, saw the car and their stuff and just took off with it."

"When did this happen?"

"A few days ago. I don't remember the exact date. Anyway, when you see Karlin, tell him Coach Conforti said thanks. He used to play for me."

"What position?"

"He was the holder for the place kicker—till he busted a finger."

"Sounds like Karlin. I'll tell him."

"Okay. See ya, detective."

Jericho went to the Case File Room. He rummaged through the Auto Theft files and found R. Cohen. The theft was reported at 4:05 p.m. on September 17, the same day Burt Cascadden drowned.

Karlin, you schmuck, he thought. *Why the hell didn't you tell me about this? Didn't it occur to you it might be connected to Burt Cascadden's disappearance? This could validate the theory that Cascadden faked his own death. But hold on. If he faked his death, he'd have planned carefully — had his own car and clothing waiting for him. He couldn't count on someone else's Jeep and clothes being parked on the beach.*

But knowing Karlin, he might've written down the wrong date.

He copied Randy Cohen's phone number from the report, and called him. The young man confirmed that his Jeep was stolen on the date specified.

Jericho returned to writing out his notes. He typed in the data on the stolen Jeep, and at the end he wrote:

Logically it doesn't seem like the Jeep is related to Cascadden's disappearance. But... on the same beach, and on the same afternoon?

CHAPTER 22

Susannah spent the rest of the day devising her plan. Her first goal was to get the negatives and any other prints Jessie had. She was hoping he kept all the damning evidence in his home, so she faced the critical problem of how to get into his apartment. She hoped nobody would be there. She doubted he lived with a woman, because no female could abide those shitty underpants, and besides, he didn't seem the type. Maybe a roommate. Hopefully not.

The next step would be to leave Jessie's belongings on the beach that night, to suggest he'd stripped to go swimming and drowned. But Susannah noticed a few blood spatters on Jessie's brown overalls. Blood on his clothing might suggest foul play, so she decided to pour Shout on the blood stains, dump the pants in her washing machine, then put them in the dryer while she went to retrieve the negatives.

The other issue was Jessie's car, a 1999 teal Hyundai Elantra, which he'd parked outside her home. Another accidental drowning on her own beach would look suspicious, so she decided to drive the Hyundai the five miles to the beach at Montauk Point, plant Jessie's clothing and personal effects on the beach, and then walk back to her house along the shore — only a two-mile stretch.

Susannah drove her BMW SUV along the dark road. West Lake Drive had no streetlamps and she flicked on her high beams to illuminate the road.

Up ahead she saw a lighted sign for Sportsman's Dock Marina. When she got closer, she could read the letters below it: Grogan's Cabins — 1 BR Efficiencies — Cable TV. No Vacancy.

She parked her car behind some trees near the marina's entrance. Her apparel was the same color as her car; black pants, shirt, and sneakers, black bandanna covering her blond hair. She carried a dance bag containing a Mag-Lite flashlight with new batteries.

She slipped on a pair of latex gloves to avoid leaving fingerprints.

The night was quiet except for the relentless shrill of cicadas. Susannah was breathing hard, her stomach doing flip-flops. *If somebody catches me, I have no excuse for why I'm prowling around here. And if I don't get those prints and negatives, the police will find them and I'll be finished.*

From the marina entrance, she saw a red neon sign reading "Liar's Saloon." The bass thump echoed from the bar's jukebox, and she could hear men's raucous laughter.

The parking area was deserted. She moved toward the cabins. Units 1 and 2 had lights on inside. She went around behind them and saw two more units. Both of them were dark. She turned on her flashlight, which lit up Unit 3.

I'd better knock, she thought. *Maybe someone's in there sleeping. If there is, I'll just have to split.*

She rapped tentatively on the door. No response. She knocked a little harder. Still nothing. On the key ring were two latch keys. She hesitated, fear gripping her.

Well, no guts, no glory.

The first key she tried didn't fit, but the second one did. She eased the door open and shone her flashlight around the darkened room. Nobody. She slipped inside and closed the door.

"Hello?" she whispered. She had no idea what she would say if someone answered. No one did.

She looked around the cabin, but it was hopeless trying to explore a dark unfamiliar space by flashlight.

118

She looked back at the door. Next to it was a window, partly covered by a Venetian blind. She had to take a chance. She lowered the blinds and flipped a wall switch. A ceramic table lamp and tilted torchiere popped on.

The living room was a lot neater than she'd expected; she figured the guy had to live in a shit hole. But except for some dirty clothes lying around, there was a sense of order. The furniture was worn but decent — lanai-style bamboo couch and chairs. At one end of the room was a Pullman kitchen with a Formica table; on the table was a Dell laptop. The sink contained a half-full coffee mug; the drainer held clean Melmac dishes.

The bathroom door was open; across from it was a door that was locked. Susannah tried the second key on Jessie's ring and the door swung open. It was a bedroom with a single window. The shade was drawn so Susannah turned on the light.

The walls were covered with framed photographs, black-and-white shots of naked and half-naked women, all lying on the beach. *Oh, my God,* thought Susannah. *So this is what that creep was up to. It looks like the shots were taken from above. He had a pilot's license, so he must've taken them from a plane, with a telephoto lens.*

She looked at the pictures one by one. The women were an odd collection of shapes and sizes, and there were no rear views. Obviously the pig wasn't concerned about beauty; all he wanted was breasts, thighs, bellies, and vaginas.

Susannah saw no photos of herself. On the dresser she noticed a cardboard Pendaflex file box. It contained hanging file folders, all neatly labeled with dates. Each held prints of nude women, and negatives stored in glassine envelopes.

At the back of the file box she found his latest folder. It had a contact sheet that was identical to the one Jessie had shown her earlier that day, but the negatives were not in the file.

It was obvious these pictures weren't taken from a plane. She surmised Jessie must've hidden near her house to get them. She pulled out the whole file folder and stuck it in her dance bag.

To be on the safe side, Susannah looked in the bureau drawers, in the wastebasket, and even under the bed. There were no more prints.

She went into the bathroom and turned on the light. The entire room glowed red from a bulb that seemed to be floating in air. The place was set up with equipment for developing and printing. She turned off the light and tried another switch. A fluorescent light flickered on.

She spotted a strip of negatives dangling from a clip on the shower rod. She held it up to the light and saw the incriminating shots. Elated, she rolled up the negatives and put them in her bag.

There was a banging on the cabin door.

"Hey, Jessie," someone yelled.

Susannah froze. It was a man's voice, slurred with alcohol. "Quit jerkin' off in there and open the fuck up." He pounded on the door again.

Then another male voice: "He's probably workin' in the darkroom. Let's go."

"Jess," the first guy yelled. "C'mon have a beer with us. We're goin' to the Liar's."

"Forget it, Norm."

"I bet he's in there spankin' the monkey," Norm said, lowering his voice. "Let's go in and catch him in the act. It'll be fuckin' hilarious."

Susannah heard the doorknob rattling. She tried to figure out where to hide.

"Damn. The door's locked."

"Norm," the other man said with annoyance. "Let him be."

The bedroom, Susannah thought. *Under the bed.*

She started to make her way to the bedroom. Then she heard Norm's voice. "I can open it with a credit card," he said. "Watch this."

Panic gripped Susannah. She retreated to the bathroom, slid behind the open door, and flattened herself against the wall.

"Screw it, Norm. Let's go. If he wants to join us later, he will."

"...Okay. Okay. You're a goddamn killjoy, ya know that?"

The voices trailed off as the men walked away. Susannah's heart was pounding. She sat down on the toilet seat, hyperventilating. It took her a while to calm down. Finally she wiped her sweating brow on her sleeve and stood up. She had to keep going.

120

In the darkroom's trash can she found another copy of the contact sheet with the photos of her. The images were washed out, underexposed in printing. She shoved the sheet into her bag, then combed the whole darkroom. There were no other prints or negatives anywhere.

On the floor was a bright yellow shopping bag with art deco lettering: East Hampton Camera Shop. It contained only a receipt for something called stop bath.

She searched the living room and kitchen. Satisfied she'd gotten everything, Susannah turned off the lights and restored the blinds to their former position. She opened the front door and peeped out. Nobody.

Susannah shut the door behind her and ripped the latex gloves off her sweating hands.

For a brief moment her tension subsided, but then the anxiety returned. There was so much more to be done.

CHAPTER 23

That night Jericho was at home on his computer, researching Burt Cascadden. He hoped to find out who his enemies were — people who might possibly want him dead.

A Google search brought up a number of news articles on Cascadden, mostly in *"The Real Deal"*, a New York City Real Estate magazine. The Bridgeview project in Brooklyn was often covered. Early articles were positive, but the most recent press was completely negative. Burt was never interviewed. Instead, his attorney, H. Quinn Healey Esq. was always his spokesman.

Healy? He must be the family lawyer Susannah mentioned in her voicemail.

Jericho decided to check Healey out on Martindale-Hubbell, an online site that gives peer ratings for all attorneys. The detective had used it occasionally in NYC, when he believed a suspect's lawyer was shady or underhanded. The site would reveal if an attorney had any ethical problems in his past.

He typed in *Martindale-Hubbell.com* and the page came up. He entered "H. Quinn Healey" pressed Search, and the screen displayed his name and rating: *Substandard — 2.0 out of 5*. He hit *"more information"* and saw a list of "Lawyers publicly censured by the Tennessee Supreme Court, as reported by the Tennessee Board of Professional Responsibility." He clicked on the hyperlink and found a page that read:

Herrold QUINN HEALEY of Memphis was publicly censured on April 7, 2002 for violating DR 1-102; DR 5-103, DR 7-102; and DR 9-102.

Healey was found guilty by the hearing panel of overdrawing his client's estate account and co-mingling personal and operating funds within. He also knowingly delayed payment of a settlement involving a client's personal injury case for several years, and misappropriated those funds for his own use.

Mitigating factors were Healey's unsullied reputation up to this point, his standing in the community, and his acknowledgment of guilt.

The Board determined a public censure was appropriate and no objection was filed by Healey.

Counselor H. Quinn Healey is clearly a slime ball, Jericho considered. *Does Susannah Cascadden know that? If she does, why is she going to him for help? If she doesn't, he could be trouble for her. If her husband is deceased, there'd surely be a will. Though Burt was in financial trouble, there'd certainly be assets Susannah would be entitled to. Maybe I should warn her. Or should I stay out of it?*

Regardless, Healey is someone I need to investigate further

CHAPTER 24

Back at her house, Susannah put on her gloves again and pulled Jessie's overalls out of the dryer. She noticed they looked too neat and clean, like they hadn't been worn. For a touch of realism, she wrinkled the overalls, brought them out to Jessie's Hyundai and rubbed them with dirt from the floor mats.

In the front seat were two cans of Bud Lite. In the back seat, Susannah saw three Ring Dings—one half-eaten—and a dirty towel.

She went back to house and returned with the rest of Jessie's clothing, plus his keys and her flashlight. Then she drove off into the night.

Montauk Point Lighthouse is up on a high hill. Its 2.5 million candlepower beacon revolves every five seconds and can be seen even in the brightest sunlight for nineteen nautical miles. On a clear night it reaches even further.

Below the lighthouse there are three distinct coastal formations. To the south is Turtle Cove, a sandy beach that is popular with bathers and surfers. The area directly under the lighthouse is a slope, terraced with huge piled-up boulders, a man-made buttress against the pounding of the surf. To the north is a flat beach covered with rocks, pebbles, and shells, which curves around past False Point and turns sandy as it reaches the Cascadden beach house. The north beach is unsuitable for swimming, but surfcasters and spear-gun-toting scuba divers love to fish its rocky waters for striped bass.

As Susannah drove Jessie's Hyundai up the hill, she could see the sweeping beam of the lighthouse beacon piercing the night sky. Her headlights illuminated a sign: *Montauk State Park — Surf Fishing Capital of the world.*

She crested the hill and saw an arrow indicating the Public Parking Lot. Opposite was another sign: *Beach Service Road — Maintenance Vehicles Only.* She swung the Hyundai onto the service road and followed its heat-cracked, bumpy macadam down the hill to Turtle Cove.

Susannah looked up and saw the moon. It was intermittently obscured by passing clouds, but there was enough light to see. Exiting the car, she trudged across the sand, carrying Jessie's clothing and the soiled towel. She put Jessie's things far back from the waterline, so they wouldn't get swept away if the tide came in.

She returned to the Hyundai and set Jessie's shoes and socks on the ground next to the car. She left his wallet and the Ring Dings in the backseat. Seeing the two cans of beer, she considered half-emptying one and putting it on the front seat, to suggest Jessie had been drinking before he went swimming.

No, she thought. *If the body washes up and it's autopsied, the medical examiner won't find alcohol in his system and he'll become suspicious.*

Then it hit her: *If his body washes up, it won't look like he drowned. His lungs will not be filled with seawater. Oh, no.*

Wait, it doesn't matter — even if the police suspect he was murdered, there'll be no connection to me. I got all the prints and negatives — I hope!

God, what if I make a mistake? I can't think of everything. And if that detective is assigned to the case...

Susannah nervously walked back up the service road. When she reached the main road, she followed it past the lighthouse and over to the snack bar and souvenir shop. She'd been there before, so she knew her way down to the north beach. She found the sandy path, but as she descended she stopped, startled by an eerie squeaking sound. She looked around and saw a children's play area, with a swing noisily swaying back

126

and forth in the breeze. A cloud passed in front of the moon, and it was suddenly pitch black.

In the total darkness, she began trembling. She felt like a helpless little girl, trapped in a lightless room, where bad things, terrible things could happen to her. Her breathing turned ragged.

Breathe. Breathe. Take deep breaths.

Slowly the panic subsided.

She reluctantly turned on her Mag-Lite and made her way down to the beach.

When she reached the beach, the cloud had passed and the moon lit her way again. But the sky was clouding over. She would have to rely on her flashlight.

The beach was so covered with rocks, stones, and shells that it was difficult to walk on. But in front of the dunes, along the thick, brambly brush, was a sandy trail, created by the 4x4's, dune buggies, and hikers that traversed the beach all summer. That would be her way home.

Susannah looked at her watch. It was 10:25 p.m. Her place was a couple of miles away; she could probably get there in under an hour.

She began her trek. For about forty minutes she made steady progress, despite the pesky insects, the horseshoe crabs, and the thorny plants that grew in the underbrush.

Then she reached a dark section of beach and heard the crashing of waves. She realized she'd made a critical mistake: the tide! It was coming in fast, and water was swirling around the natural rock barrier that kept people away from her own private beach.

Going back to the lighthouse would take forty minutes, and then she'd have to walk five miles along the highway to get to her house. That was not an option. Not only was she getting tired, but if she was spotted walking on that dark road in the dead of night, how could she explain it?

The thick undergrowth on the dunes precluded walking around the rocks. She considered jumping into the ocean and attempting to swim, but she knew she'd be pulled out to sea by the current. And she didn't want to wait the tide out, because it could be as much as six hours before it receded enough. Six hours on that bug-infested, crab-ridden beach? No way. She had to try to make it through on foot.

Susannah stepped cautiously into the churning water. She felt the slippery rocks under her sneakers. She began taking small steps, feeling around for solid footing as she went. She trained the flashlight on the water to pick up any large rocks that might impede her. Her ankle twisted when she slipped on some slick stones, but she was able to shift her weight and avoid a sprain.

A surging wave leaped out of the night and knocked her legs out from under her. She fell backward into the swirling water. Her flashlight flew out of her hands and disappeared, leaving Susannah in darkness. In the grip of the rip current, she was being pulled relentlessly toward the open sea. It was as if the deep had decided to claim her, as punishment for her evil deeds.

Then, with a sudden change of heart, the ocean receded and released her. Susannah struggled onto her hands and knees and tried to orient herself. In the distance she could see the lighthouse beam sweeping through the sky. She turned in the opposite direction, and after a few moments she could make out a twinkling light off in the distance; it had to be her house. Thank God she'd left the deck light on.

She felt a slicing pain in the palm of her left hand and knew she'd cut it on the sharp edge of a rock. It was clear — the safest way to move forward now was by crawling. Only a low center of gravity could keep her from losing her balance. She reached in her pocket and pulled out her latex gloves. They might make her grip more slippery but hopefully they'd prevent her hands from getting further lacerated.

Keeping her eyes on the beacon of her deck light, she moved forward once more, crawling, dragging herself along, battling the rocks and the waves. Her hand stung, her belly still ached from Jessie's punch, and her strength was failing. Still she persevered.

At last she felt a smooth surface under her hands and knees. It was soft wet sand, devoid of rocks and pebbles. She rose to her feet. Her house was now visible on the dunes only a few hundred yards away.

Susannah stood up and walked to the house. As she climbed the deck steps she saw the statue of the flute-playing Krishna. For a startling moment she thought she heard him playing his flute. But it was just the wind.

Susannah took a hot shower and put a Band-Aid on her hand. Dressed in a bathrobe, she went out to the living room bar and poured herself a large snifter of Grand Armagnac.

She sat down on the couch in front of the fireplace. On the coffee table she noticed the Monopoly game Burt had sent her after their first date.

She thought of the night she'd invited Blanche and Maurezio out to the beach house. After dinner, Burt insisted they all play Monopoly, and he played like a cutthroat, win-at-all-costs asshole. It brought back all her memories of his smugness, his arrogance, his megalomania.

She picked up Jessie's negatives and contact sheets and examined the twenty-four shots of her killing her husband.

She sipped her cognac, thinking about what would happen if the police got their hands on these pictures. She would *Go To Jail, Go Directly to jail, and never Pass Go* — never have a moment in her life of joy or fulfillment.

Susannah placed the photos and negatives in the fireplace, doused them with brandy, and lit them. She sat back and watched them burn. They gave off a warm, comforting glow.

Incriminating evidence flambé, she thought, with a touch of levity.

But the light-hearted moment was brief. It was replaced by a mantra that from now on she could never quite repress: *I've taken the lives of two human beings. I've taken the lives of two human beings.*

CHAPTER 25

In the morning Susannah decided to have breakfast at the Amagansett Farmer's Market. It was one of her favorite places; she often went there to have coffee and muffins, sitting at a picnic table under a canopy of oak and maple trees. After the trauma of last night, she thought it best to do a normal activity, hoping to normalize her life. It was no easy task.

She had the *Sunday Times* with her and decided to do the crossword puzzle. When she opened the magazine section, she saw an ad for a mattress company. It said: "Call 1-800 M-A-T-T-R-E-S. Leave off the last S for Savings."

She turned the page in annoyance, thinking — I'm sick of all these alphabet phone numbers; 1-800 CAR-SALE, 1-800 MORTGAGE ...

Then it hit her: *Letters stand for numbers. A-BE-DEGHI?*

She took out a pen and scribbled in the margin of the magazine. *Let's see, A(1) — B(2) E(5) — D(4) E(5) G(7) H(8) I(9) 1-25-45789. That could definitely be the number of Burt's Singapore bank account!*

She pulled out her iPhone and looked up UBAF bank. It listed a contact phone number and she tapped it into her keyboard. The call was answered by a recording in various languages, finally telling her to press "four" for English. Another recording announced that the bank was closed and would re-open at nine in the morning.

Of course, time difference, she thought.

"Press 'two', the voice intoned, "to be connected to a twenty-four hour service line."

A woman with a polished English accent answered.

"Good evening," Susannah said. "I'd like to check my account balance. Account number 1-25-45789."

"Name?"

"Cascadden." She spelled it out.

"Just a moment while I pull up that account. ...Yes, I have it. Your PIN number, please."

"Um, I don't have that at the moment. I'm Mr. Cascadden's wife."

"I'm sorry, Madam. Without a PIN number I can't give out any information."

"My husband is deceased."

"Oh, I am sorry. But without a PIN number, we'll have to see a death certificate and probated will."

"Photocopies?"

"No. We require the originals. In these types of cases, we ask that the surviving party bring the documents and appear at our office in person. As you can imagine, we take great care in protecting privacy, and guarding against fraud."

"Of course," Susannah said, concealing her frustration. "I'll get back to you on that. Thank you."

As she hung up, she heard a child's voice shouting.

"Susannah, Susannah."

She looked up and saw Katie, her five-year-old dance pupil, dashing toward her.

"Hiya, Katie-did," Susannah said, waving.

She held out her arms and the child fairly flew into them. Then Katie turned her head and called out, "Daddy."

Jericho approached the table, carrying a white paper bag.

"This is my dance teacher, Daddy."

132

"Detective Jericho," Susannah exclaimed. "I didn't realize... "

"Katie uses her stepfather's last name," Jericho explained.

"Oh."

"Honey, get off Mrs. Cascadden's lap," Jericho said to Katie. "Sorry. She gets a little overexuberant sometimes."

"No, no," Susannah said smiling. "I prefer to call it high energy."

"Can we sit with her?" Katie begged her father. "Please."

"No, honey. I'm sure Mrs. Cascadden would like to read the paper."

"There aren't any free tables," the child said.

Jericho looked around and saw she was right. "Let's go, Katie. We can have our cookies in the car."

"Don't be silly," Susannah said. "Please join me." Katie immediately slid off Susannah's lap and sat in the chair next to her. Jericho shrugged and sat down. Susannah smiled. *Terrific,* she thought. *Here I am having breakfast with the detective who could nail me for homicide. "Please join me!" What was I thinking? Obviously I wasn't.*

Jericho handed Katie an oatmeal raisin cookie and a Coke. He took out a container of caffe latte and some biscotti for himself.

There was an awkward silence.

"I, uh, I've talked to your wife a few times," Susannah said. "She's very nice."

"They're divorced," Katie jumped in. "I live with my mom and Irwin. Daddy visitates me every weekend."

Jericho reached over and stroked his daughter's curly brown hair. "Yep," he said with a grin "I moved out here from New York so I could 'visitate' her. Katie's the light of my life."

Susannah saw the love in the detective's eyes as he looked at his daughter. There was a tenderness about him that was so unlike the tough cop she'd been dealing with.

"Y'know, Katie could become a dancer some day, if she wants to," Susannah said. "She's very strong and has excellent kinetic rhythm."

"Could I get on "Dancing with the Stars?""

"It's possible."

Jericho hugged his daughter. "What star would you pick for your partner?,"

"Maybe *I* could be the star!" said Katie.

Susannah laughed. Jericho was glowing. Here he was, with his daughter and another woman, and it felt comfortable and wonderful almost like a family.

His cell phone rang.

Susannah flinched. It was chirping *Für Elise* just like Burt's Blackberry. She hoped the detective didn't notice her reaction.

"Yes, Chief." Jericho frowned. "Where?"

He listened for a while. "Okay, but why can't Randall take it? All right, all right," he said. "Turtle Cove. Got it."

"Oh my God, Turtle Cove," Susannah thought. *"They've found the Hyundai!"*

"Okay," Jericho said. "I just have to drop my daughter off at home. I'll get there soon as I can."

He turned to Katie. "C'mon, Sweetie. Daddy's gotta go to work."

"But we're supposed to rent 'Toy Story 3' and watch it at your house."

"I'll make it up to you, I promise."

Katie got up and took her father's hand. "Bye-bye, Susannah."

"Bye, Katie. See you next week."

"Thanks for letting us sit with you," Jericho said. "I'm sure we'll talk soon."

"Sorry you have to work."

He nodded sadly. "A policeman's lot is not a happy one."

Hmm — a cop quoting Gilbert & Sullivan? Susannah thought as she watched them leave hand in hand. *But soon Daddy will resume his*

134

role as Detective Jericho, inspecting the abandoned Hyundai and Virgil's clothing on Turtle Cove beach, looking for clues.

I hope to God I've thought of everything.

When Susannah got home she found a message on her machine from Gretchen's husband, Arnold Lewis. He said he'd be happy to represent Susannah and help with any legal matters that might arise. Susannah called the lawyer back, thanked him, and told him about Quinn Healey's reluctance to show her Burt's will.

"Have you looked for a copy around the house?" Arnold asked.

She said she'd searched Burt's desk and computer hard drive in the city, and his office and laptop at the beach house and had no luck.

"I'll just write Healey a letter," Arnold said. "He knows he has to produce the will posthaste or face a court order."

"Wouldn't it be better to call?"

"No."

"Oh, okay. I just thought — "

"Lawyers prefer letters because they're evidentiary."

"Do you want Healey's contact info?"

"I'll find it online."

Susannah had only known Arnold socially and found him to be genial and funny. Now, in his role as an attorney he was cold and humorless.

Arnold asked for her home and e-mail addresses and promised to send her a copy of Burt's will soon as it arrived.

"Listen," Susannah said, "I expect to pay you for this work."

"You'll get a bill."

Well, that was kind of abrupt, she thought.

After a moment she spoke. "Um...um...that'll be fine."

"I'll get back to you."

"Say hi to Gretchen."

135

"Right."

He hung up. She shook her head. *Well, at least he's no Quinn Healey.*

CHAPTER 26

Jericho was finishing up his investigation on Turtle Cove beach. He had interviewed the maintenance worker who'd found the abandoned Hyundai. The workman had been sent to the beach because some asshole had removed a sign saying *"Piping Plover Nesting Area — Do Not Disturb."* It was replaced with a sign reading: "Piping Plover Tastes Like Chicken."

Jericho inventoried the physical evidence. The missing man's wallet identified him as Jessie Russell, residing at Grogan's Cabins, Montauk.

The similarity to Burt Cascadden's disappearance was startling. *There must be a connection*, he thought. *Does Jessie Russell have anything to do with Cascadden? Is Russell alive or dead? If he's dead, could this be the work of a serial killer? Jesus, as far as I know, there's never been a serial killer out here.*

On the scene was Teddy Karlin, Jericho's least favorite patrolman. Karlin was dying to dust for prints, but Jericho feared he'd smudge everything, so he did it himself.

"Hey, Jericho," Karlin said, holding up a half-eaten cream-filled devil's food cake. "Found a bunch of these on the back seat. He musta had a thing for Ring Dings."

"I wouldn't be talking about him in the past tense just yet," Jericho said.

"But it sure looks like he took off his clothes, went for a dip, and drowned."

"Appearances can be deceiving," Jericho said patiently. "Stick those Ring Dings in the bag with the other stuff. The half-eaten one might give us bite marks later, for identification."

"Wait a minute," Jericho went on. "Hand me the evidence bag." Karlin complied and Jericho reached into it and pulled out a sock. He smelled it gingerly and made a face. "There's enough organic material in athlete's foot to give us a shit-load of DNA if we need it. Gimme a zip baggie." Jericho placed both socks in the baggie, sealed it, and put it back with the other evidence.

Jericho photographed the scene, then ordered Karlin to call for a tow truck. "Oh, and tell them to bring a CrimeScope. When they come, have 'em take the Hundai to the station house, then meet me at Russell's place. And bring the CrimeScope."

"No problem."

"That means there'll be a problem," Jericho thought wryly.

"Grogan's Cabins over on West Lake, right?"

"Right. I'll go over there now — see if he's showed up, or if there's any clue as to his whereabouts."

"Mrs. Grogan'll let you in the cabin. Tell her you're a friend of mine."

"Okay."

"From the picture on his pilot's license," Karlin said, "I'd figure the missing guy's a Mexican — or maybe some kind of Hispanic."

Jericho ignored the Archie Bunker-ism. "With a name like Russell?"

"He coulda changed it. You know these illegals."

"Let me ask you something, Teddy," Jericho said. Karlin was an idiot, but he was a Bonacker, the name given to natives of the area, so he had a good knowledge of local happenings. "Two disappearances that appear to be drownings within a few days does that seem odd to you?"

"Nah," Karlin replied. "Especially this time of year when the rip is so strong. The weather's nice and people tend to ignore the no-

138

swimmin' flags. I remember when I was a rookie, two kids, one from the high school and a surfer from Mineola got sucked away in the space of a couple days. Later we found the kid floatin' off Georgica Beach, and a week after that, part of a ribcage washed up. Chief Manos said there coulda been three floaters, because the ribcage had entirely different DMA."

"D-*N*-A."

"Yeah. We never did find the other bodies. Sharks coulda got 'em."

CHAPTER 27

Mrs. Grogan willingly handed Jericho the missing man's room key. "Is that Indian in trouble?" she asked.

"He's a Native-American?"

"Yeah. Shinnecock. And he drinks like an Indian too."

"Well, he seems to have gone missing," Jericho said. "What can you tell me about him?"

Mrs. Grogan had nothing good to say about Jessie Russell, except that he paid his rent on time. She said Jessie had a job flying airplanes, and that his hobby was photography.

"He's always boasting about how he develops his own pictures, like he was some kind of genius."

"So he has his own darkroom?"

"I guess so. I never go into his place. He won't let anybody in. It's kinda creepy."

She went on. "He's a regular at the Liar's. After three beers he becomes an obnoxious loudmouth. And if I refuse to serve him, he gets real belligerent. He has two drinkin' buddies who work at the airport, Norm Blechner and Bernie Traywick."

"You know anything about his family?"

"Nah," she said. "Well, only that his mother died last year, back at the reservation in Hampton Bays. Jessie took it pretty hard. For weeks afterward he'd come in and git soused every night."

Jericho entered the cabin and took a cursory look around the living room. He headed to the back, where he saw two rooms across from each other. One was a bathroom turned darkroom. He turned on its light and looked around. There was all the standard developing and printing equipment. He thought it unusual, in this digital age, for someone still to be working with analog gear.

He could find no negatives, and there were no prints, even in the trash basket.

Jericho crossed over into Jessie's bedroom. He was surprised by the collection of framed photographs on the wall. *Jessie must've shot them from his plane. Voyeurism taken to new heights,* he mused.

There was a shot of a woman with vivid white bikini lines across her breasts and groin, emphasizing the dark suntan on the rest of her body. Another was a full-figured lady with thunder thighs and large breasts pillowing out upon her chest. There was a shot of a nude blonde and Jericho wondered if it might be Susannah, but the woman's hair was short and her body wasn't that great. Right above Jessie's bed was a double-header; a photo that looked like a mother and her prepubescent daughter lying out in the sun together. The mother had angular hips and her breasts were flattened out by her supine position. At first she appeared to be wearing a bathing suit bottom, but then Jericho realized it was the woman's pubic hair, a dark black triangle at her crotch. Lying next to her, the young girl's body was undeveloped and undefined, except for the hairless delta that specified her gender.

"*Por favor ... Por favor.*" Jericho heard the words echoing in his mind again. *A woman's words, flowing into a whimper that becomes a never-ending wail. He sees the little girl's pale white body writhing as her limbs flail about, hands clawing the air. He sees the diaper-covered triangle at the junction of her legs. Above it, where the navel should be, a spike protrudes, its sharp point jutting up through the flesh. Blood is everywhere, enveloping the little girl, covering the detective.*

One step too many. One step too many.

All is red now, incarnadine liquid flowing over his vision, sweeping over mind and consciousness, then dissolving rapidly into total darkness ...

142

"Jericho? You in there?"

Jericho heard Karlin's voice as if coming from a far distance. "Jericho?"

There was a pounding on the door.

Jericho opened his eyes and realized he was lying on a bed.

"Yeah, yeah, Karlin," he said hoarsely. "Hold on."

He sat up and looked around. He saw the women's pictures on the wall. He knew he'd blacked out.

Jesus. How long have I been unconscious?

He got up and walked unsteadily toward the kitchen. He turned on the cold water, and splashed it on his face.

"Be right there," he called out to Karlin.

He dried his face with a paper towel, walked to the door and opened it. "Come on in, Teddy," he said. Then, wanting to find out how long he'd been out, Jericho asked, "How long did you have to wait for the tow truck?"

"I dunno. Twenty minutes."

Plus fifteen minutes to get here, he figured. *That's over half an hour unaccounted for. Damn.*

Karlin entered. He was carrying the latent print spray can, and a CrimeScope, a black device with a light source on it.

"Put on your gloves," Jericho said. "We've got work to do."

Karlin complied.

"Let's start with the bedroom," Jericho said. "Wait'll you see what this guy does for kicks."

Jericho gave Karlin his first work assignment — "Sit down and stay outta my way."

The detective took numerous photos of the scene.

143

He discovered an address book with a listing for "Mom." The phone number had the Southampton prefix *283*. Since next of kin had to be notified about a missing person, Jericho copied the number so he could call it later.

The bedroom was clean and neat. The nude prints and negatives were filed in a Pendaflex. Even the videotapes and DVDs in the cabinet — all action/adventure and martial arts — were lined up alphabetically.

Jericho booted up the computer. No password, so Jericho had no problem logging on. He checked out Jessie's browsing history — mostly XXX-rated sites: PornerBros.com, MammaryLane.com, Blowjobs'R'Us.com.

In the bedroom closet was an assortment of cheap clothing. He noticed one He-Man brand denim bib overalls — blue, like the brown one Jericho had found in the Hyundai. Both were size 40 regular. On the bib of the blue one, Jericho saw a few dark spots that looked like blood.

"Teddy," he called out. "Bring the CrimeScope in here."

Karlin focused the CrimeScope light on the spots. Blood doesn't glow in normal light, but when Karlin tuned the machine to blood's unique color range, it showed up nicely, confirming Jericho's guess.

"If it's the missing guy's blood," Karlin said, "we should be thinkin' foul play."

Jericho rolled his eyes. "So you're saying somebody stabbed or shot him, pulled off his *blue* overalls, then took him and his *brown* overalls to the beach and dumped him?"

Karlin was speechless.

"Who knows?", Jericho said. "He might have cut himself shaving." He grabbed the overalls and put them in an evidence bag. "Or — it might not even be *his* blood. It could be a red herring."

"Y'know," Karlin said. "I never really understood what that means."

"It means it's a misleading clue. Supposedly, in Jolly Old England, escaping convicts would drag a bloody herring across their trail, to put bloodhounds off the scent."

"Wow! That's really interesting!"

144

"But it's probably apocryphal."

"Fer sure."

"Okay, Teddy," Jericho said. "We're done here. Have you got any crime scene tape with you?"

"In the truck."

"Good. We oughta seal up."

CHAPTER 28

Susannah sat down at her computer. She'd forgotten to RSVP to her friend Shirley that she'd be unable to attend their high school reunion. She logged on to Gmail and saw Shirley's message she'd Saved As New. There was another message in her In box. It was from *Auto64372@Anonymail.com.*

She opened it.

The message was succinct and absolutely terrifying: *YOU DID A BAD THING.*

In a panic, Susannah went to the *Anonymail.com website,* hoping to find out who had e-mailed her. The Web page explained how the service worked:

You, the visitor send an e-mail using our Web interface. No trace of your identity is given to Anonymail nor to the e-mail's intended recipient. Your identity is concealed because all trails lead back to Anonymail, not the sender. Thus, it is truly Anonymous e-mail.

Users often ask — Is there any possible way the recipient of my e-mail can find out my identity? The answer is NO. However (sorry, there is a however), Anonymail cooperates with law enforcement agencies, and in the investigation of a crime we could supply them the name of your Internet Service Provider (ISP) and from that the FBI or the police can dig deeper and probably track you down. So please — don't use us to do anything illegal.

The last thing Susannah could do was go to the police. And the sender knew that. *But who could it be?*

Maybe someone else had seen her kill her husband, or witnessed what happened with Jessie Russell.

What was the purpose of the e-mail? Obviously to scare me. But to what end? Possibly the sender just suspected or was guessing about what I'd done, and the e-mail was meant to unnerve me, cause me to make a slip.

Or...was it a precursor to blackmail?

She tried to think of all the people who could have sent the e-mail.

It sounds like Burt, but he's dead. It could be Jessie Russell, but he's dead, too. Detective Jericho? That would make no sense. Quinn Healey? Well, he's a lawyer so anything is possible. Who else? God, it could be anybody. Who else knows my e-mail address? Doesn't matter, any one with computer smarts could easily find me.

She was getting nowhere. But whoever did this was clearly trying to mess with her mind. And succeeding.

There wasn't a damn thing she could do. She could only wait for the sender's next move — which she knew would come soon.

CHAPTER 29

Back at the precinct house, Jericho called the number for "Mom" listed in Jessie's address book. A woman answered and said she was Jessie's sister Margaret. The detective told her that he was notifying her, as next of kin, of her brother's disappearance.

"We found his car and clothing on a beach."

"Do you think he's dead?" she asked.

"I'm afraid it's a strong possibility."

"Good," she said. "He can rot in hell."

She hung up.

Jericho drove to East Hampton Airport. Norm Blechner, the radio dispatcher, was on duty. He said he'd known Jessie for four years, ever since Jessie started towing banner for the Fly-by-Day Aerial Advertising Company,

"Yeah," Norm said, "me and Bernie went down the Liar's about nine-thirty last night. We figured Jessie was home 'cause his light was on, so we banged on his door and tried to get him to come with us. But he must've been in the darkroom or somethin', 'cause he didn't answer the door."

"Did you see him inside?"

"The shade was down."

"Did you see his car?"

"No."

"Then you don't really know if he was home."

"No. I guess not."

"Okay, thanks, Mr. Blechner."

"Detective?" the dispatcher said.

"Yes?"

"Do you think Jessie drowned?"

"Could be."

"That's weird."

"Why?"

"Well, you say you found his stuff on the beach and it looked like he went for a midnight swim."

"Yes."

"Well, Jessie had this thing about sharks," Norm said. "He was scared shitless of 'em. Seems he saw *Jaws* when he was a kid and never got over it. The last thing he'd ever do, I mean, in my opinion, would be go jump in the ocean in the middle of the night."

Wait a minute, Jericho thought, *Blechner says the lights were on in Russell's cabin the night he and his pal went to the Liar's Saloon. Were they on or off when I searched his cabin?*

They were on. But did I throw the wall switch when I entered the place?

Dammit! That was right before I blacked out — I can't remember!

Am I losing my edge here?

Maybe that idiot Karlin was right, Jericho thought. *The facts do seem to be indicating foul play.*

150

CHAPTER 30

Patrolman Karlin drew search duty the next morning. At 8 a.m. he was driving an open-top Jeep slowly along the water's edge at Turtle Cove Beach.

He saw two chunky women on a blanket, drinking coffee and reading different sections of the *East Hampton Star*.

Carpet-munchers, he said under his breath. *I can always tell.*

A dude carrying a surfboard, dressed in floppy trunks that hung below his knees, gave the cop a two-fingered peace sign as he passed. Karlin wanted to respond with a single digit, but that was against regulations.

Don't gimme that Beach Boys "Good Vibrations" crap. Get a job.

He heard a crunching sound under his left front tire.

"Fuck was that?"

He stopped the Jeep, backed up a few yards, and got out. On the sand was a spinal column. It had been broken in two; he could see the tire track where the Jeep had run over the vertebrae. At first Karlin thought it was a fish, but once he looked closer he recognized it as human. For one thing, there were neck bones, and he'd cleaned enough fish to know fish didn't have necks. The spine had bits of ghastly white skin and some other kind of mung hanging from it. He'd goofed by running over it, but nobody had to know that, and besides, there was enough bone and stuff to get the genetics, which was all that mattered. In fact, Chief Manos would surely commend him for his great police work, and apologize for his recent criticism, which was that Karlin was a numb-nuts.

He got back into the Jeep and called the precinct house.

When Susannah woke up, she went immediately to her computer. There was another message from Anonymail. It read: *YOU DID A BAD BAD THING.*

Her stomach churned with fear.

This was torture. These e-mails were a perfect form of harassment — they were simultaneously an accusation, a threat, and a punishment.

On the beach, Jericho watched as Dr. John Alvarez, the assistant medical examiner from Hauppauge examined the fragments of spinal column. These bones signified a death, and the AME was required to add it to the list of Suffolk County unidentified bodies.

"John Doe No. 27," Alvarez dictated into a digital recorder. Alvarez was a tall, thin Latino man who looked as cadaverous as his clientele. He was wearing the usual latex gloves.

"John Doe?" Jericho asked. "How do you know it's from a man?"

Alvarez stopped his recorder and explained patiently. "Vertebral width and disc-facet depth are significantly greater in men."

Jericho nodded. He noted the subtle sing-song in Alvarez's accent that indicated a Mexican-American background.

The AME spoke again into his recorder. "Two spinal sections. One comprised of C-3 through T-4. The other, T-5 through L-2. No sacral or coccygeal vertebrae. Some bits of epidermal and lipoid tissue remain."

"Got any idea of time of death?" Jericho asked.

Alvarez shook his head no. "Sea water's no friend to forensics. Lab work may tell us something."

152

He signaled to the driver of the ME truck, who got out and walked toward them.

"Let me just get a few photos," Alvarez said to his driver. "Then we're outta here." He turned to Jericho. "There's a suicide waiting for us in Speonk, and later this afternoon I'm scheduled to do a cut-up."

"We've got two possible drownings in Montauk," Jericho said. "These fragments could belong to either one of them."

"You have any genetic material from the missing persons?" asked Alvarez.

"I'm working on it." Since there had been no real evidence of foul play, he hadn't collected anything yet.

"You get anything that might be a DNA match, make sure you run it over to the crime lab yourself. Y'know, chain of evidence."

"Right."

"You know what to look for?"

"Yes."

"Hair is always good. But remember, no hair shafts without *follicles*."

I know that, putz, is what Jericho thought, but instead he just nodded. He wanted to stay on Alvarez's good side. AME's can get you lab results real quick if they like you.

"I'm kinda new around here," Jericho said, ingenuously. "Is the crime lab in Hauppauge?"

"Yeah. Same building as the ME office."

The driver was carrying what looked like a Bloomingdale's Big Brown Bag. Alvarez picked up the two pieces of spinal column and put them in it. Then the driver sealed the bag with evidence tape. Alvarez signed and dated the tape with a felt pen.

"Well," Jericho said, "thanks for getting here so fast. And I really appreciate your help. You sure know the drill." Big smile.

"No problem." Alvarez said and turned to the driver. "Gino, give Detective Jericho a PL9 Form."

"That would be?" Jericho asked, feigning ignorance.

153

"Evidence Analysis Request," Alvarez replied. "If you do find any genetic material, things'll go a lot faster if you make out the paper work in triplicate before you drive over. Good luck."

He likes me, thought Jericho. *He really likes me.*

Jericho was confident the blood spots on the blue overalls in Jessie's closet would yield DNA. But he couldn't be sure if it was Jessie's blood.

They were close to Jessie's place, so he drove over there to look for a comb or brush that might have hair samples. There was a comb in the bathroom but it seemed to have nothing on it. He tagged it and bagged it anyway, just in case. He checked the sink and bathtub drains. They contained some gunk which didn't look promising, but he scraped a sample into a baggie.

He went back into the living room and saw the Dell computer. Next to it was a wastebasket. Recalling Jessie's predilection for XXX-rated websites, Jericho kneeled down and looked in the basket. There were a bunch of crumpled Kleenex tissues. Jericho put on his gloves and picked one up.

Snot or semen? My money's on semen. Either way, they're bodily fluids, loaded with DNA. With this, and Jessie's stinky socks, I've got what I need.

Susannah was nervous about Jericho coming over. He'd explained only that he needed her help with something.

She took a quick shower, washed her hair, and put on a little makeup, hoping her looks might keep him from noticing how upset she was about the anonymous e-mails.

When Jericho arrived, she served him some fresh-brewed coffee. Sitting across from her at the kitchen counter, he explained why he was there.

"We found fragments of a human spinal column out at Turtle Cove Beach. It's possible that it's your husband's. I need to get a sample of his genetic material to see if it matches the DNA from the spine."

"Oh, I see."

154

"The easiest thing would be a sample of his hair." Jericho said. "Do you have a comb or a brush he used?"

She led him to Burt's bathroom. Jericho snapped on a pair of latex gloves. Susannah swallowed hard.

"Are you all right, Mrs. Cascadden?"

"Yes. Why?"

"You look a little upset."

"This isn't easy."

"Of course." Jericho picked up Burt's hairbrush, a Jean-Pierre Prestige model. It had numerous black hairs straggling from its boar bristles. There were follicles galore.

"Dyed hair, correct?"

"Yes."

Jericho opened the medicine cabinet and saw a bottle of Just For Men Shampoo-In Hair Color — Natural Jet Black.

He took out an evidence bag and dumped the hair dye and the hairbrush into it.

"This'll do fine," he said as he sealed the bag.

They returned to the living room in silence.

"Thanks, Mrs. Cascadden."

"I just hope you find out something. This — this not knowing is really getting to me."

"I should tell you," Jericho said. "This DNA could match somebody else. There's been another possible drowning."

"Oh, Gosh... I don't know what to hope for."

"I understand. But it's always better to know."

"How long before we find out anything?" she asked.

"About a week if I can pull strings. I'll do my best. When I hear, you'll hear."

He smiled compassionately at her. She smiled back. For a moment Susannah felt a warm connection between them. Then Jericho looked away. The moment passed.

After Jericho left, Susannah's mind stayed on the detective. For the first time she'd picked up a genuine sense of concern from him. And it felt good.

But he was the last person she could turn to for reassurance.

CHAPTER 31

In the morning Jericho went to the Chief's office. He needed permission to go "up-island," the local phrase meaning west of Riverhead.

He'd brought two bags with him. One contained Jessie's socks and Kleenex. In the other was Burt Cascadden's hair, hair dye, and hairbrush.

The Chief okayed his trip to the Hauppauge crime lab, and Jericho updated him on the Cascadden and Russell investigations.

"So," the Chief said, "If the Indian was scared to swim in the ocean, there's a good chance he was murdered."

"Yes."

"Motive?"

"My first thought was the nude pictures — somebody could've been pissed off about them, a husband, a boyfriend, maybe the woman herself.

"Maybe Jessie was blackmailing someone."

"But nude pictures are no big deal these days. Who would pay to keep the pictures from being seen?"

"Maybe the blackmailer threatened to have them published," Dominick said. "Like, if the woman was a celebrity, or the wife of a celebrity. Remember *Hustler* magazine's nudie shots of Jackie Kennedy?"

"That was back in the Seventies, old-timer. Today? Hell, you can go on the Internet and see naked pictures of almost anybody famous. Who'd go so far as to *kill* to keep the pictures out of the media?"

"I dunno. Maybe an old-timer like me."

Jericho smiled. "That does suggest another possibility," he said. "Maybe Russell did sell nude pictures to a magazine and an angry husband found out and killed Jessie. No blackmail, just revenge."

Manos nodded. "So — you've got some possible motives, but nothing concrete."

"Not yet."

The Chief didn't hide his annoyance. "Any progress on the Cascadden thing?" he asked.

"So far it's an accidental drowning."

The Chief looked thoughtful. "Lemme ask you something," he said. "You think Cascadden could've been murdered?"

"It's possible."

"You think the wife could've done it?"

"The wife?" Jericho said, his voice rising.

"Yes."

The idea upset him. "Yes, she could be a suspect," he said, hiding his feelings. "But so far it doesn't seem likely."

Manos looked at him quizzically. "The husband had big bucks. There's her motive."

"Chief," he said, "he was in deep financial trouble, heading to bankruptcy."

"But the wife might not've known that," he said.

The detective didn't respond.

"Jericho," the Chief said, "I'm getting a funny vibe from you. What's wrong?"

"Nothing's wrong," he responded calmly. "I just mean, at this point there's no evidence of homicide. Maybe if the bones turn out to be Cascadden's, there could be some forensic indication of murder. But they

158

probably won't show anything. There's only two spinal sections, and the seawater's cleaned 'em up pretty good."

"So you've got nothing going in either case."

"Nothing concrete. But maybe these DNA comparisons will..."

"Jericho," Manos interrupted, frowning. "You're the hotshot Manhattan homicide dick. Why do you think I gave you the shield?"

Jericho was silent.

"I don't want a repeat of what happened with the Ted Ammon murder. You remember that, back in 2001?"

Manos was referring to East Hampton's one recent high profile homicide case. Ammon was a multi-millionaire, who was bludgeoned to death in his Middle Lane mansion.

"Yes," Jericho said. "It got tons of media coverage in the city. As I remember, Ammon's estranged wife got her slime-ball boyfriend to whack him, so she'd inherit his fortune. What was her name? — Generosa."

"Yeah. Funny name for a greedy bitch," said Manos. "The D.A. assigned the case to the Suffolk County police, saying we weren't capable of handling a big murder investigation. I don't want that reputation on my watch."

"I understand."

"Detective," Manos said, "I would very much like you to clear up the death of that Indian. And *soon.*"

Jericho didn't even flinch this time when Manos used the very politically incorrect term. "I'm on it."

"And resolve the Cascadden case."

Jericho nodded. He picked up the evidence bags and went out to his car; a used, black Toyota Camry. It was about an hour's drive to Hauppauge.

As he drove, Jericho remembered the Chief's question — "You think the wife could've done it?" He chastised himself for the way he reacted.

159

I'm losing my objectivity, he thought, *and that's the worst thing a detective can do. Still, I haven't seen anything to suggest homicide in the disappearance of Burton Cascadden. Except, possibly, that track in the sand in front of the beach house — which Susannah had no trouble explaining.*

CHAPTER 32

As Jericho approached Southampton on Route 27, he remembered the angry words of Jessie's sister: "He can rot in hell." Jericho needed to find a suspect, perhaps someone who hated Jessie Russell. His sister Margaret was certainly worth talking to. So he decided a stop on his way to delivering the DNA evidence was in order.

He pulled off the highway at Tuckahoe Road and headed for the Shinnecock reservation.

Next to the entrance was the Shinnecock Indian Trading Post and Smoke Shop, with the requisite totem pole in front, feathered headdresses hung from the roof rafters, plus loads of cornball Indian souvenirs available for heap big wampum.

The Shinnecock are a state-recognized tribe, but they're not, with some exceptions, recognized by the federal government. This enables them to sell low-tax cigarettes, but it also prevents them from receiving federal funds for health and education, or getting assistance from the Bureau of Indian Affairs to clean up their contaminated water supply and investigate their soaring cancer rates. And without federal support, they can't establish a gambling casino like Foxwoods, the gravy train of the Mashantuket Pequots in Connecticut.

Lately though, NY State had begun to see casino gambling as a badly needed source of revenue, but between politics, red tape, lobbying from Atlantic City, and competition from other powerful gaming corporations, it would likely be a long time before anyone pulled a slot machine lever for the benefit of the Shinnecocks.

Jericho flashed his badge and ID to the uniformed guard at the entrance to the reservation. Big mistake.

"Sorry, detective. Can't let you in. You got no jurisdiction here."

"I'm investigating a possible homicide," Jericho said. "Southampton PD will okay it. Just call."

"This ain't their jurisdiction, either. This is state land. We're under the State Police. You'll need written authorization from them."

"Look, I just want to talk to Margaret Russell. I'll go in as a private citizen."

"No way."

"Her brother Jessie is dead and I'm trying to — "

"Jessie Russell is dead?"

"Did you know him?"

"Sure. Is that the homicide you're lookin' into?"

"Yes."

"Well, I hope whoever snuffed him cut off his balls first and shoved 'em up his ass."

"His sister Margaret seems to share your opinion of him."

"If you want a list of people who want Jessie dead, it'll include every person on the rez."

"Why? What did he do?"

"Raped a fifteen-year-old girl — Carrie Hall. Sweetest thing you ever saw. One afternoon she was home alone, doin' her lessons while her mother was at work. Jessie — he was here visitin' his mom — sneaked in and did the girl, then told her he'd kill her if she talked. Took the poor kid a year before she worked up the courage to say what happened. Mrs. Hall refused to press charges; she didn't want to put her daughter through any more grief. So Jessie got off. But her whole family swore they'd get him."

"How long ago was this?"

"Maybe five years."

"You think someone'd kill him after all this time?"

162

"They been arguin' about it for years in the Tribal Council. Some people sayin' an eye for an eye, others sayin' no — 'cause we're livin' in a country of laws. Like that's done a lotta friggin' good for our people. But anyone in Carrie's family, especially her three brothers, mighta got fed up and decided to smoke the prick."

"Guess I'll have to get an okay from the State Police. What are the names of the brothers?"

The guard shook his head. "You can talk to them, or anybody else," he said, "but you won't get nowhere. On the rez we all cover for each other. It's the Red Wall of Silence."

Jericho got back into his car and drove away frustrated. He knew it wouldn't matter if he got the State Police, every cop in Suffolk County, and even the FBI in on the investigation. If a member of the Shinnecock tribe had killed Jessie Russell, the case would likely never be cleared.

He swung his car onto the Montauk Highway and headed west to the crime lab.

CHAPTER 33

The morning e-mail ratcheted up the pressure on Susannah. "YOU DID A BAD THING. CONFESS. CONFESS, OR I'LL MAKE YOU PAY!"

CONFESS? Why does the sender want me to confess? I'LL MAKE YOU PAY. Pay what? Pay money? Pay... with my life?

The mantra of guilt began playing in her mind again: *I've taken the lives of two human beings.*

The fax phone rang. Susannah walked into Burt's office and saw papers filling the tray of the fax machine.

The top sheet was from Arnold Lewis, and a copy of Burt's will followed. The language was surprisingly simple and straightforward: upon Burt's demise, his entire estate should be given to his wife, Susannah Dahlgren Cascadden.

The next paragraph stated: "If the above-named beneficiary (my wife) dies before me, declines the inheritance, or is ineligible for it (together referred to as predeceased), I direct that my entire estate be given to my friend and attorney H. Quinn Healey, Esq., of 21 East 44 Street, NY NY 10017."

Susannah got it immediately: *If I were convicted of murdering my husband, clearly I'd no longer have a legal claim on his estate — I'd be "ineligible for it." I'd go to prison, and the estate — the three or four million from the sale of the beach house, plus Burt's offshore money, if Healey knows about it — would go to the attorney.*

Who would profit if I confessed? Of course — it's Quinn! No wonder he was reluctant to show me the will. So Healey is the most logical anonymous e-mailer. But how does he know I "did a bad thing"? Could he possibly know I killed Burt? Maybe he's just guessing. Maybe he's bluffing. Could he somehow have gotten a copy of Jessie's photographs? Could Jessie have sent him the pictures? No, that makes no sense. Still, everything points to Healey. Whether he's guessing, bluffing, or has hard evidence against me, he's the one with the motive.

Suddenly Susannah was seized with anger and an intense desire to fight back.

She picked up the phone and made an appointment to see Healey that afternoon.

Before she left for the city, she dressed to the nines and wore some of her most expensive jewelry.

"Nice to see you, Susannah," Healey said as she entered his office. "Hope you didn't hit traffic on the way in."

"I took the plane."

"Oh. Oh yes. That's the only way to fly."

She watched him smile the way men do when they try to act cool but instead say something stupid.

"Please sit down," he said. "I'm glad you're here. We've got some things to go over."

On his desk she noticed a framed photograph of a matronly woman and two teenage boys, posing in front of a tan Mercedes-Benz.

Healey saw Susannah looking at the photograph.

"That's my pride and joy," he said. "1972 300 SEL 4.5."

"Terrific." She sat down in a wooden spindle armchair with a Dartmouth seal on the back crown.

"First of all," Susannah said, "I want you to know I've retained my own attorney, I think, under the circumstances..."

Healey interrupted her. "I think that's a very wise decision. I had a close emotional tie to your husband, so you may justifiably feel I can't be objective with you. Comfort is critical in the attorney-client relationship, and if you feel comfortable with your lawyer, then I'm comfortable with that."

Susannah nodded.

"But there are many details to be settled," Healey went on, "and it'll be better if you and I sit down and work them out together. I'm sure you don't want your lawyer billing you for all the hours it'll take. Susannah — I promise you'll never get a bill from me, no matter how long things drag on. And believe me, they tend to drag on."

"Thank you."

"All right," he said. "Now, let me tell you where things stand. I filed for Chapter 11, and all Burt's assets are now in receivership. The townhouse is foreclosed. "

"But they can't touch the beach house, right?" Susannah asked.

"Correct. As I said, that's yours," he said. "But you know, it'll take a while if Burt — "

He broke off.

"If his body isn't found," she said.

He nodded somberly, like a funeral director. "I know you're concerned about how you're going to manage," he said, "but I want you to know something. I say this in all sincerity — you can count on me."

"That's very nice."

"No. I mean it, Susannah. I'd like to be a friend to you, and help you through these trying times." He smiled.

"There are a few things I'd like to discuss," Susannah said firmly. "Friend to friend."

"Tell me."

"First of all, I know about Tennessee."

"What?"

"About your censure for unethical conduct."

The glib lawyer was speechless.

"It would be a shame if all your clients heard about that," she said. "They won't, of course, unless I find myself being interviewed by the police or the press. Then I'll find a way to get that information out."

"Why would you want to do that?"

"Self-defense."

"I don't understand."

Susannah went on. "That's not all. Anonymous e-mail isn't anonymous if it's involved in a crime. The police will investigate and find out who the sender is. They'll find out it was you."

Healey looked puzzled. "E-mail?"

"'Confess.' That's harassment. 'Confess or I'll make you pay.' That's extortion. I'd love to see you try to collect the money from Burt's estate, with harassment and extortion charges hanging over you, and your previous censure for ripping off an estate in Tennessee. Plus one thing's for sure — your law career will be finished."

Healey threw up his hands in confusion. "I'm sorry. I don't get it."

"What I'm saying is," Susannah said, "if I go down, you go down."

"Susannah," he said, "have you done something wrong? Are you in trouble? Do you need my help?"

He's good, thought Susannah.

Healey spoke softly. "I know this is a difficult time for you."

He got up, went to where she was sitting, and put a sympathetic hand on her shoulder.

"My dear Susannah," he said. "I understand how hard it is coming to grips with bereavement. In my lifetime I've lost many who are dear to me. And now we share a mutual burden — the death of a man we both loved. I can see how disoriented you've become, how confused, how frightened. But this will pass, darling. Just give it time. Trust me on that."

His hand was gently massaging her neck. She pulled away from him in revulsion, and stood up.

168

"I hope I've made my point," she said.

"Of course you have."

She turned to leave.

"Wait," he said. He scribbled something on a business card and handed it to her.

"This is my private number. I want you to call if you feel like talking. And I'd like to suggest we get together for dinner next week. I think it'll be good for both of us. Sort of therapy."

"Goodbye, Mr. Healey." She handed him back the card but he refused it.

"Please, Susannah. You may find you need it. Read what it says."

She read "Quinn — 917-587-4332. Any time." She stuck the card in her purse.

"Remember, Sweetie," he said. "You can count on me."

She left.

Healey is slick, she thought. *He gave no indication that he knew what I was talking about. But if he does have evidence against me, my threats ought to make him think twice before turning me in.*

I sure as hell hope so...—"Sweetie!"

The next morning brought another message from Anonymail. It was the same: "YOU DID A BAD THING. CONFESS, OR I'LL MAKE YOU PAY."

Healey is still e-mailing, she reasoned, *because he figures if he stops, I'll know he's the sender. He wants to keep me guessing.*
Just as she was about to press delete, the house phone rang. It was Healy.

"Sweetie! I was thinking you should came into the city and I can treat you to a nice dinner at Le Bernardin"

Susannah couldn't believe he was calling her. "Quinn, if you have anything to say to me, you can call my lawyer."

When he asked, "Why don't I come out there?" she hung up on him.

CHAPTER 34

Mort set up his wooden French-style easel on a high dune facing the beach. The easel was perfect for working outside, with its slide-out drawer to hold the watercolor paints, and clamp for his water jar.

Painting was Mort's hobby, and he was delighted with this opportunity to combine business with pleasure.

He was dressed in olive Bermuda shorts and a painter's smock. He wore black knee socks and sneakers, and a broad-brimmed Panama hat tied under his chin so it wouldn't blow off.

After unfolding his aluminum and canvas stool, Mort sat down and surveyed the area. Below him, off to the left, was the Cascadden house, a blindingly white concrete structure set into the dunes, its large teakwood deck facing the sea. Mort's painter's eye was drawn to the red geraniums planted in half whiskey barrels around the entrance. It would require a precise mixture of cadmium red and scarlet lake to capture their essence.

But this morning he was more fascinated by the sky, a vast luminous expanse of changing blues; cerulean, aquamarine, cobalt. It reminded him of a Childe Hassam painting: *Morning on the beach at Wellfleet, Cape Cod.*

Mort set his watercolor paper block on the easel and adjusted the holder to a 10-degree angle. It was heavy paper, the 300 lb. Lanaquarelle, because he worked aggressively with washes and layering, and the external sizing took it well.

He began in pencil, lightly sketching in the clouds, trying to capture the rhythms of their patterns as they floated across the sky.

When he was satisfied, he opened his water jar, dipped in a sable brush, and washed the water in broad strokes across the paper. Then he tilted the block up slightly, loaded the brush with cobalt blue, and drew it slowly along the edge of wetness, letting the blue bleed down for a graded sky effect. It was a good start.

That was the thing he loved about watercolor. You couldn't paint over, you couldn't erase. You had to know precisely where the paint would go, how the paper would take it, when it would dry, and what your next step would be. That was what his whole life was about: technique, precision, expertise.

After a while, he squeezed a small amount of violet onto his palette. He would need to add the pale purple to the clouds, to give them visual depth. Now in his mind he already saw the whole picture, complete in every detail. It was going to be lovely.

After a sleepless night, Susannah got out of bed and put on a swimsuit and an old men's button-down shirt. She checked her e-mail and there was nothing from Anonymail. *What if the e-mails have stopped?*

The fear of impending doom seized her.

No e-mails is worse, she realized. *What if Healey's not worried about my threats? What if he's decided to turn me over to the police? What do I do now?*

She rinsed the dishes, straightened up the kitchen, then filled a watering can. She went to the angled bay window next to the front door and watered the potted coleus plants that sat on the window seat. As she did, she caught sight of the painter up on the dunes. It was surprising, she'd never seen anyone on those dunes before.

She decided to get a closer look while she watered the geraniums. She put on her sunglasses and went outside.

As she uncoiled the garden hose, she glanced up at the painter. His presence made her nervous. She felt her heart start to pound in her chest. She took a deep breath.

He looks okay, she thought, trying to reassure herself. *He's not on my property. So he has a right to be there.*

She looked up at the blue sky and wondered how anyone could capture its full radiance with paint and brush.

She turned the spigot and felt the hose stiffen with water. It was going to be a hot day, so she was careful to water only the soil and not splash the leaves or blossoms. Otherwise they would get scorched under the midday sun.

As she watered, she smelled the characteristically bitter scent of geraniums. *Strange,* she thought, *that such gorgeous flowers give off such an ugly odor.*

Strange, too, that on a sunny day like this, her mind was clouded with fear.

"Excuse me, madam."

She looked up with a start and saw the painter walking up the driveway. He was carrying his water jar.

"I'm sorry to bother you," he said, in his clipped English/Algerian accent, "but I wonder if you could let me have a bit of your water. This needs freshening."

"Sure," she said. "Hang on."

Susannah bent over the spigot to turn down the water pressure.

Wait a minute, she thought. There's something familiar about that voice. Now where have I –?

The last thing Susannah heard before she blacked out was a large thump.

Mort watched his victim collapse, like a puppet with severed strings. He had brought his sap sharply down on the back of Susannah's head, with enough force to knock her out yet not kill her. The cause of death had to be drowning. She'd have to be breathing when he held her under, so her lungs would fill with sea water.

He knew from experience she'd be out for five to six minutes. He put the sap back in his pocket and put the empty water jar in the other. Then he picked up Susannah and carried her through the house and out on the deck. He surveyed the beach. It was empty.

173

He looked around for a towel and saw one lying on the deck mat. He set Susannah down briefly in a deck chair, grabbed the towel, and put it around her neck. Then he picked her up and descended the stairs to the beach. He walked straight to the water's edge and lowered Susannah to the sand. He placed the towel and her sunglasses next to her.

He heard a faint moan that told him she'd soon be coming to. He lifted her in his arms and waded in the shallow water. He softly whistled the tune "Oh, Susannah." He glanced down at her lovely face, the eyelids fluttering and then blinking. The shock of cold water would revive her, but it would be too late. Way too late.

"Police. Freeze."

Mort turned his head and saw Jericho, who was crouched low on the beach, with his gun in a two-handed grip.

"Put her down," Jericho shouted. "Gently. Do it. Now!"

Jericho watched the man turn to face him and walk back up to dry land, carrying Susannah. He bent over and deposited her on the beach. Then he angled his body slightly away from the detective, and made a sudden movement. Jericho went on instant alert.

"Glock party!" Mort shouted as he spun and fired.

In the same instant, Jericho dropped to the sand and got off three quick shots. One blew a bloody hole below the man's sternum, the second punctured a lung, and the third pierced his heart.

Mort's bullet thudded harmlessly into a sand dune.

Susannah heard the shots as her unconscious haze lifted. She opened her eyes and saw Mort lying beside her, his chest covered with blood. His abdomen was rising and falling spasmodically. A sound was coming from his mouth, a kind of "Eh, eh, eh, eh," which ended in a gurgle. His head flopped to the side and he stopped breathing.

Jericho leaned over her. "You okay?"

"...Yes. I think so."

"Good."

"What's going on?"

"This guy was about to drown you."

174

"Oh, my God," Susannah said. "How did you — "

"I'll explain later."

The detective bent over the body and pulled the crumpled Panama hat away from Mort's face.

Jericho recognized Mort immediately. "Holy shit," he exclaimed. His picture had been distributed frequently by the FBI, Secret Service, and Interpol, warning all police officers to be on the lookout for him, especially during visits to the Big Apple by foreign dignitaries, the President, even the Pope.

"Do you know who this guy is?" he asked Susannah.

"No."

"He's an internationally known assassin who goes by the name of Mort. You have any idea why he was after you?"

"No. None at all."

But even as Susannah answered, she realized who had probably hired the hitman — Quinn Healey. I bet he knows Mort through Burt. And he pockets at least three million if I'm dead. Maybe more if he knows how to access Burt's off-shore bank account.

Jericho examined Mort's pistol without touching it. He noted it was a Glock 50 caliber semiautomatic with a Scorpion silencer.

"Gee, my head hurts," Susannah moaned.

Jericho felt the pocket of the dead man's smock. Then, using a handkerchief to avoid leaving fingerprints, he reached into the pocket. "Yeah. Here's why."

He held up the sap. Susannah touched the back of her head and grimaced. "Ow. It's really swelling up."

"We should get some ice on it. Wait a minute, what's this?"

With his hanky-covered hand he pulled the water jar out of Mort's other pocket.

"Oh, he was pretending to be a watercolor artist," Susannah said. "He set up an easel on the hill next to my house."

"I'll check it out when the support crew gets here. Let me just call in."

He phoned the precinct house on his cell and reported the incident to Chief Manos.

"I'm not kiddin' you, Dominick," Jericho said. "It's Mr. Mort himself. He was about to drown Mrs. Cascadden... Yeah, it might be related to her husband's disappearance, but I don't know anything yet. I just got here."

The Chief said he'd come out personally.

"Fine. Oh, and you better notify Alvarez at the ME's office. He'll get out here right away, I'm sure."

As Jericho gave his boss the address and directions to the Cascadden house, Susannah took advantage of the detective's distraction. Furtively, she slipped something into the corpse's Bermuda shorts pocket.

CHAPTER 35

Up at the house, Jericho waited on the sun deck while Susannah went into the kitchen and got some ice. "I'd get it for you," he'd said, "But I'm required to keep the body in sight till support arrives."

Susannah came out pressing an ice pack to the back of her head. She settled into a deck chair while Jericho sat on the end of a lounger.

"Mrs. Cascadden..." Jericho said.

"Please call me Susannah," she said. "After all, you did save my life... Oh gosh, I'm sorry — I haven't even thanked you."

"Hey, I'm just glad I got here in time."

"What's your first name?"

"Actually, department regulations don't allow us to use our given names. They like us to be formal with the public."

"I'm not the public. I'm the victim of a crime."

"Doesn't matter. Besides, I'm not too crazy about my given name."

"I understand. Thank you, Jericho," Susannah said with sincerity.

After a moment, she spoke again. "I guess...there's no news on my husband."

"No, but actually, that's why I came out here. We're putting him in the FBI's missing person's database, which requires a photograph whenever possible. Do you have one?"

"Um, no."

"None at all?"

"No. He...we weren't sentimental that way."

"Well, we can use his driver's license. I saw it in his wallet when I was here before."

"Oh. Oh yes. I'll get it for you."

Susannah got up and went inside to get it.

When she returned, she handed the license to Jericho. He looked at the photo of Burt with interest.

What's with those lips? he thought.

"This'll do." he said. He put the license in his jacket pocket.

"Now we have to figure out who wants you dead." Jericho said. "You have no idea who'd put a contract on your life?"

"No. It must've been a mistake."

"Mort is the best in the business. He doesn't make mistakes."

"Except today," Susannah said, "When he was just a tad slow on the draw."

Jericho's warm, self-effacing smile made her understand why damsels in distress cry out, "My hero!"

Their eyes locked, and for a moment an electric spark seemed to crackle between them.

Susannah averted her eyes, then stood up. "Wait a minute," she said. "I just had a thought."

She went back into the house and returned with two documents.

"This is a copy of my husband's will," she said. "You can see in paragraph 4 that if I die, Burt's entire estate goes to his lawyer, Quinn Healey."

As Jericho read the paragraph, she sat down beside him on the lounger.

178

"So," he said. "You think it's possible the lawyer ordered this hit on you?"

"It does give him a motive. My husband had financial difficulties, but there's still this house, the cars, and probably an off-shore bank account."

"That would be, what, in the millions?"

Susannah nodded. "And here's something I found on the Internet."

He read the second document.

"Well," he said, "previous public censure probably wouldn't be allowed in court, but it shows he ain't no angel."

"So, you think he could be a suspect?"

"Could be," Jericho said. "But this'll be a tough case. See, a professional like Mort is super careful about being linked to anybody. Every aspect of his identity is covert. He'll have a false passport, all kinds of phony ID. I saw a car outside your house, but I'm sure it's rented with a fake driver's license and paid for in cash. He's constantly on the move and I doubt we'll ever find out where he's been living. And he certainly would keep no written records. So we'll have to investigate the lawyer himself to link him to the killer."

"But — you'll do that."

"Of course," Jericho said. "Can I keep this copy of your husband's will?"

"Sure," Susannah said. "I have my own lawyer now and he can send me another copy."

They were sitting close enough now that she could look into her rescuer's eyes. There was a sadness in them; somehow they looked older than he was.

"Jericho," she said. "I just keep thinking that I wouldn't exist any more if it weren't for you."

"Well, I'm glad you still exist." He reached over and touched the top of her hand.

Susannah felt his warm palm, pressing gently. She slowly turned her hand over, till her palm faced his. Suddenly they were aware of being skin to skin, hotness to hotness.

The doorbell rang. They pulled apart.

"That must be your support team," she said breathlessly.

"Yes," Jericho replied. He could feel his face flushing. "I'll get it."

He rose to his feet and went to answer the door.

Soon the place was crawling with cops. Susannah watched from the deck as they pounded stakes into the sand and surrounded the area with bright yellow crime scene tape.

Some obvious bigwig was strutting around like General Patton, giving orders. He shooed away a couple of beach joggers who stopped to gawk. Jericho was kneeling beside the hitman's corpse, searching through his clothing and dictating to a patrolman with a notebook.

A cop with a rake was systematically dragging it through the sand, looking for evidence.

The bigwig appeared on Susannah's deck and said he'd like to get a statement.

"Detective Jericho knows what happened," she said.

"He's the shooter, that's why it's better if I do it. I'm Dominick Manos, Chief of Police."

Susannah looked at the rosacea on his nose and wondered if it was from drinking or a Bill Clinton kind of thing.

"How do you do, Chief. I'm Susannah Cascadden."

"Cascadden? Like the guy who used to play for the Jets?"

"Who?"

"Chad Cascadden. Number 51. Outside linebacker."

Susannah shrugged.

"Doesn't matter. Tell me what went down this morning."

180

He took out an investigation notebook. She spoke quickly and he wrote furiously. Occasionally he had to hold up his hand and stop her until he caught up. As they were finishing, Jericho joined them on the deck.

"Excuse me, Chief," he said. "I found something interesting."

He held up a business card. "This was in Mort's pocket — H. Quinn Healey, Esquire. It's got a handwritten phone number on the back, and it's signed with Healey's first name."

Susannah noticed Jericho was wearing latex gloves.

My fingerprints on the card! she thought.

"Quinn Healey?" she said with surprise. "Let me see that." She snatched the card from the detective and looked at it.

"Mrs. Cascadden," Jericho shouted. "That's evidence. You're contaminating it with your fingerprints."

"Oh, gee. I'm so sorry," she said. "I just wasn't thinking."

She handed Healey's business card back. She was definitely thinking.

"Healey?" the Chief said. "You know who that is?"

"Yes." Jericho answered. "Mrs. Cascadden showed me a copy of her husband's will. If she dies, his estate goes to his lawyer, Quinn Healey."

"So the lawyer may have hired the hitman."

"Right," Jericho said. "But I'm surprised."

"About what?"

"Well, a world class hitman doesn't usually leave a paper trail."

"Sometimes you get lucky. Did he have phony IDs?"

"Of course."

"What name was he using?"

"John Tod, with one D. He was a noted punster."

"Huh?"

"*Tod* means death in German," Jericho explained. "And of course *Mort* — "

Susannah jumped in. "*Mort* means death in French."

The Chief tried to look like he knew that.

"Mrs. Cascadden," Jericho said, "I must ask you not to discuss this investigation with anyone. Especially the possible involvement of Mr. Healey."

"I won't."

"A case like this is very tricky."

"But you've got the handwritten phone number."

"We're not even positive it's the lawyer's writing. As I said, do not discuss this case."

Parolman Teddy Karlin approached them."

"Chief," he said, "the medical examiner radioed that he's on his way over. Helicopter should be here in twenty minutes. He says someone from EHPD has to sign off on the body."

"I'll wait for him," Chief Manos said. Jericho could see his boss wanted to connect as much as possible to this high profile case. Jericho couldn't have cared less.

If Healey hired the Mort, Jericho thought, *he also could've hired the hitman to kill Burton Cascadden. He needed both Susannah and her husband dead in order to inherit the estate. Definitely something to consider.*

He turned and went down the steps to the beach, Susannah called to him, "Jericho, thank you again for saving my life."

"Any time."

He walked back to the crime scene berating himself. *What the hell was I doing, touching her like that? And what was she doing when she reciprocated?*

Oh, come on, it was only a handshake.

But maybe it meant more.

Stop it! If I start thinking that way I risk not only compromising this investigation but also getting myself in deep trouble.

182

So why am I thinking at this very moment that I can't wait to see her again?

CHAPTER 36

Officer Karlin's assignment was to drive Mort's rental car back to the precinct house, and also bring the easel and stool with him.

When he got to the automobile, which was parked in front of the beach house, he took out his phone and called his pal Nicholas Rhinelander at *Long Island Newsday*. He had a deal with the columnist — any tips he delivered on criminal activity in East Hampton or Montauk would be rewarded on a sliding scale, from fifty bucks for a publishable misdemeanor up to five hundred for a major scoop.

"Nicky," Karlin said into the phone. "You owe me five hundred clams."

Afterward, he was so excited about the money that he just drove the car back to town, forgetting all about the easel and the stool.

Susannah decided to go to bed early that night. Around nine she took a long hot bath, hoping the warm water and fragrant bath oil would calm her unsettled feelings. But her anxious thoughts kept intruding:

Planting Healey's phone number on the body was a smart move. But what if it doesn't work? What if they can't nail him for hiring the hitman?

Healey would realize I'd given the police his business card. What would he do about it?

How well did I cover up my...my...what I did to Burt? And to Jessie Russell?

Any mistake could destroy me. And it seems like the longer this ordeal goes on, the more mistakes I could make.

There's so much I can't anticipate or control.

And what about that moment when I touched Jericho's hand? It was so warm, so strong.

What does he want? What do I want? What could a woman who has killed two human beings dare to want?

She had no answers.

CHAPTER 37

HITMAN HIT BY COP

EAST HAMPTON DETECTIVE IN SHOOTOUT

WITH HIRED KILLER

The desk sergeant thrust *Newsday*'s front page in Jericho's face as he entered the precinct house.

"Congrats, detective," the sergeant said. "You da man."

Chief Manos strode out of his office with two men.

"Jericho," he said. "This is Nicholas Rhinelander, I'm sure you read his column. He's here to get a few pictures."

Rhinelander smiled.

Jericho didn't.

Rhinelander looked like a toad, a smiling toad.

"Get them in front of the American flag?" Rhinelander said to the photographer. "Chief, move in real close to him."

Jericho found himself next to Manos, staring sourly at the camera while his boss beamed. Strobe flashes went off.

"So tell me, detective," Rhinelander said. "How come you were on the beach when this Mort character was doin' his thing?"

"Sorry," Jericho replied. "I can't give out any information. It's too early in the investigation."

"Sources tell me the intended victim was a Mrs. Cascadden. Why was she? — "

"Who are your sources?"

"You know I can't reveal that."

"And I can't reveal anything about this case," Jericho said. He turned, walked into his office and shut the door.

"Jesus!" Manos shouted at Rhinelander, "I said you could get a few pictures. I didn't say you could interview him."

"Sorry. It's the newshound in me."

Manos' secretary called out to him. "*Eyewitness News* on the phone. They're sending a TV truck."

Rhinelander grabbed the photographer. "Let's go, Leon. We're done here."

"Don't go messin' up my case, Mr. Rhinelander," Manos said.

"Not to worry. But you're gonna be up to your ass in media by this afternoon."

Manos made a beeline for Jericho's office and barged in.

"Somebody must've tipped off *Newsday*," Manos said.

"Yeah. Some fink made a few bucks with his big mouth."

"Doesn't really matter," Manos said. "This kinda story you can't hide. But don't worry. I'll handle the media. You're gonna have your hands full — bein' a detective and a suspect in the same case."

"Who'll be investigating me?"

"Yours truly, representing Homicide. And Harburg from Internal Affairs. He'll be here this afternoon."

"You know him?"

"Yeah. Usual IA type, holier than thou. But I've got your statement and Mrs. Cascadden's statement. Hopefully he'll accept them both and go home."

"When do you think the DA will present to the grand jury?"

"A few days at the most," Manos said. "And don't worry, they'll come up with a 'no bill.' Nobody's lookin' to nail you for whackin' one of the World's Most Wanted. You're a goddamn hero."

Jericho nodded. "Listen," he said. "I've got a comparison exemplar of the Cascadden lawyer's signature. Looks like a match with the one on his business card."

"The card you found on Mort's body?"

"Yes. Who do you use for document forensics?"

"Place called Handwriting Synergistics. My secretary'll give you the address. It's in Georgia."

"Georgia? Chief, it'll take for fucking ever. NYPD has their own handwriting guys. I can — "

"Jericho. You're under scrutiny now. You gotta do everything by the book. Don't go playin' rogue cop on me, even in a small detail. Got me?"

"Yeah."

"Anyway," Manos went on, "the two signatures are enough to get a search warrant on Healey. I know Judge Rakoff. He won't give us any grief. Write in your affidavit that in your professional opinion the signatures match, and send him Xerox copies of both samples."

"Okay," Jericho said, "I better get going on this paperwork."

"I'm assigning Anderson and Grenci to work with you on this case. We'll all get together after you meet with IA."

"Okay."

"I hated doing it," Manos said, "but I'm handing off the Jessie Russell investigation to the State Police. We don't have the manpower. You've got the names of possible suspects in the Shinnecock tribe?"

"Could be anyone in Russell's family. But nobody there will talk."

"Ya never know. Anyway it's NYSP's jurisdiction. Write out a summary of your notes, fax it to them."

"Right."

189

I'll get to it when I get to it, Jericho said to himself. *Which might not be too soon. This is still my fucking case!*

CHAPTER 38

Susannah was about to leave the house for her dance class when the phone rang.

"Hello?"

"Susannah, hi, this is Quinn. Quinn Healey."

Shocked, she said nothing.

"I read about the hitman in *Newsday* this morning," he said. "Terrible thing. How are you?"

Newsday? she thought. *I can't believe this made the papers already.*

"Any idea who hired the guy?" he asked.

"I'm not supposed to discuss it."

"Of course." There was a pause. "Susannah, I'm very concerned about you. How about if I come out tomorrow? I'll take you to dinner at Nick & Tony's and we can — "

"I told you not to call me, Quinn. I meant it."

She hung up.

What the hell is he doing? she asked herself. *He can't know about the business card. But he must assume I'll be questioned in this case. I guess he figures he's so well covered that it's best to behave normally, play the part of family attorney and concerned friend. And maybe he's so egotistical he thinks he can still get laid. What a jerk. Wait till he finds out his handwritten name and phone number was found on the hitman's body. He won't be so cocky then.*

But what if he's found another hitman, or he's planning kill me himself? Jesus!

Maybe this dinner invitation was part of his plan? If he had the nerve to call me, who knows what he's got in mind?

She threw her dance bag over her shoulder and opened the front door. As she walked to her car, she saw two men coming toward her. They looked menacing. She was too far from her house to run back inside. She panicked and froze.

"Mrs. Cascadden," one of them called out.

Susannah made a dash for her SUV. As she opened the car door she heard the *click-whirr* of a camera shutter.

"Mrs. Cascadden," the man shouted, "You're better off letting us getting a decent shot of you. Otherwise you're on the front page looking like a scared rabbit."

She was inside her car now, doors and windows locked. She saw the camera pointed at her, and put up a hand to shield her face. *Click-whirr.*

The other man was leaning over the windshield, waving a picture ID with the word *Press* on it.

"Nicholas Rhinelander," he shouted. *"Long Island Newsday."*

Okay, maybe they're not hired killers, she thought. *But I'm taking no chances.*

She started the car and backed quickly out of the driveway, forcing the newsmen to jump out of the way. She drove off, tires squealing.

In her mind, Susannah tried to make sense of her panic. *Am I being paranoid? No. Paranoid means being unreasonably suspicious of other people's thoughts or intentions. There's nothing unreasonable about my fears.*

192

As Susannah taught her dance class, she kept watching Katie. She noticed the little girl had the same serious look as her father, when total concentration was required.

After class, Katie ran over and gave her a hug. "You sure are a good teacher," she exclaimed. For a brief moment Susannah felt like the person she used to be.

Then Katie spied her mother and ran to her. Susannah looked at Jericho's ex-wife . *Hmm,* she thought. *Quite attractive*

As Susannah walked down the hall, Gretchen appeared and said she'd like to talk to her.

Gretchen's husband was waiting in the office. "Susannah," he said warmly, "How are you feeling?"

Arnold was no longer the cold-ass attorney. He was back to being Mr. Congeniality.

"I'm managing," Susannah replied.

"Sit down, honey," Gretchen said. "We've been so worried about you. God, what a thing to go through."

Susannah nodded.

"The paper said he was a hitman," Gretchen said.

"Yes."

"I know you're not supposed to talk about what happened," Arnold said. "We just want you to know we're here for you."

"I appreciate that."

"Susannah," Arnold said, "you've probably figured this out on your own, but clearly Quinn Healey had a motive to put out a contract on you."

"Yes," she said. "The police are looking into that."

"Good."

"Suze," Gretchen said, "Arnie and I talked it over and we'd like you to come and stay with us for a while. We've got a guest room over our garage, so you can come and go as you please."

"Oh, thanks," Susannah said. "I appreciate it, but I'm fine."

"But you've been through so much; this is a time to be with friends. And you'll be much safer staying with us. Maybe this thing isn't over. What if — "

"Thanks, Gretch. But really, I'll be okay. I won't be driven out of my own home."

"Well, if you change your mind," Arnold said, "just let us know."

"Thanks. I will."

"Any word from the police on your husband's disappearance?" Arnold asked.

"Sort of. They told me they found a spinal column washed up on the beach, and that it might belong to Burt. They're DNA testing it right now."

"Oh, honey," Gretchen said. "This must be so awful for you."

"Forgive me for asking," Arnold said. "But did your husband have any life insurance?"

"Gee, I don't know."

"Because, if it turns out your husband is deceased, that's important information. If you put in a claim, the insurance company might dispute it, even take it to court. In fact, your whole inheritance could be delayed for years, if there's no proof of death. These are tricky legal issues that I might be able to help you with."

"Well, thanks, but — "

"Also," Arnold went on, "I hate to say this, but as sole beneficiary in Burt's will you stand to profit from his death — so you might fall under suspicion."

Susannah struggled to keep her voice calm. "Just because I'm in the will?"

"Especially if foul play is suggested,"

"Foul play?" Susannah said. "The police never suggested that."

"But who knows? They may find evidence of it later. And if they do — you could possibly be a suspect."

194

"...Me?"

"I'm just trying to cover all bases," Arnold went on. "If you'd like, I'll fax you an agreement authorizing me to act on your behalf, for whatever comes up."

"But, I don't think..."

"Arnie," Gretchen said to her husband. "Tell her what we discussed last night!"

"Oh, yes," the lawyer said. "All my legal work for you will be *pro bono.*"

"Don't even think about paying," Gretchen said. "We're your friends!"

"I know I said I'd bill you," Arnold said. "But I wasn't thinking. It was reflexive lawyer talk. Forgive me."

"Thanks," Susannah said. "That's really nice of you."

Gretchen smiled and hugged Susannah. Arnold extended his hand for a handshake, but Susannah kissed him on the cheek.

It was reassuring to know they were her friends.

CHAPTER 39

That night Jericho received a call at home from his ex-wife Sarah. She had something important to discuss and wanted to come over.

Jericho lived on Pocahontas Lane, in a wooded area near the Indian cemetery, about five miles from Montauk Point. It was cheap, and a twenty-minute drive to where Katie lived with Sarah and Irwin.

Jericho straightened up the place as best he could. The A-frame house had once been an artist's atelier. When Jericho was first shown the house, the realtor pointed with pride at the splatters of oil paint all over the floors — very Jackson Pollack, she'd said. Actually it was a sloppy mess, but after Jericho moved in he grew fond of it. Nobody else ever came to visit but Katie, and she thought it was cool.

As he slid the vacuum cleaner under the bed, Jericho questioned his sudden need to do housework, an activity he had disdained during his marriage. Maybe it was to show Sarah he had his act together.

When Sarah arrived, she showed no interest in the lack of dust bunnies. She looked grim.

"What's up, Sarah?"

"Can we sit down?"

"Sure."

Sarah had once been rail thin, but the pound a year she'd put on over the last ten was quite becoming to her. She settled into an armchair, and as she leaned forward her blouse fell open. Jericho caught himself trying to glom a glimpse of her breasts.

What the hell am I doing? he asked himself. *She's my ex-wife, and I'm ogling her like a hyper-hormonal teenager. Get a grip.*

"Would you like a drink?" Jericho asked. "I've got some white wine."

"I thought you quit."

"Oh, absolutely. But I keep a bottle in the fridge, in case — y'know, for company."

"No, thanks. I'm good."

"So, what did you want to talk to me about?"

"It's about Katie."

Jericho felt suddenly anxious. "Has something happened to her?"

"No. She's fine, Neil."

He was always startled when he heard his first name. Sarah was the only one who used it.

She paused to collect herself. "The thing is, Irwin's father is retiring — y'know, he's got this big construction company — anyway, he wants Irwin to take over the business. It would mean — us moving to Washington."

"D.C.?"

"State. Tacoma."

Jericho's heart sank.

"It's a great opportunity for Irwin," she said. "He's gone as far as he can here in Montauk. And y'know, since I've been working at the health food store, I've gotten very interested in nutritional healing. There's a school of naturopathic medicine close by in Seattle. I could get a degree and — "

"You can't do this," Jericho said angrily.

"Please, Neil, I'm sorry — "

"Jesus Christ," he shouted. "You know what Katie means to me. When you moved out here, I relocated to be with her. I had to start at the bottom with the East Hampton police, but it didn't matter, because the important thing was to be near her."

"I know that, Neil."

"Sarah, we have joint custody."

"But I have *residual* custody. She has to live with me."

"You can't just pick up and move out of state. I can go to court."

"Please," Sarah said. "I know what you're feeling. But you know you can't win in court. You'd have to try to get residual custody for yourself, and you don't have the kind of schedule where you could take care of her. The court puts the welfare of the child first, and you know they'd decide Katie should be with her mother."

"For God's sake, Sarah," Jericho said, "we agreed we'd always be reasonable and fair when it comes to Katie. This is totally *un*fair. "

"Neil," she said gently. "We didn't plan for this to happen. Irwin's dad always said he'd work till he dropped. But now he's giving us a wonderful opportunity. Irwin'll be making much more money, and Katie will live in a great neighborhood and have the finest schooling."

"So what happens to my visitation rights?"

"Irwin made a suggestion. He's offering to pay for your airfare, as many trips as you want. It's only a five-hour flight. You can come out every weekend. You'll have to red-eye it but – "

"Christ, Sarah."

"And if your child support becomes a hardship — "

"I'll always pay Katie's child support," Jericho said firmly.

"Okay, okay," she said. "Anyway, you can have her for Christmas, Easter, four weeks in the summer."

"Summer is the busy season out here. I won't have that much free time."

"I know," Sarah said compassionately. "but we'll work it out somehow."

Jericho sighed, knowing there was nothing he could do. "When would you be leaving?" he asked.

"Right after Thanksgiving."

"Oh, no."

"I'm really sorry, Neil."

"You'll be uprooting Katie, taking her away from all her friends."

Sarah gave him a compassionate look. "Please try to understand."

"Have you told Katie about this?"

"Not yet."

"It's gonna kill her."

"Kids are resilient. They're stronger than we think."

"Well, I'm not."

"You're the strongest man I've ever known."

He could see she meant it. It didn't help. He felt the tears coming.

"Please, Neil," Sarah said. "It'll be okay."

He rose and walked into the kitchen. He grabbed a dishtowel and wiped his eyes.

"Listen," he called out. "I think I need some time alone with this."

"Of course. Call me later if you want to talk."

He heard Sarah moving toward the door.

"Neil. I — I'm truly sorry."

Jericho opened the refrigerator and took out the bottle of wine. He sat down at the kitchen table and stared at it.

I know I'm not an alcoholic, he told himself. *It was easy to quit once I got away from all the crap in New York. So what the hell if I take a little sip of Chardonnay, to calm myself down?*

He got a corkscrew from the table drawer, stripped off the plastic from the neck of the bottle, and began to open it.

As he did, he heard a far off rumble of thunder.

200

He struggled to sort things out in his mind. *Why did this have to happen? Everything was going so well. Things with Katie and me are great, I'm doing okay in my job, and I'm even starting to think maybe something could develop with Susannah. Not now of course, but maybe, after this case is cleared...*

He picked up the wine bottle.

I need this. Christ, yes. I need this! One drink won't hurt.

Bottle in hand, he opened the kitchen door and stepped out into the black night.

He heard the thunder closer now, resounding like a tympani roll.

He raised the bottle to his lips, hesitated a moment, then took a big slug of wine.

Immediately he felt the familiar warmth in his system, the fulfillment of a long-denied need. His head started spinning and he held onto the back porch rail for support.

A thunder clap echoed in the sky. A lightening flash illuminated the woods around him. It was like a warning from heaven. He was about to take another swig when it hit him. *One more swallow of this stuff and I'm lost!*

He could hear the first spatter of raindrops on the porch roof.

Mocked by the cheeping of crickets, he realized how weak and vulnerable he was.

Abruptly he hurled the bottle into the forest. "No!" he shouted as it shattered.

The rain began coming down in earnest, drenching him from head to toe.

Jericho walked back into the house, the alcohol still dizzying his brain and body.

I'll get on with my life, he told himself. *Do the best I can. But I need something good to happen for me. Goddammit, I need something good!*

CHAPTER 40

Susannah was in bed, reading *Dance Magazine*. The rain was falling in torrents, pounding the roof above her, pelting her bedroom window.

She heard the familiar ding from the laptop on her nightstand, indicating she had an e-mail.

She sat up, swung onto the edge of her bed and opened Gmail. The e-mail was all in caps:

IT'S ME AGAIN. YOU DID A BAD THING.

YOU ARE BEING WATCHED!

It was signed with a smiley face emoticon.

The fear gripped her once more.

I thought this e-mail thing was over. Now this. What does it mean? Someone is trying to harass me, frighten me. But who? Someone... evil.

She got up, feeling suddenly exposed because she was wearing only a t-shirt. She put on a robe, and looked out the window into the dark, rainy night. She saw nothing.

What did I expect to see? she thought.

She'd said she wouldn't cry any more, but there was no holding back.

The tears came, flooding her eyes. She threw herself down on the bed, her body racked with sobs. She lay there, frightened, overwhelmed by the feeling that her life was beyond her control. And she felt terribly alone.

The doorbell rang. She sat up, wiping her eyes.

The doorbell rang again, more urgently.

Susannah looked at her alarm clock. It was just after midnight.

She went to the top of the stairs and called down.

"Who's there?"

"Police. Open up!"

She thought she recognized the detective's voice. Descending the stairs, she called out.

"Detective Jericho?"

"Yes."

She went to the bay window, where she could see him at the door. She wanted to make sure.

She opened the door.

Jericho stood there in the rain, holding a large umbrella over him. He looked disheveled and very intense.

"Detective. What are you?..."

"Susannah," he interrupted her.

"First name?"

"It's...I'm not here as a cop."

"Do you want to come in?"

"Please."

He closed his umbrella and left it outside. He kicked off his sneakers, and entered.

"Those sneakers'll get ruined," she said.

"They're old canvas Topsiders. I've worn them wet before."

For a moment they stood facing each other in silence. He smiled. Seeing him, the terror that had seized her only a few minutes before seemed to ease away.

"I'm sorry to bother you," Jericho said. "I just needed to talk."

"About what?"

"Something personal."

She could see Jericho was troubled. "Are you okay?"

Jericho saw the face of this beautiful woman, looking at him with warmth and genuine concern.

"What is it?" she said softly, placing her hand tentatively on his cheek.

Jericho pulled her to him and kissed her. The spark of connection that had flashed between them over the past few weeks burst into an engulfing flame.

Jericho was amazed at the softness of her lips. It had been so long since he'd kissed a woman. And when her tongue slid tentatively into his mouth, he was momentarily back in high school, experiencing the wonder of his first kiss.

She melted against him, adoring his strength. In his arms she felt protected, like nothing bad could happen to her. She could feel the heat start to pool within her as his lips left her mouth, trailing wetly along her cheek. She moaned and pulled away.

"This isn't a good idea."

"I know."

His hands still held her around the waist. She could have backed away further, but she didn't. She could feel his burgeoning manhood pressing against her thigh. "Do you want to come upstairs?"

"Very much."

Jericho followed her up the stairway to her bedroom. As Susannah climbed the steps, she removed her robe and trailed it behind her. Above her naked buttocks were two gently indented dimples. It was the most erotic sight Jericho had ever seen.

She lay naked on the bed and watched him undress. She admired his well-defined arms and chest. He was thick around the middle, but his upper abdomen still showed muscle beneath. *A two-pack,* she thought.

He stripped off his pants and briefs, and dropped belly down beside her. He reached for her and she stopped him.

"Do you have a condom?"

"Uh, gee, no."

"Neither do I."

"I'm sorry."

"Oh, well. Don't worry about it.

"You mean — "

"We'll just have to improvise."

"Improvise?"

"Y'know, explore alternative possibilities."

"Sounds promising".

"Me first," she said.

Gently she pushed him over on his back.

He felt her long hair trailing along his torso as her head moved toward his genitals. Then she was there, dragging her tresses back and forth, making his penis rise and thicken.

Jericho's eyes were closed so he didn't see Susannah swing her body over him. But he felt her breasts pressing on his thighs.

Her fingernails dug into his belly muscles as her mouth took him. She was all wetness and enveloping warmth, her tongue a soft whip of pleasure, swirling and slithering over the length of him.

God, I love how he feels in my mouth, she thought. *So hard, hot, and slippery smooth.* Jericho moaned softly, and knowing she was giving him pleasure made Susannah wet with her own desire.

One of her hands was stroking his shaft now. The other was on the sac below, caressing, coaxing. For long moments she kept him on the edge, teasing him, controlling him. Finally Jericho felt the delicious flow of orgasmic tension begin to rise. The sensation built, and built, then abruptly peaked. His back arched, his hips lifted and fell and lifted again, but her mouth stayed with him, striving to contain his essence.

He collapsed back on the damp bedclothes. Susannah rested her head on her hand, watching his softening member. She kissed it lightly, affectionately, then wriggled up to lie beside him. Jericho pulled her close and for a while they rested in silence.

"It's only in moments like this," Susannah said, "that I regret giving up cigarettes."

Jericho laughed. "I'd like to ask you something," he said. "Don't answer if you don't want to."

"What is it?"

"Did you love your husband?"

"No."

He waited for her to explain more. She didn't.

"I noticed you've got separate bedrooms," Jericho said.

Susannah hesitated before answering. "We...well, it's complicated.

"None of my business," he said. "I'm sorry."

She leaned over and kissed him on the lips to tell him it was all right.

"Were you a dancer before you became a teacher?" he asked.

"Yes."

"Ballet? Modern?"

"Modern."

"Martha Graham?"

"How did you know?"

"I'm a detective. I deduce things."

"C'mon."

"Okay," he said smiling. "Martha Graham's the only name I know in modern dance."

"Did you ever see her?"

"I saw the company. When I was a kid my mom used to drag me into the city for concerts, dance, theatre. I liked Martha Graham because the ladies kept pumpin' their pelvises. Guess I was a horny little devil back then."

"As opposed to now?"

Jericho grinned.

"How long have you been a detective?" she asked.

"Fifteen years. But only a couple in East Hampton. Before that I was in the city. Twenty-third Precinct, East Harlem."

"Why did you leave?"

Jericho paused before he answered. "I got burned out."

"I guess it's pretty rough, what a city cop has to deal with on a day-to-day basis."

"Yeah."

"So you moved out here to be with Katie?"

Jericho nodded.

"She's a doll," Susannah said.

He smiled but there was that sadness in his eyes.

"So," she said, "was there one thing that led you to quit the police department, or was it just everything?"

"Everything," Jericho answered. "But there was one event that triggered it, and it didn't really involve police work."

Jericho sat up and propped some pillows behind his head.

"I was walking home after work one night," he said, "when I saw a restaurant delivery boy on a bike, coming straight at me. Bicycles on the sidewalk always pissed me off, because on patrol I'd seen plenty of pedestrians creamed by these kamikazes. So this delivery boy was bearing down on me, full speed ahead. He was avoiding eye contact; they always do — I guess on the theory that if they don't acknowledge you, it forces *you* to take responsibility for not getting hit. As the kid passed, he grazed my jacket sleeve, and without thinking I stuck out my elbow and shoved hard. The bike wobbled, skidded out of control, then smashed into a light pole. The kid went flying over the handlebars and landed on the sidewalk."

He paused and let out a self-derisive sigh.

"Susannah, I watched it all with a sense of amusement, like it was a movie cartoon. I mean, I'm a cop and I just stood there. I didn't even go to the aid of an injured person."

"A couple people on the street went to help him. I watched them pull the banged-up kid to his feet, and he went limping over to his wrecked bike. After that I turned around and went home. A week later I quit the force."

Susannah could see the memory was upsetting. She reached over and gently stroked his hair. He closed his eyes; it had been a long time since anyone had soothed him. After a while Susannah spoke seductively.

"How would you feel about a little more improvisation?"

"Sounds good. But this time it's my turn."

"Have at it."

"I must warn you, though — I'm a little out of practice."

"Hey, it's like riding a bicycle."

Jericho slid down to the juncture of her thighs. She felt his tongue, moist and warm, beginning to explore. Like all the men she'd known, he was tentative and cautious, hoping to find his way into her mysterious center of desire. After a while he found the right spot, and she began to shudder against his wet mouth and stroking tongue. *Yes. Yes,* she whispered. That was all the coaching he needed.

Before long, she wanted to tell him he would qualify for the Tour de France.

At last they fell asleep, spoon style.

Jericho awoke when Susannah shifted her body. The rain had ended and the skies were clear. The moonlight from the window gave her naked form a ghostly pallor. Her limbs were spread out, her breasts barely discernible mounds on her chest. As Jericho watched, her hands reached up into the air, perhaps responding to something in an unknowable dream. Then they fell to the mattress.

Jericho felt a stab of anguish. After covering her with the bed sheet, he rolled over and fell into a deep sleep.

Jericho hears a baby crying. Then a woman's pleading voice: "Por favor ... Por favor."

Jericho and his partner draw their guns.

Luis Ramos holds the naked baby in his hands, dangling her out a wide-open window.

"Come any closer and the kid's history."

The baby is shrieking incessantly.

Jericho speaks calmly: "Luis, if you kill that kid, you'll get life in the joint. If you hand me the baby, all you'll face is drug charges. You'll probably end up with five to ten. It's a much better deal."

"Drop your guns or I drop the baby."

The mother calls out softly. "Madre de Dios, por favor... Por favor..."

The two cops put down their guns. Ramos pulls out a switchblade and holds it to the baby's throat.

"Now I'm gonna walk outta here. And I'll kill the kid if you try to stop me."

The whoop of police sirens echoes from the street.

"That's backup," Jericho says. "They'll surround the building. Sharpshooters'll blow your head off the moment you show your face. Even if you do get through, you'll have a kidnapping charge hanging over you. Then you're really fucked. Believe me, you're better off surrendering."

Jericho edges toward Ramos. "Give me the baby."

The drug dealer backs away.

"Come on, Luis. It's for the best."

"Stay away from me."

Jericho takes a step closer.

210

"Don't do that," Ramos shouts and retreats in panic. He backs into a low windowsill and topples backward; in an instant he and the baby are gone.

"Rosario," the mother screams. "Ay, mi niña, no ..."

The two detectives dash down the three flights of stairs and out into the street. A crowd is gathering. Ramos is a crumpled mess on the pavement, dead in a pool of blood. The baby girl is impaled on an iron fence in front of the building. Her body is face-up with a spike protruding from her navel. Her arms and legs move slowly for a while, then stop.

Jericho hears the child's mother whimpering, then she lets out a long agonized wail of grief.

And it hits him — Oh, Jesus. That little girl would still be alive if I hadn't taken one step too many!

Jericho cried out in his sleep — "One step too many! One step..."

He awoke and sat up.

Susannah spoke groggily. "Jericho, what is it? You all right?"

"...Yeah. Just a bad dream."

"You want to talk about it?"

"No, I'm fine."

"Sometimes it's good to talk about bad stuff."

He wanted to. When it happened it was too painful. He never brought it up with his wife. Even he and his partner didn't discuss it — it was an unspoken thing; let sleeping dogs lie. In their reports they called it an accident. Rosario's mother was interviewed but she was incoherent.

"I'm sorry, Susannah," Jericho said. "I — it was nothing, just a dream. Go back to sleep."

He waited till he heard Susannah's even breathing. Then, careful not to disturb her, he got up.

When the first daylight filtered into the bedroom, Susannah woke and saw Jericho wasn't there. She put on her robe and went to find him.

Jericho was lying in a lounger out on the deck, watching the sunrise over the Atlantic. He had his clothes on, though his feet were bare.

"Good morning," she said, caressing his head.

"Hi, beautiful."

"Couldn't sleep?"

"Too much excitement, I guess."

She sat down beside him. For a while they watched the sunrise in silence.

There were dense clouds on the horizon, obscuring the sun. But its rays were gradually lightening the sky, imparting a pink glow to the feathery clouds that floated high above the sea.

"Susannah," Jericho said, "last night — "

"Yes?"

"You were a wonder."

"Takes one to know one."

He took her hand. "Maybe next time you'll let me go *all the way*."

"What kind of a girl do you think I am?"

"The best."

He leaned over and kissed her on the cheek.

"Susannah — I won't be able to see you for a while," he said.

She looked at him questioningly.

"See, when a cop shoots someone it sets in motion a whole bunch of procedures. Technically, I'm now a suspect in a homicide. Internal Affairs will investigate the shooting, and so will the DA. Then the case'll be presented to a grand jury, and they'll decide whether it was justifiable homicide."

"But you were saving my life," she said. "And the guy you shot was a notorious assassin. What could be more justifiable than that?"

"If this happened in my old precinct, it would be cleared up in no time," Jericho said. "Sadly, police shootings are so common in East

212

Harlem they're just not as rigid about it. But East *Hampton* is a different deal. The Chief made it clear to me — the big money residents of Georgica and Further Lane came out here for peace and quiet. They don't like the idea of police violence of any kind. And they can raise quite a stink. So we have to go by the letter of the law."

"That's so unfair. You're a hero."

"It'll be fine," Jericho said. "You're the only eyewitness, and I'm sure you told Chief Manos exactly what happened."

"I did."

"But until the matter is adjudicated, I'm assigned 'no contact' status, which means I've gotta stay in the station house."

"Can you still work on the case?"

"Yeah. But only from my desk. I should be returned to active duty in a week or so. In the meantime, any contact with you would compromise your status as a credible witness. Internal Affairs will interview me today, and after that they could be nosing around anywhere, any time."

"I understand."

"I'm sorry, Susannah. I should've told you all this last night, before I — "

"I wouldn't have cared," she said, reaching for his hand.

They were silent for a few moments.

The Susannah spoke. "Can I ask you something...about the, uh, investigation?"

"You're not supposed to, but...okay."

"Healey's signature on the will," Susannah said. "Is it a problem that it's a fax, not the original?".

"Not for our purposes," Jericho explained. "We just want to establish high probability."

"Then you can arrest Healey?"

"No, no. Even if the signatures match, that wouldn't be enough. If that's our only evidence, the DA would say forget it. Even if he got an indictment, no jury would convict if all we've got is two signatures."

"But he had a motive. Remember — if I'm dead, he's the sole heir of my husband's estate, which is quite a lot of money."

Jericho looked thoughtful for a moment.

"That's a solid motive," he said. "But I'm afraid it's still not a strong case. Murder-for-hire cases are difficult. For one thing, the person doing the hiring always has an alibi for when the killing goes down. We'll have to establish Healey's contact with the hitman, maybe find an eyewitness, check phone records, e-mails."

Oh, God. Not e-mails, she thought. *'Anonymail cooperates with law enforcement'*.

"But a pro like Mort covers his tracks," Jericho went on. "Like I said, I'm surprised that phone number was in his pocket."

"Okay," she said. "But, what if you brought Healey into the station house, y'know, for questioning? How would he explain it?"

"I doubt he'd come in."

"But doesn't he have to?"

"Susannah, that's a common misconception. You can't bring an unwilling person in for questioning. And if you go to their house to interview them, they can slam the door in your face. Or hang up on you when you try to phone. Fact is, the police can't force someone to answer questions under any circumstances. If you arrest them, they have their Miranda right to remain silent. And if you take them to trial, they have the Constitutional right not to testify. Healey is an attorney. He of all people would know that."

"Jericho, I'm scared," Susannah said. "What if Healey tries to have me killed again?"

"That's not likely."

"But it's possible."

"Well, remember, at this point we don't have proof that he did hire Mort. But assuming he did, we can prevent him from trying it again."

"How?"

"I'll make sure he knows about the business card. That'll certainly deter him."

214

"How can you do that?"

"We'll be sending men into the city to interview him, probably today."

"But you said he could refuse to talk."

"He'd refuse to come out here to the station house," Jericho said. "But if we send our men to his office to speak with him, he'll probably act real cooperative, like he has nothing to hide. He'll answer a few questions, and establish an alibi. Then they'll show him a photocopy of his business card and ask why it was found on the hitman's body. He'll say 'I have no idea' and then refer us to a lawyer."

"What if he won't look at the card?"

"I'll e-mail him a JPG of it and request an explanation."

"That sounds good, but still..."

"Susannah," Jericho said with intensity, "Once Healey knows he's under suspicion, he won't dare to harm you. I promise — I won't let anything happen to you."

"When you say it, I believe it," she said. "Now it would be good if you kissed me."

He grabbed her and did an excellent job of it. Then he stood up.

"Well," he said, "I better get home. I need a shower before work."

"You can shower here."

"I'd like to change clothes too."

"Want some coffee before you leave?"

"No, that's okay. What've you got on for today?"

"Nothing much. I'm teaching at noon."

"Kiss Katie for me. I'll try to call you later — in *an unofficial capacity.*"

She nodded.

"You've got my card, don't you?" Jericho asked.

"Yes."

"My cell's always on, so you can reach me any time."

"Thanks," she said. "Can I give you something to make sure you remember last night?"

"Sure."

Susannah reached in her robe pocket and pulled out Jericho's damp sweat socks. Jericho laughed and stuffed them in his pocket.

Outside on the porch, Susannah watched as Jericho put on his still rain-soaked sneakers. Then he grabbed his umbrella and started walking toward his car. His Topsiders squished with every step.

Susannah giggled at the sound. Then she had a distressing thought — *I won't be seeing him for a week or so. I miss him already.*

Jericho stopped, looked up at the sandy hill in front of the house and saw Mort's wooden easel. It was on its side, having been toppled over in the night's rainstorm.

That idiot Karlin screwed up again, he thought. *He was supposed to bring in that stuff.*

Irritated, Jericho climbed the hill, intending to do it himself. When he got to the top, he realized he couldn't because he wasn't supposed to be there in the first place. Well, he could leave them be — the easel and stool were listed on the evidence manifest, and Montrose, the property clerk, would notice those items were missing and send somebody to get them.

He crossed over to the easel, curious to look at the painting. The rain had washed the paper on the watercolor block clean, except for some streaks of pale green and blue.

As Jericho descended the hill, he noticed a flash of color under a clump of beach grass. He went over and kneeled down. It was a piece of red, orange, and blue cellophane wrapper with a picture of a duck wearing a chef's hat. There was printing on it — the letters R-I-N-G.

Drake's Ring Dings, he thought. *Like the snacks we found in Jessie Russell's Hyundai.*

WTF?

He carefully wrapped the cake wrapper in his handkerchief to preserve fingerprints, and put it in his pocket.

CHAPTER 41

Jericho's afternoon meeting with the Internal Affairs officer went well. Harburg had no problem with Jericho's action; Mrs. Cascadden's statement made it clear he'd had no choice but to shoot to kill. Harburg even congratulated Jericho, calling him Dead-eye for outdrawing a famous hitman.

Later, Jericho attended a meeting in the Chief's office with Officers Grenci and Thompson.

"Gentlemen," Chief Manos said, "Detective Jericho here will be heading up the hitman investigation. He's on desk duty for a while, so keep him informed at all times. Now, this is a pretty big case for a small department like ours, but I know if we all put our pedal to the metal we're gonna make East Hampton proud of us. Right?"

Everybody grunted in assent.

"All right, Grenci," the Chief said to his eager-beaver subordinate, "today you and Thompson will go into the city and interview Healey at his office. Don't tell him he's a suspect — you just want to know if he has any idea who'd want to kill Mrs. Cascadden. Chances are you'll get nothing from him, but probe, probe, ya never know. And while you're there, get his fingerprints so we can check 'em against whatever's on the business card."

"How are we supposed get his prints?" Grenci asked. "I mean — till we get a warrant, we can't take anything from his office. Right?"

"Just hand Healey your ID wallet," Manos said, winking at Jericho. "Make sure he grabs it by the plastic photo window. Plastic retains a good sample."

"Cool," Grenci said.

Waste of time, Chief, thought Jericho. *We already have matching signatures. By tomorrow you'll have a search warrant from Judge Rakoff. You'll be confiscating his computers, which will have his prints all over them, so why bother with the wallet bit?*

Jericho kept his mouth shut.

"Jericho," Manos said. "since you're grounded, why don't you check the phone companies and get hold of Healey's telephone records?"

Jericho hated that he couldn't interview Healey himself, but there was nothing he could do about it.

Oh, and Chief, he thought, *if I'm in charge of this investigation, how come you're giving all the orders? I'm sorry to tell you this, Dominick — but you're in way over your head.*

Jericho went to his office. To protect Susannah, he had to make sure Healey knew he was under suspicion. On his computer, Jericho accessed *NY State Unified Court System.* In *Attorney Search* he entered H. Quinn Healey. This yielded Healey's contact information, including his fax number and e-mail address.

He scanned Healey's business card, saved it as a JPG and e-mailed it to the lawyer, along with a request for an explanation from Detective Jericho, East Hampton Town Police.

Then, just to be extra sure, he sent the same thing to Healey by fax.

As he finished at the fax machine, Officer Karlin passed by. Jericho grabbed him by the arm.

"You fucked up, Karlin. Sergeant Montrose called me from the evidence room this morning. He says the hitman's easel and stool are missing. You were supposed to bring them in yesterday.

"Oh, Jeez," Karlin said. "I'll go back and get them right now. Jericho, I sincerely apologize. I know I messed up. And listen, if there's anything I can do to help you, just say the word. I really admire your detective work, and I know I could learn a lot from you."

"Karlin, working with you is a real adventure."

Karlin left, thinking — *Detective Jericho digs me. We could be, like, a team.*

Jericho returned to the pile of paperwork on his desk. But he couldn't concentrate; his mind was on overload. And the incompetence around him made things worse.

He took the Ring Ding wrapper out of his pocket.

What does this mean? he asked himself. *Unless the hitman also ate Ring Dings, this wrapper places Jessie Russell up on Susannah's hill at some point. Maybe he was spying on her, trying to get some nude pictures.*

But Russell's MO was to take photos from a plane. Why would he have changed it? If he did get pictures of Susannah, had he tried to blackmail her? Why would she pay? Hold on, there were no nude pictures or negatives of Susannah at Jessie's place, so blackmail is unlikely.

Why am I worried about the Jessie Russell case? That's the responsibility of the State Police. But if it involves Susannah, I'm damn well making it my responsibility!

Jesus, I'm running around in circles, getting nowhere.

Jericho closed his eyes and leaned back in his chair.

He thought of his old partner, Mickey "Mouse" Davis. *Miss you, dude*, he thought. *I could sure use a little feedback.*

When they were stymied on a case, Mouse used to say, "Let's erase our minds like a blackboard, then look at the clean slate. And remember — what's unlikely is still possible."

Okay, he reasoned, *let's look at Jessie Russell. I'm assuming he's dead, but what if he's not? What if he faked his death? Maybe he found out the Shinnecocks were going to kill him for revenge, or they came after him and he got away. Then, so he'd be free of them, he faked his drowning death at the Montauk beach. He left his car on the beach and then walked the six miles to town and caught an early train into the city. It's complicated, but it's possible.*

219

"What else?" Mouse would have asked, "Have we checked out every lead?"

No. Not the Ring Ding wrapper, Jericho thought. *It suggests some connection between Jessie Russell and Susannah. What could it be? I don't know, but I need to ask her about it. I can't go out to her house. She'll have to come in to the precinct house.*

He felt uncomfortable about calling Susannah, so he asked the Chief's secretary to do it.

"Oh, and Ada," Jericho said. "please bring me the Jessie Russell file."

CHAPTER 42

Susannah came to Jericho's office late that afternoon.

"Please sit down, Susannah," he said with formality when she entered. She was wearing her usual men's shirt over jeans, but her hair was tied up in a chignon. He'd never seen it like that. *She always looks so damn beautiful.*

"It's... really nice to see you," he said, after clearing his throat.

"This is weird."

"I know."

There was an awkward pause.

"Sorry it has to be in an official capacity," Jericho said. "But there's something I have to ask you."

"What?"

"Well, I've been investigating another drowning death that happened three days after your husband died. The victim's name was Jessie Russell. Does that name mean anything to you?"

"No, should it?" she responded.

As she spoke, Susannah reached up and touched the side of her nose. Jericho recognized the classic "Pinocchio Tell", a sign that a person is lying. He also knew it was far from foolproof.

"Well, there's some indication that he knew you," he said. "Or at least had an interest in you."

"I don't understand."

"We have physical evidence suggesting he was up on the hill next to your house, the same hill where the hitman set up his easel."

"What kind of evidence?"

"That's classified. But the guy was a known peeping tom, and was probably spying on you."

"Ugh, how creepy."

"So — you have no knowledge of this Jessie Russell?"

"No."

"Susannah," Jericho said. "Jessie Russell is not a very nice man. In addition to being a voyeur, he's also a rapist. And we're not entirely sure he's dead. There's always a chance he could come after you."

"Oh, God."

"Just be to on the safe side", Jericho said calmly, "you should probably lock all your doors and windows. Do you have an alarm system?"

"No."

"Well, I'd get one right away. AHS Home Security is good."

"OK."

"And be on the lookout for any sign of him."

"I will." *Careful,* she thought, *I'm not supposed to know what he looks like.*

"What does he look like?," she asked. "Do you have a description?"

Jericho reached into the file on his desk and pulled out Jessie Russell's pilot's license, encased in a clear plastic envelope.

"He's Native American," Jericho said, handing it to Susannah. "Mid-thirties, long black hair, dark complexion."

Susannah looked at Jessie's menacing face. She gasped as the horrifying memory of his brutal sexual attack flashed in her mind.

"You okay?" Jericho asked.

222

"Yes...yes," she said "It's just...the idea of what he's done to women."

"I understand."

"He really looks scary."

"Look, he may not even be alive," Jericho said. "But you need to be on guard."

"Believe me, I will be."

"Call me if you need me."

"I will."

"And remember about the alarm system."

She smiled at him. "Thanks for worrying about me."

Susannah stood up. They shook hands awkwardly, and she left.

As Susannah drove home, she thought: *Jesus, Jessie Russell can't be alive. His skull was bashed in, and he never moved, even when I dragged him into the ocean.*

But...what if, by some quirk, he managed to survive? Then I'm in real danger. What if he has another set of photographs stashed somewhere? What if he sends them to the police? What if he comes back for revenge — to rape me, kill me?

And what about Jericho? Maybe he knows more than he's telling me. He's a good detective — did he believe me?

Last night was magical, she thought. *I'm really falling for Detective Jericho. This man, this wonderful man who saved my life. But I mustn't forget — he can just as easily destroy it.*

She sighed heavily.

CHAPTER 43

That night, as she got ready for bed, Susannah put Jericho's number on speed dial on her landline.

He might be getting too close for comfort, she thought. *But I can still count on him to protect me if I need him.*

She entered his number in Location 1, replacing Burt's office number.

She couldn't sleep. All the doors and windows were locked, but still she didn't feel safe. She'd called AHS and they said they come tomorrow to install a home security system.

Her mind was racing. *What if Jessie Russell is lurking outside? What if Jericho is wrong about Quinn Healey? What if Healey's hired another assassin, or he's planning to kill me himself? As Jericho said — people are unpredictable.*

Since nobody in Montauk worried much about break-ins, the locks on the Cascadden beach house were the basic household variety, easily broken or jimmied.

Susannah remembered Burt's gun. She turned on her bedside lamp, got up, and went to Burt's bedroom. She took out the automatic pistol and hefted it in her hand. It was fairly light. Embossed on the barrel was: *HECKLER & KOCH GMBH — OBERNDORF — Mod HK 4 Made in Germany.*

Jesus, she thought, *I've never fired a gun in my life. I hate these things.*

She went back to her bedroom and examined the weapon. She noticed the thumb safety. Next to it was a white dot. Gingerly she pushed the lever forward. Now she could see a red dot. That would be Safety Off. She swiveled it back to *On.*

Now, where are the bullets? she wondered. *They've gotta be in the handle.*

After some fiddling, she found a lever that released the magazine. She turned it over and emptied the cartridges into her palm. There were seven .38 caliber bullets. Then she reinserted them. With a downward pressure, each one locked into place.

Once the magazine was back in the gun, she got up and went over to her full-length mirror. She was wearing floppy powder blue pajamas. Taking a two-handed stance, she crouched and aimed it at herself.

You look like a damn idiot, she told herself. *You have no idea what you're doing. Girl, this weapon has no protective value unless you know how to fire it.*

She put on a robe, went downstairs, and unlocked the sliding door to the deck. It was 2 a.m. The beach was deserted.

The black sky was dotted with stars, and grains of wind-blown sand stung her face. She could hear the surf crashing and the plaintive cry of gulls.

Susannah raised the pistol in both hands and pointed it at the sliver of moon that hung over the horizon. She pulled the trigger.

Nothing.

"Oh, shit," she said out loud. She'd forgotten to turn off the safety. This was obviously not her thing.

She flicked the lever forward, aimed the pistol again, and fired.

The gun jumped wildly in her hand, but she hung onto it.

With satisfaction she returned the safety to *On* and walked back into the house.

There were six bullets left — enough to fix anybody who tried to mess with her.

She placed the gun in her nightstand drawer, nestled among the panties, bras, and nightgowns. She left the drawer open.

Jericho couldn't sleep either.

He kept thinking about Susannah, about how much she mattered to him. He remembered when he saw her at the Farmer's Market while he was with Katie; the three of them almost like a family. But it was more than that. Susannah was great looking, smart, sexy, and loving. And she made him feel like a whole person — not just a cop with an empty life, trying to be a father to the daughter he'd lost because he'd been an irresponsible jerk.

But...I'm still a cop, he reminded himself. *And there's that unanswered question: was there any connection between Susannah and Jessie Russell?*

CHAPTER 44

Taking a break from his morning patrol, Officer Teddy Karlin stopped at Mr. John's Steak & Pancake house in Montauk.

As he sat having coffee and a Krispy Kreme, his mind was on Detective Jericho.

Yeah, he thought, *I'm learning a lot from Jericho. If I play it cool, hang with him, be like, his assistant, he could be my ticket to getting a gold shield. Of course, I have to learn to think like a detective. Use my imagination. Come up with stuff, theories.*

All right, let's take the Jessie Russell case. What theory could I come up with? How about — the lady's husband, what's his name? Cascadden. Maybe Cascadden finds out the Indian is porking his wife, so he kills him in a jealous rage. Then Cascadden fakes his own death and disappears. Nah, that sucks. Cascadden died before the Indian. Shit! All right. How about the Cascadden case? Haven't heard much about that investigation. Just that the guy drowned. But what if it wasn't an accident. Maybe his wife killed him. Shot him, stabbed him, poisoned him, bashed in his head — whatever, and dumped him in the ocean. Then she makes it look like a swimming accident. Motive? Obvious: her husband's a multimillionaire so she'd inherit big bucks. Hmm, not bad. Maybe I oughta investigate.

"Hey, Jericho. It's lucky you came in this morning," Sergeant Trevor Montrose said in the evidence room. "State cops are gonna pick the stuff up later today."

Montrose, one of the few black men in the EHTPD, spoke with the lilting accent of his native Barbados.

"Best be puttin' on the hand-condoms, mon" he said, giving Jericho latex gloves.

Jericho snapped them on. "What you got?"

Montrose went to a stack of three-by-four-foot cubbyholes behind him and pulled out an A&P carton containing Jessie Russell's keys, cash, wallet, shoes and socks, T-shirt, towel, and Ring-Dings. Jericho carefully scrutinized each item.

"What you lookin' for?" Montrose asked.

"Something that'll tell me something."

"That numb-nuts Karlin finally brought in the hitman's paintin' stuff. You want to see it?"

"No. What else you got?"

The evidence clerk picked up a clipboard with a manifest on it.

"Only thing left is the coveralls," he said, using the West Indian term. "Hold on — that's two coveralls. He-Man brand."

"Right," Jericho said. "One's from the beach, the other's from Russell's cabin."

"They right behind you," Montrose said. "Hangin' on the rod, next to that humongous brassiere."

Jericho turned and saw the two pairs of overalls, one blue, one brown, each on a separate hanger

"I happened to notice," Montrose said, "the blue one might have blood stains on the bib."

"Very observant, Trev. Yeah, the State Police'll run a lab report on it."

When Jericho picked up the two hangers, he noticed something odd about the brown overalls. He pulled them off the hanger and laid them out on the counter.

"Hey, Trev," he said. "Something's hinky here."

"Whatchu mean, mon?"

230

"Russell supposedly drove his car to the beach while wearing them. But look at the crotch and waist. There should be creases there, from the guy sitting down."

"You right."

"They're wrinkled up," Jericho said, "but not in a natural way. And look at this dirt on the knees and the fly. It looks like somebody rubbed it in. There's no reason for overalls to get dirty that way."

"So somebody must've washed 'em."

"Looks like it," Jericho said. "We were meant to think Russell was wearing them before he went swimming and drowned."

"Ah, but the clean jeans tell a different story," Trevor said. "We could be lookin' at homicide."

"Very likely," Jericho said. "My guess is Russell was killed earlier, causing bloodstains on his overalls. The killer washed them out before he planted them at the beach."

"But what about the blood stains on the blue overalls?"

"I dunno," Jericho said. "They could be unrelated. Maybe Russell cut himself."

"So, should I give the State Police the blue ones, too?"

"Umm. Let me think."

This pretty much rules out the Shinnecocks as Jessie Russell's murderers. They wouldn't have killed him, thrown his corpse in their car, driven the thirty miles back to the reservation to wash the overalls, then come all the way back to the beach and dump the body. They could've used the Montauk Laundromat, but I doubt it. They'd want to lie low if they'd just killed a man. More likely whoever did this was a local resident.

The idea hit Jericho so hard he felt his face twitch.

Susannah! Oh, Jesus. Is that possible?

His mind started racing. He recalled Susannah touching her nose when she said she didn't know Jessie Russell.

But why would Susannah have killed Russell? The answer came swiftly. *Rape. That makes sense — Jessie tried to rape her and she killed him in the struggle. Self defense.*

But then she would've had to do this whole cover up, drive Jessie's car down to the beach, stage the drowning...

My God, he thought. *I know Susannah. Is she really capable of all that?*

She's a strong woman. Maybe she did what she had to do — But...why the cover-up if she killed in self-defense?

Jericho spoke calmly to Montrose. "Yeah, give the State cops both overalls," he said. "I'll fax them a report this afternoon, explaining everything to them."

I'll have to stall the State Police, he told himself. *The two overalls will confuse them. I'll be vague about which is which. Eventually their detectives may notice the brown ones have been washed. Or maybe they won't. Meanwhile, I'm buying time. I hope I'm wrong, but Susannah's a suspect and I want to investigate her myself, so I can help her if it turns out badly. But that'll have to wait till I'm back on active duty. For now, I'll point the State Police in the direction of the Shinnecock tribe.*

When Susannah got up in the morning, there was a message on her answering machine: "Hi, this is Maggie from AHS Home Security. Turns out our East Hampton installation man has come down with Lyme Disease and can't work for a while. We keep telling our guys the grass around here is loaded with deer ticks, but sometimes they just don't listen. Anyway, the thing is, we'll have to bring a tech over from our Riverhead office, and he can't do the job on your house till tomorrow. 9 A.M. If that's okay with you, no need to call. Otherwise you can ring me at 516-307-8300. 'Bye now."

Susannah moaned in frustration.

The phone rang.

"Hello?"

"Darlin'," her mother said in an anxious voice, "I'm settin' here readin' the *Times-Picayune* and there's an article about you gettin' attacked by a hired killer."

Susannah couldn't believe it had already made the national wire services.

"Oh, um," Susannah stammered, "Yes. It was a mistake. Seems he was after somebody else."

"Are you all right?"

"Fine, Mama. Doin' jes' just fine," Susannah replied, unconsciously reverting to a Southern accent. "I'm very lucky. A policeman rescued me in the nick o' time."

"Well, that's a relief. Why didn't you call me?"

"Didn't want you to worry. You've got enough on your mind. How's Daddy doin'?"

"Pretty poor, I'm afraid. He's in a coma mostly. Wakes up once in a while, but even then he's out of it."

"Oh, Mama. That's terrible."

"Listen, honey," her mother said. "I hate to bother you, but the check didn't come this month, and — "

"Gosh, I'm sorry, I'll take care of it right away."

"Guess you've had a lot on your mind."

"Yes, but that's no excuse."

"How's Burt?"

"Huh?"

"I said how's Burt?"

This was definitely not the time to tell her.

"He...he's away on business. A long trip."

"Where?"

"Um, Singapore. Some multinational somethin' or other."

"Well, tell him I said hey."

"I will, Mama."

"Listen, honey, if you feel like comin' down for a visit, I wouldn't mind a little company.

"Wish I could. But my teaching schedule's kinda tight right now. Maybe in a week or so.

"Okay. You won't forget about the check?"

"No, I won't," Susannah said. "Promise."

"Thank you, darlin'," said Ethel. "I love you."

"Love you too, Mama."

Susannah thought about how to get her mom the money. Her bank balance was only around $2,000 and Ethel was expecting $7,000. It would be best to take the cash from the $60,000 she'd stashed in Burt's desk, and send a postal money order. It was better than putting the money in her account and writing a check — she didn't want bank records of a large cash deposit.

She had gone downstairs to Burt's office when the front doorbell rang.

She approached the door and called out.

"Who is it?"

"East Hampton Town Police."

"What do you want?"

"Just to ask a few questions, M'am."

She was about to open the door, when her stomach flip-flopped with fear.

What if it's not a cop? What if it's a trick — someone out to get me?

She moved over to the bay window, where she could peek out and see whoever was standing at the door. He did look like a policeman. He had the blue uniform and the silver shield. Gun? Did he have a gun? No, she didn't see one. But she did see a nightstick hanging from a holder on his belt. What if he was a fake cop? He could use the nightstick on her. He could kill her.

"M'am?" the man called out.

She went back to the front door and yelled through it.

234

"Slip your ID under the door."

After a brief delay, she saw an ID card sliding beneath the door. She picked it up. It read *Patrolman Theodore S. Karlin. EHTPD.* His dim-bulb face in the photo made him look like a convict.

Cautiously she opened the door. Squinting into the bright sunlight she looked at the cop. He was grinning. She handed him back his ID card.

"Mind if I come in?"

"Yes."

Karlin started to move towards her. She stopped in with her hand.

"Yes, I do mind," she said. "What do you want?"

"Mrs. Cascadden," he said. "I'm here investigating your husband's death."

"I thought Detective Jericho was handling that."

"He's tied up, so I'm doin' some legwork for him."

Oh, that's right, she thought. *No-contact status.*

"Maybe you remember me," Karlin said. "I was here on the hitman case, assisting Detective Jericho."

Susanna nodded noncommittally.

"So," the cop went on, "where were you when your husband drowned?"

"Here."

"On the beach or in the house?"

"The house. In my statement I — "

"Is there anyone who could collaborate that?"

Did he say "collaborate"? she asked herself.

"No," she answered.

"Mrs. Cascadden," Karlin said. "Do you know of any reason someone might want to kill your husband?"

She shrugged.

He pressed on. "Of course, there's one person who I know would benefit from his death. That person would be — you."

God, she thought. *They must suspect something. Do they have some new evidence? Did Jericho send this guy?*

Karlin pressed on. "I'll bet you'd inherit a tidy sum if..."

"Officer," she cut in. "I have nothing further to say."

"Ma'm, you're required to answer my questions."

Susannah gave him an obdurate look.

"Look," Karlin went on, "I don't want to have to take you down the station house."

"I won't go," she said casually. "Unless you're arresting me. Are you arresting me?"

"Mrs. Cascadden," he said emphatically, using her name as if it were a threat.

She smiled. "Of course if you do arrest me, you'll have to Mirandize me. Then I have the right to remain silent, so that won't work."

Officer Karlin looked stunned.

"Uh, well, thank you for your time," he mumbled. "I'll get back to you on this."

He turned and walked back toward his squad car. Then he stopped.

"Mrs. Cascadden," he said. "You're not under arrest but you *are* under suspicion. I'm going to have to ask you not to leave town."

Karlin gave her an intimidating look and drove off.

Susannah felt her throat start to close up. It was as if a noose were tightening around her neck.

CHAPTER 45

That afternoon Teddy Karlin came to Jericho's office. He had a copy of *Newsday* with him.

"Jericho. You see this morning's paper?"

"Only the sports."

"Check this out."

In Nicholas Rhinelander's column was a picture of Susannah, taken through her car window. She was attempting to cover her face with her hand, and her eyes were wide with fright. The caption read: "The elusive Mrs. Cascadden. What does she know about her husband's disappearance? Is the investigation on the slow track?"

"In the picture she looks guilty," Karlin said. "Makes ya think, huh?"

"This is why I hate journalists," Jericho grumbled.

"Yeah," Karlin agreed, "that Nicky Rhinelander is the worst."

Nicky? Jericho thought. *Nobody would call Nicholas Rhinelander "Nicky," except someone who knew him really well. And if Teddy Karlin knows "Nicky" really well, the conclusion is obvious.*

"Teddy," Jericho said. "The one thing I hate more than journalists is cops who take money from them."

"Huh?"

Teddy's eyes darted. It was the look of a guilty man.

"Don't bother to deny it," Jericho said. "I know you tipped off your pal Nicky about me shooting Mort on the beach. You've been feeding him scoops for years now, for a nice payola, haven't you?"

"That's not true — "

"Shut up," Jericho said. "I'm gonna see to it that you pull midnight-to-four shifts for the next twelve months, and that'll involve night foot patrol at the town dump."

"But I didn't do anything."

"It'll be smelly, cold, lonely, boring work, but you'll have plenty of time to think — think about never taking another penny from Nicholas Rhinelander. Got me?"

"C'mon, Jericho," Karlin pleaded.

"Now get the hell out of here, Teddy."

After Karlin left, Jericho went to the Chief's office and explained what Karlin had done. Manos had seen the *Newsday* photo and was furious at Rhinelander's implication that the investigation had stalled. He promised to make patrolman Karlin's life a nightmare.

"But I've got some good news for you," Manos said. "I just spoke to Harburg. IA's giving you a clean bill."

"Nice of 'em," Jericho replied.

"And the grand jury hearing will just be pro forma. You'll be back on active duty inside of a week. Contingent on the psychiatric report, of course."

"What?"

"Departmental regulations. You gotta go see a shrink."

"Are you kidding?"

"You must've had the same deal in the city," Manos said. "Whenever a police officer kills someone, he has to — "

"Sure. But you mean to tell me East Hampton Town Police has a shrink on staff?"

"Not on staff, but on call. She has a private practice over in Sag Harbor. It's rare, but we do use her when a cop's involved with a fatality

— a car crash, a death in a house fire, particularly if there's a kid involved."

"Oh, Christ."

"It's no big deal. I made you an appointment tomorrow morning. You go in, you say you're real sad about taking the life of another human being, but you're coping. Y'know, you're trained for it, it's part of the job, blah, blah, blah."

"Dammit," Jericho shouted. "I haven't got time for that shit."

Chief Manos could see that Jericho was upset. "Jericho," he said with concern, "have you — did you ever kill somebody before, in the line of duty?"

"...No."

"Well, look, maybe the shrink'll do you some good. Anyway you gotta go. And when you gotta go — "

"I know," Jericho said resignedly. "What time?"

"Ten-forty-five, tomorrow morning. Her name is Dr. Patel. Wait a minute, I wrote it down for you." He started searching in his pockets.

"Do you know her?" Jericho asked.

"Yeah. On 9/11, me and Trev Montrose volunteered to go down to Ground Zero and help with the digging. I got pretty shook up. I went to Dr. Patel for a couple months after that. She helped me put things in perspective."

He found the notepaper. "Here it is — Dr. Chandrakala Patel."

"Chandrakala?" Jericho said.

"She's Indian. Not American Indian. Indian Indian."

Jericho nodded.

"Well," Manos said, handing Jericho the name and address, "enjoy, enjoy."

"Fuck you, fuck you."

Susannah had taken $7,000 from the envelope in Burt's desk and left the rest in the back of the drawer.

She went to the Montauk Post Office and asked for a $7,000 money order but $1,000 was the limit. The postal worker said she could bypass the rule by sending additional $1,000 money orders from the post offices in Amagansett, East Hampton, Sagaponack, Bridgehampton, Water Mill, and Southampton. It was *Seinfeld*-ian.

So she spent the next few hours visiting six East End post offices. She felt like a drug dealer laundering money.

That night Susannah made sure all the doors and windows were locked, and went to bed. Since the home alarm system was not yet in place, she left her nightstand drawer open, with the pistol within easy reach.

Under the sea, the current swirls, flowing around the bones of a man. Susannah sees the bones, resting on the sludgy bottom, undulating gently in the dark water. They begin to coalesce into a skeletal figure.

The bone man stands up.

He glides along the murky sea floor, stirring up muddy particles that rise and cling to him, taking on the shape of legs, arms, torso, head — a grotesque corporeal entity.

The figure pushes off the bottom, arms caressing the water with a sensual breaststroke. The legs kick frog-like, propelling him upward to the ocean surface. His head splashes up out of the water, ghostly in the pale moonlight. Tendrils of slimy brown seaweed hang down over his face, hiding all his features, except the glowing green eyes.

The creature snorts and rolls over onto his back, floating on the waves as they carry him to the shore. Covered in seaweed, he rides the surface like a bed of kelp, each breaker tossing him on its whitecaps as it surges toward landfall.

When the water is knee deep, the creature turns over, stands up, and wades to shore. The moonlight illuminates his flesh — inky and mottled, the color of the muddy bottom. Sea vegetation dangles from his shoulders and arms. As he emerges from the surf he shakes droplets of water off the flaccid, hose-like protuberance at his groin —— the pride of Burton Lloyd Cascadden.

240

The dream scene changes. Susannah is in her bed, staring up at the large, menacing figure of her husband. Burt's voice is harsh, guttural. "Sweetie. Sweetie." His head is ghastly, his features shapeless, as if decayed. The eyes glow with green hatred. "How lovely you look," he says ominously. "Like a shining angel — no, like the Good Fairy. But your beauty deceives. Your sweet appearance conceals your murderous heart. You must pay — pay for the evil within you."

Burt reaches down and pinches her nostrils tight shut...

Susannah woke up, gasping ragged breaths through her mouth. The bedroom was dark.

"Who's there? Is anybody there?"

Silence.

Trembling, she reached for her bedside lamp. *Click.* The bright light assaulted her eyes. She squinted in the harsh glare, trying to focus.

The room was empty. Susannah grabbed the pistol from the nightstand drawer.

"I've got a gun," she shouted, flipping off the safety. Then louder, "If you don't get the hell outta here you're dead."

Nothing.

I must have been dreaming, she thought. *Or was I? Is someone still in the house? If so, who could it be? I couldn't see his face.*

Gripping the gun, she went to check her bathroom.

Nobody.

Her heart was still racing. Cautiously she descended the stairs. At the bottom was a light switch.

Click.

All the lamps in the living room went on.

Nothing.

The front door was locked. So were the living room windows and the glass door to the deck.

She checked the guest bathroom. Empty. Window locked.

The kitchen and pantry were clear as well. Burt's bedroom and bath, and his office, were deserted.

Oh, my God, the closets.

She tightened her grip on the gun. Pulse pounding, she swung Burt's closet door open. Nothing. She went to her bedroom, opened the closet door, and slapped at the clothes on their hangers. Nobody.

She checked every other closet. Finally she was sure there was no one in the house.

It was all a dream. A scary dream.

She hoped.

CHAPTER 46

Jericho parked on Main Street in front of the Sag Harbor movie theatre, with its streamlined thirties styling and Art Deco neon signage.

Two years before, when he was looking for a place to live, Jericho had answered an ad for a cottage rental in Sag Harbor — on Gull Rock Road. He took an immediate liking to the old whaling village, built on steep hills leading down to the bay. Unlike East Hampton, with its chic boutiques and trendy art galleries, Sag Harbor had a family-owned food market, a variety store called Schmidt's 5&10, a barbershop with a barber pole, and a park with a dusty softball field. Jericho understood why its funky, unpretentious quality appealed to artists and writers, who refer to it as the *Un*-Hampton.

Later, Trevor Montrose told him Sag Harbor also has a beachfront community of African-Americans, who like to call it the *Lionel* Hampton.

Jericho had chosen to live in Montauk because it was closer to Katie, but he always enjoyed driving over to Sag when he got the chance.

Except this morning.

He walked down Main Street and turned right at the Bay Street Playhouse. Dr. Patel's office was on Bay Street in a gray-shingled salt box facing the marina.

A high wind was blowing off the water, causing the masts of the docked sailboats to sway back and forth. Jericho was irritated by the incessant hollow clanking of the sailboat lines, slapping against their masts.

Outside Dr. Patel's office were two wooden shingles hanging from a post. One read: *Dr. Chandrakala Patel, PHD, MSW.* Below it a smaller sign: *Eastern Suffolk County Rape Crisis Center.*

Jericho rang the doorbell and Dr. Patel answered. She was a short, fiftyish woman and her plump body was encased in a mauve polyester pantsuit. Jericho was immediately transfixed by her dark almond-shaped eyes. She had smooth brown skin, a full mouth, and coal black hair drawn up in a knot.

She ushered Jericho into her small office, which was dominated by a tapestry depicting a fat man holding a bowl, sitting in a spread-kneed yoga position. Jericho noticed that Dr. Patel was wearing one piece of Indian jewelry — an ornately detailed silver *Om* pendant. Buddhist, he thought, not Hindu.

The room smelled faintly of old house, and sandalwood incense.

"You can take that rocker-recliner over there," Dr. Patel said. "Some people like to sit up straight or rock, others prefer to be laid back, so to speak. Your call."

"Sitting'll be fine," Jericho said in a hoarse voice. He cleared his throat.

The therapist eased herself down into an Eames chair about six feet across from him.

Jericho felt disoriented and dizzy.

"You okay, Mr. Jericho?"

Jericho squirmed awkwardly. He felt like a schoolboy summoned to the principal's office.

"I'm good."

"There's a bottle of Evian on the end table next to you. Help yourself."

Jericho unscrewed the plastic bottle and took a swig.

Dr. Patel smiled. "Everyone feels uncomfortable when they come here for the first time," she said. "Actually, I'm uncomfortable myself, I'm just more experienced at hiding it."

Jericho smiled back.

"As you know," she said, "I've been asked to evaluate you, find out what effect your recent actions have had on your ability to resume active duty. So I'm going to ask you some questions. Try to remember two things. One — there is no right or wrong answer. Two — being truthful is the only way to go. In other words, don't bullshit me."

Jericho nodded.

Dr. Patel took out a notebook. She began by asking him for some background. Jericho told her how long he'd been in the EHTPD, about his previous service with NYPD, his divorce. He admitted to a drinking problem that had adversely affected his marriage, but said he hadn't had a drink since he left New York. (He figured the one gulp of wine he had after his encounter with Sarah didn't count.) Then he talked about his relationship with Katie.

"Sounds like you're very attached to your daughter," the therapist said.

"Yes, I am. She — unfortunately my wife and her second husband are moving to Washington state in a few months. I'm really having a tough time with that."

"I'll bet."

"I'm handling it, though."

Dr. Patel scribbled in her notebook. She looked up.

"How are you handling the fact that you killed that hitman?"

Jericho gathered himself before answering.

"It's not an easy thing, taking a human life," he said carefully. "We're trained for it, though. On the first day at the academy they tell you it's something you may have to do, that it comes with the territory. Basically I feel good about it. After all, I killed a professional killer, a man with no conscience, who took who knows how many human lives simply for profit."

"Yes," Dr. Patel said. "And you also saved a woman's life. You should feel proud."

"I was doing what I was trained to do," Jericho said simply.

"Have you ever had to kill someone before this?"

"No."

She nodded. "How do your feelings now compare with what you went through in East Harlem?"

"East Harlem?"

"I understand you were on the scene at the death of an infant girl there."

Jericho was stunned. "How do you know about that?" he said angrily. "My NYPD records are confidential. You can't get access without a court order — "

"Mr. Jericho," Dr. Patel said. "I haven't seen your file. I looked you up online. Just doing my homework. The *Daily News* archives have a number of articles about the incident."

Jericho took a deep breath. "Well," he said, "It was a terrible thing. The guy who held her hostage killed her. It was a tragic accident."

"Yes. I read about it," she said. "Did you see a police psychologist afterwards?"

"Yes."

"How did that go?"

"Fine."

"How often did you see him?"

"Once."

"Only once?"

"He said there was no need for extended therapy."

Dr. Patel looked at him long and hard.

"Y'know, Detective Jericho," she said, "one of my specialties is dealing with posttraumatic stress. I do a lot of work with victims of sexual assault, mostly women but some men too. After going through deeply shocking and disturbing experiences, victims react by trying to reprogram their brains, reinterpret the event, block out the memory of it. That's a natural response, a normal reaction to an abnormal situation. But those coping mechanisms can generate a host of emotional problems."

Dr. Patel leaned forward in her chair.

246

"Mr. Jericho," she said. "As a police officer, you're often exposed to stressful incidents. In fact, you probably thrive on the kind of stress most folks would avoid at all costs. And it's lucky for society there are people like you."

"But you pay a price," she went on. "No matter how tough you are, these incidents affect you deeply. You're trained to set aside your feelings, deal with the incident and move one. Your job, maybe even your survival, depends on it. And there's that macho cop thing — don't talk about it, don't show your emotions. Fahgeddaboudit. Trouble is, Mr. Jericho, these memories have been imprinted on your brain. A memory like killing another human being, or witnessing the death of a child, can be devastating. Do you see what I'm saying?"

"Yes."

"I'm satisfied that you're not bothered by shooting that hitman. But this business with the little girl in New York, that's much more troubling. According to the newspaper, a drug dealer had taken a child hostage, and you and your partner had drawn your guns on him."

"Correct."

"And the drug dealer fell out a window with the baby girl?"

"Yes."

"Witnessing that had to be shattering," she said. "Do you think your drinking problem was related to it?"

"Hard to say."

"Have you had any subsequent sleep disturbances?"

"I sleep okay."

"Any nightmares of the event?"

"No."

"How about intrusive memories? Flashbacks?"

"No."

"Blackouts?"

"No."

"So it's like it never happened," she said.

"I didn't say that."

"Mr. Jericho, you have a young daughter yourself. It's hard to believe witnessing a baby girl's violent death wouldn't leave you with *some* symptoms of post traumatic stress."

Jericho felt rage churning inside him. He struggled to suppress it.

"Look," he said. "I think about that girl's death a lot. I haven't gotten over it — not by a long shot. But I'm here because of what happened on the beach last week. I think I'm pretty together about that, and I gather you think so too. This is about whether I can go back on active duty or not, and I don't think something that went down six years ago should have a bearing on it."

"But it does."

"Believe me, doctor," Jericho said, "I've come to terms with what happened."

"I think we need to go a little further with that."

Dr. Patel looked thoughtful for a moment. "How long since you've been back to your old precinct?" she asked.

"A coupla years."

"Your partner, what's his name?"

"Davis. Mickey Davis."

"Is he still there?"

"Yes."

"I think it would be useful for you to go back there — back to the scene of the tragedy. Visit the building where it happened, try to find the mother. Do you remember her name?"

"Yes, but — "

"Good. Try to find her, talk to her. Then go meet with your old partner. Get his memories of what happened. Compare them with yours."

"Are you saying I have to do this before you give me clearance?"

"Detective Jericho," Dr. Patel said calmly, "I have a feeling there's a lot more going on here."

"Like what?"

248

"I'm not sure. Possibly there's a component of guilt involved. But I don't want to get into it until you reconnect with these events in your past."

Jericho pressed his lips into a tight line of resentment. He said nothing.

"I think it would be best to get on this right away," the therapist said.

"How soon before I can return to active duty?"

Dr. Patel hesitated before answering. "That depends," she said. "I know you want to get back, and I have no desire to stand in your way. I just want to make sure you're not repressing feelings that could cause you to act irresponsibly."

Jericho's anger burst out of him. "God damn it! You have no right to..."

Dr. Patel interrupted calmly. "I understand your frustration."

"Fine. Are we finished now?"

"Yes. Give me a call after you've done what I suggested."

Jericho got up to leave.

"Detective Jericho," Dr. Patel said, "I don't mean to sound parental, but this is for your own good."

He left, annoyed with himself.

I screwed up with that shrink. I should've played along instead of getting pissed. Thing is, I couldn't tell her about the blackouts and the flashbacks. If I did — no way she'd release me from desk duty. Best thing now is just to do what she said, and then go back and tell her I followed her instructions, saying how it was upsetting but that I'm glad I did it because now I see things more clearly. I realize I was repressing my memory of the trauma, and now I have some closure, ya-dah, ya-dah, ya-dah.

When he got to his car, he called Chief Manos on his cell and got permission to take the rest of the day off, go to the city and follow Dr. Patel's orders.

As he started the car he grumbled out loud, "Might as well get this shit over with!"

CHAPTER 47

At nine in the morning, the AHS technician arrived at Susannah's house and set up the wireless home security system. It took about three hours. He installed entry sensors which would trigger an alarm if one of the doors or windows were opened. He added motion sensors as a second line of defense, should anyone find a way to bypass these deterrents. Any breach would trigger a loud alarm and activate flashing strobe lights inside and outside the house. It would also signal the AHS office, which would immediately alert East Hampton police. The technician explained that EHTP always had a squad car patrolling the Montauk area, and they'd be within five or ten minutes of Susannah's house.

"I'll still need my house-key to unlock the door, right?"

"Yes," the AHS man replied.

"What if I want to keep a window open?" she asked.

"Well, first you'd have to disable the alarm, then open the window, then re-set the alarm. Same thing in reverse if you want to close the window. It's a pain in the butt, but hey, that's the price of safety. If you mess up, all hell will break loose."

He installed a digital control panel inside the house, next to the door, which could be activated or deactivated by a remote on a special keychain, or manually by using the alpha-numeric keyboard. Susannah chose her mother's name: E-T-H-E-L as a code. Also, the system could be enabled/disabled from outside by typing the code on her cell phone keypad while pointing the phone at the doorway. Inside there was an indicator light — green for *system on*, red for *system off*.

In addition, there were AHS decals placed on all windows and doors, and a large *DayGlo* sign at the front entrance, which read: PROPERTY PROTECTED BY AMERICAN HOME SECURITY WIRELESS SYSTEMS. "DON'T EVEN <u>THINK</u> ABOUT IT."

As the AHS man left, Susannah thanked him, then said, "I feel like a prisoner in my own home."

"Yeah," the installer retorted, "but nobody ever breaks into a prison."

Susannah had been unable to do her Martha Graham stretching routine since Jessie attacked her. After the security man left, she was determined to give it a try. She put on the music, lay down on the mat, and began. But immediately, the memories of that awful episode flooded back into her mind — Jessie's sweaty body pressing against her, his hands, his foul breath, his wet, sloppy mouth...

She sat up and turned off the music.

She took a deep breath and went inside to gather her things for her upcoming dance class.

The traffic was moving well on the LIE as Jericho drove into the city.

As he passed a Queens shopping center, a large billboard caught his eye. It showed a little girl grinning happily at a large pepperoni pizza. The lettering said: "It's Not Delivery — It's DiGiorno".

He remembered what his daughter had said to him the night before. Katie was at Jericho's house for dinner and they were polishing off a frozen pizza, when she suddenly brought up the move to Tacoma.

"I'm gonna miss you, Daddy."

"Me, too. When did Mommy tell you?"

"Yesterday." Katie said, "She and Irwin sat me down and told me they had good news. Well, they tried to make it sound like good

252

news, like I was gonna make new friends and go to a great school, but it was lousy news and they knew it."

"Well, I'll come to see you often. But it's far away."

"I know. Mommy told me you'd get a red eye from doing it, but you wouldn't mind."

"I'll come whenever I can."

"And she said you could have me for the summer. Maybe even the whole summer."

"Well, I'll try," Jericho said. "But I don't get vacation time in the summer. That's when it's real busy out here."

"You could see me at night. And get somebody to watch me in the day. Our neighbor, Mrs. Blinken, she's crazy about me. She could mind me."

"Not every day."

"Well, some days I have dance class. And my dance teacher Susannah, she likes me. I bet she wouldn't mind taking care of me. Wait a minute, you know her. Remember, Daddy, we all had breakfast at the 'Gansett Market?"

"Yes, I remember."

"I think she likes you," Katie said knowingly. "Maybe you could ask her."

Jericho hugged his daughter and gave her the parent's classic noncommittal response: "We'll see."

A half hour later Jericho was crossing the Triboro Bridge into Manhattan. It was bittersweet, seeing the rust-red buildings of the Roosevelt Housing Project along the Harlem River, the decaying piers jutting out into the water, the steeple of the *Iglesia Pentacostal de la Virgen* rising above the slums on the ironically named Pleasant Avenue.

This used to be my turf, he thought.

He'd called Detective Mickey "Mouse" Davis and told him he was coming in. He hadn't seen Mouse since leaving the NYPD but they talked occasionally on the phone.

Jericho didn't feel like making a return visit to the squad room, seeing his old pals and doing the usual hey-buddy-how're-they-hangin'? bullshit. Mouse understood. They agreed to meet at the Nuevo Korean Kitchin (*sic*), their old hangout.

Jericho drove down Second Avenue, past the familiar bodegas, cantinas, storefront churches, tattoo and hair-braiding parlors. It was a warm afternoon and East Harlem's main drag was crowded with Latinos, Blacks, Caucasians, Arabs, Asians, and various combinations thereof. Jericho was reminded of a Langston Hughes poem in a book Mouse had given him: "Black and white / Gold and brown / Chocolate custard pie of a town."

He stopped at a light at East 119th Street. Salsa music was blaring out of the corner record store. Hip-hop resounded from the fifteen-inch subwoofers of a double-parked Chevy Tahoe with tinted windows. An ice cream truck pulled up, its tinkly bells playing the theme from *The Flintstones*. The sweet cacophony of the ghetto.

Damn. I've missed this.

CHAPTER 48

Before his meeting with Mouse, Jericho revisited what Dr. Patel had called "the scene of the tragedy." The house was on 118th between First and Pleasant Avenues. Jericho saw a parking space when he turned left off Second, so he pulled his car in and began walking east.

His nostalgia was replaced by anxiety. After crossing First Avenue he heard a woman yelling, "*Por favor, por favor* ... " Was it real or was it memory? He got dizzy and had to grab onto a lamppost for support.

Jericho pushed forward along the shady street, fixing his eyes on the house numbers — 378, 380, 382. He'd never forgotten the address — 390 East 118th.

Abruptly his eyes were jolted by bright sunlight. He was standing in front of a chain link fence. The building was gone. In its place was a community garden, lush with shade trees, pine bushes, petunias, marigolds, and sunflowers.

On the fence hung a sign: *Jardín Conmemorativo de Rosario — Rosario's Memorial Garden.*

Jericho figured the city had condemned the dilapidated crack house and torn it down. Many such gardens had sprung up on weedy, garbage-littered vacant lots, the result of a civic project called Green Thumb.

Then he saw it — on the sidewalk. The wreckers had left standing a section of the building's wrought iron fencing, with five sharp-pointed spears thrusting skyward. One had a reddish stain on its point — it was rust, but it looked like blood. Jericho had to turn away.

"Intrusive memories? flashbacks?"

"No."

Yes — the little girl's pale white body writhing as the limbs flail about, hands clawing the air. The diapered triangle at the junction of her legs. Above it, where the naval should be, a spike protrudes.

"Detective Jericho, is that you?"

One step too many ...

Jericho saw a thirtyish woman wearing gardening gloves coming toward him. He pulled himself together.

"Hey, Paloma," Jericho said.

"Long time don't see."

"Likewise."

"I'd shake hands," she said, "but mine are sweaty as you-know-what from these gloves."

She gave him a warm smile. Paloma, who was born in Peru, had a classic Inca face. As a teenager, Jericho recalled, she'd had a certain elegance. He noticed she was wearing a wedding ring.

"Nice garden," Jericho said.

"Yeah," she said. "It's a shame it has to honor Rosario. *Pobrecita*, but hey." She shrugged.

Jericho nodded.

"Heard you was working out in Hamptons," the woman said. "What's a matter, you too good for *El Barrio* now?"

"Barrio's too good for me."

She smiled.

"You know where Mrs. Colón is?" Jericho asked.

"Rosario's mama? Ay." She shook her head. "She never get over it. She went, how you say? *Catatónico*. Never talk again. They put her in the Bellevue. Finally her grandma come and take her back to Santurce."

256

Paloma's eyes got weepy. Jericho took the woman in his arms and held her. She'd once been a prostitute, and Jericho had been with her a couple of times. That was years ago. He wondered if she even remembered. In those days she was strung out on crack most of the time. He'd helped her get straight.

"Yeah," she said, stroking the back of his neck, "long time don't see."

She remembered.

CHAPTER 49

After teaching her class, Susannah went to Gretchen's office to pick up her paycheck.

Gretchen smiled from her desk as her friend entered. "Hi, Hon."

"Hey, Gretch."

"I've got your check right here."

"Thanks."

"Have you thought any more about staying with us for a while?"

"Thanks, but I'm fine."

"Listen, why don't you come over for dinner tonight? We can have drinks out on our deck. Oh, you haven't seen our new deck, have you?"

"No."

"It's cantilevered over the cliffs. The view is spectacular!"

Susannah pictured the jagged, sandstone cliffs that abutted the beach at Ditch Plains.

"Those cliffs are maybe a hundred feet high", she said. "Isn't it scary?"

"No. It feels like you're flying."

"Well, if you say so."

"See you at around seven, okay?"

"Sounds good", Susannah replied.

"Listen, before you go..." Gretchen said. She pulled a document out of her desk drawer. "Arnold finished this last night and asked me to give it to you."

"What is it?"

"Some kind of authorization — so he can go to court for you if it's necessary, and, y'know, get a ruling on Burt's death. He wants you to sign it."

"I thought he was going to fax it to me."

"Yes. But he knew I'd see you today, and he says an original is always preferable to a copy."

Susannah picked up the letter. It read:

Dear Susannah Cascadden:

You have asked me to represent you in connection with all matters regarding the disappearance/death of your husband, Burton L. Cascadden. You authorize me to contact state and town authorities, if required, for the purpose of obtaining insurance policies, and/or a death certificate and letters of administration for your husband's estate.

I am enclosing a form of Power of Attorney designating me as your legally authorized representative...

"Doesn't it have to be notarized?" Susannah asked.

"Yes," Gretchen said. "I can do it. You know I help out in Arnold's office when things get busy, so I became a notary public to expedite the paper work. Let me just get my stamp. Meanwhile you can sign."

Susannah signed the power of attorney.

Gretchen went to her purse, brought out the stamp and notarized the document. "Oh," she said, "I almost forgot. I have pictures for you."

She brought out a yellow shopping bag with Art Deco lettering: East Hampton Camera Shop. Susannah had a flash of memory – she'd seen a similar bag in Jessie's dark room.

"These are the shots of the kids I took in class the other day," Gretchen said.

260

"Thanks. I'll look at them when I get home. I've got a bunch of errands to do now."

"Okay. See you tonight."

Susannah got in her car. Setting the East Hampton Camera Shop bag next to her, she felt a frisson of fear.

Does Gretchen have some connection with that camera shop? she asked herself. *Could the shop have another set of prints of me killing Burt?*

That's ridiculous. Jessie did his own developing and printing.

Jesus, I'm really getting paranoid. But what if Gretchen and Arnold do have incriminating pictures and they're in cahoots with Healey to split Burt's estate? — there's this house, the cars, and probably Healey knows how to access Burt's off-shore funds.

That's motive enough for all three of them to want me dead.

That power of attorney I signed, I didn't read it too carefully. That could've been a huge mistake.

She visualized those high Ditch Plains sandstone cliffs, and suddenly remembered that Burt's first wife had been pushed off those very cliffs. She visualized herself being shoved off the cantilevered deck by Gretchen and her husband. Falling... falling...

Is this my imagination running wild? Or maybe it's my instinct for self-preservation. But it's my gut feeling and I'd be a fool to ignore it. I can't go over there for dinner. I just can't!

CHAPTER 50

The Nuevo Korean Kitchin, on First Avenue and 117th, was essentially a coffee shop. Jericho slid into a booth and called Mouse on his cell. The station house was just up the block, and his former partner said he'd be there in a few minutes.

The place looked pretty much the same. Shiny turquoise walls, a big chalkboard menu featuring a weird assortment of dishes: *Espaguetti con Pollo, Hamburg/Chessburg, Bistec Kang Suh, Toast'd English.*

The only difference was that now the cashier and the waitress were Pakistanis. Jericho had seen it often — when Korean delis and grocery stores became successful, they immediately hired Pakistani help. Interesting pecking order.

Detective Mickey Davis walked in the door. He was a tall black man with white hair frizzing up over his high-domed forehead. He'd gotten much thinner in the past two years. And his hair was whiter. He wore rimless glasses, through which peered his startling gray-green eyes. "Musta been a honky in the woodpile," he used to say.

"'Sup, Mouse," Jericho said.

"Hey, hey, hotshot," Mouse said. "Nice goin', smokin' that Most Wanted dude on the beach. What's his name again?"

"Mort."

"Yeah, Mort. I read about it in the *Post*. Headline said 'Hero Cop Kills — ''"

"Hero-schmeero," Jericho said. "It was pretty routine."

"Battle, you're full of crap, as usual."

Jericho smiled. It had been a long time since he'd heard his cop nickname, derived from the way he introduced himself: "Jericho — like in the Battle."

Mouse sat down and the waitress immediately took their orders. Jericho had his customary sweet roll and coffee. Mouse asked for tuna salad — no mayo.

"No more Chessburgs?" Jericho asked.

Mouse yanked up his colorful *Guayabera* shirt, showing off a narrow pale scar bisecting his pectorals.

"I had a little blockage in my coronary artery," he explained. "They call it 'the bypass zipper'. Doctors say I'm only allowed fat-free food. I'm on the NoMo diet."

"NoMo?"

"No Mo' burgers, No Mo' fries, No Mo' soul food," he explained. "Last night Keisha made me chitlins 'n' black-eyed peas cooked without *lard*. Man, you know what that taste like — without lard?"

"Not really."

"Taste like goat pellets."

"Taste like that anyway."

Neither man laughed. To them, kidding around was a game with one unspoken rule: first guy who laughs loses.

They had re-bonded instantly. For a while they chatted, catching up on each other's lives. Mouse's two boys were now at Brooklyn College; Jericho described his work in East Hampton, talked about Katie, her upcoming move to the Coast.

Mouse nodded compassionately. "In life, ain't but one thing certain," he said. "Change."

"So," Jericho said, "how's the desk duty working out?"

"Sucks," Mouse stated succinctly. "My wife, of course, is thrilled. She says — better to have one of your leg veins in your heart than a bullet.

"Can't argue with that."

Mouse did allow that the stress from working the streets all these years had caught up with him.

"You the smart one," he said, "movin' to the Hamptons, where there's nothin' but rich folks with zoning violations and tax problems."

"Plenty of regular people live out there too," Jericho said. "There's working-class communities like Sag Harbor, Springs, Montauk."

"I went to Montauk once. Nice place. When I was in high school my Daddy drove out with me and my brother, and we went on a party boat to catch fluke. Didn't catch nothin' though — except for one blowfish. Damn thing inflated and looked like a balloon with a fish face on one end."

The waitress brought their order. Neither man was hungry — they both picked at their food.

"Man," Jericho said, "seems like only yesterday we were sitting here eating this crap."

"Tempus fuggit," Mouse said.

"True dat."

"So, Battle," Mouse said. "You said you had something you wanted to discuss. Something important?"

Jericho stared down at his sweet roll, thinking — I don't want to do this. "I've got a situation," he finally said.

"Yeah?"

"Well, after I shot that hitman, I was required to go see a shrink. You know the drill."

"Sure."

"I can't go back on the street till the doc clears me."

"So what's the problem?" Mouse asked. "You s'posed to be all shook up about icin' a hired killer?"

"Thing is," Jericho said, "she knows about the whole deal with, y'know, what happened on 118th Street."

"What does that have to do with anything?"

"That's what *I* said."

"What was her answer?"

"Well, the shrink's a rape crisis counselor, so I guess she tends to think about everything in terms of post-traumatic stress. She seems to feel I could be traumatized about, y'know, what happened. That it might affect my work. So she ordered me to go back to where it all went down. Said I should talk to you about it, take a little trip down memory lane."

Mouse looked grim. "That's not a fun trip."

"No."

"What does she think you're gonna find out?"

"Who the hell knows?" Jericho growled. "She said I might have 'a component of guilt over the incident.'"

"Guilt?" Mouse said. "What have you got to feel guilty about?"

"You kiddin' me?"

"Well, shit, it was *me* who spooked the guy."

"No," Jericho said. "I took a couple of steps toward him, and he backed up and toppled out the window."

"Is that what you been thinkin' all this time?"

"Yeah."

"Jericho, I went for my gun."

"What?"

"Remember, he made us put our guns on the floor?"

"Of course I remember."

"The way he was holdin' the little girl," Mouse explained, "I saw I had a clean shot at him — I thought I could take him down. He was looking at you, 'cause you were talking to him, and I figured I could grab my weapon without him seeing. But as I grabbed my gun, he noticed me and yelled, 'Don't do that.' Then he backed away from me and they fell out the window."

Jericho looked at him incredulously. "It wasn't because I stepped toward him?"

"No," Mouse said. "I thought you knew that. I never talked about it, because it hurt too much."

"My God." Jericho said in amazement. Then his breath wooshed out in a sigh of relief.

"Lemme tell you somethin'," his partner said. "I saw the department shrink for a year after the incident. And I still have nightmares about it. Truth is, that child's death was probably the main cause of my heart problems. It's something you really never get over."

"Jesus, Mouse. That's terrible," Jericho said quietly. "But look, man, you weren't responsible. You were trying to save her — you did your best. And what if we'd let that drug freak get away with little Rosario? What would he have done to her?"

"What if?" Mouse said, his gray-green eyes getting moist, "That's the question I keep asking myself. And I always get the same answer: Who knows?"

CHAPTER 51

At sundown Jericho was heading home on the Long Island Expressway. He felt good — partly because he'd reconnected with his partner, but mostly because he knew he hadn't caused Rosario Colón's death. A heavy burden lifted. At last, he hoped, the flashbacks, nightmares, and blackouts would stop.

He hated to admit it, but Dr. Patel was right. Revisiting the scene of the tragedy was definitely for his own good.

But when his thoughts turned to Mouse, his mood changed. His friend had tried to save Rosario and was rewarded with lifelong guilt that had seized his soul and attacked his heart.

I'm okay but my partner's screwed, he thought. A policeman's lot is not a happy one — it sucks.

A mile past the Douglaston Interchange. Jericho found himself stuck in a massive traffic jam. The entire eastbound lane was blocked for repairs, and the cars had been diverted to the westbound side of the highway, which was itself down to one lane due to a fender bender.

The traffic heading west, toward the city, was now re-routed onto the westbound service road.

The driver in front of Jericho kept riding his brakes, the tail lights flashing off and on like a pinball machine gone berserk. *Asshole.*

After a five minute complete stop, the traffic started to move again, albeit at a snail's pace. Jericho looked over at the cars coming toward him on the westbound service road. Now they were all stopped, stuck in some fresh gridlock hell. *The damn LIE. It'll getcha comin' and goin'.*

The imagery of two-way traffic threw a switch in Jericho's mind. A memory surfaced, along with a doubt that had nagged him since this whole Cascadden case began.

The track in the sand.

I asked Susannah about it that first day, he remembered, *saying it looked like something had been dragged from her house into the water. She explained it was from her swim-raft, that she'd hauled it down to the ocean to go swimming. But when she climbed on it, she said, she got caught in the rip tide. She claimed she rode the raft parallel to the shore until she was out of the rip. Then she paddled back to the beach. That meant Susannah would've waded ashore far down the beach. Dragging the raft back to the house would have left another track.*

Two-way traffic — comin' and goin'.

So there should have been two tracks in the sand.

But there was only one.

A couple of hours later Jericho was driving past the pond on the East Hampton town commons, watching two gracefully gliding white swans who, illuminated by the pink toned street lamps, looked almost like flamingos. His cell phone rang. It was Chief Manos.

"Jericho, where are you?"

"Just hitting town."

"Good. Get your ass in here. There's something I want you to see."

"What?"

"You'll see when you get here."

Five minutes later Jericho walked into the Chief's office. John Alvarez, the medical examiner, was laying out some 2"x3" photographs on Dominick's desk. He turned to greet Jericho.

270

"I'm glad you're here, Detective," Alvarez said. "I brought these over myself — I thought you and the Chief would want to see them right away."

"Let's take a look," said Manos.

He and Jericho had to lean over and squint to see the photos.

"The light was bad." Alvarez said, "so they're a little hard to see, but anyway..."

The photos were all of a nude dead man. The front views showed him sprawled out on some kind of plastic sheeting. A surgeon's scalpel lay beside him. The rear views revealed a nasty gash in the victim's lower spine, and a bloody head wound.

"Where was he found?" Jericho asked.

"Park ranger spotted him this afternoon, at Camp Hero," Manos replied. "I responded to the call. The body was in a quicksand bog."

"Quicksand? Wouldn't a body be permanently sunk?..."

Alvarez interrupted him. "Remember it rained very heavily the other night. See, quicksand is just a specific mixture of sand and underground saltwater, in which the friction between the sand particles and the water is reduced, creating a mushy mixture that can't support any weight. The heavy rain diluted the quicksand, and the body floated up, just as it would in seawater. Clearly somebody dumped this man here expecting he'd never be found."

"Any ID?"

"No," Alvarez said. "But I'd say he's Mexican. Besides his Latino features, he's wearing a silver crucifix pendant marked TC-92 on the back. That's the current marking system for Mexican silver. The T stands for Taxco. My dad wears one very much like it."

"Guy could be one of those illegals," Manos said. "If he is, we might never solve this murder. Those people are so afraid of cops they usually don't even report crimes."

"But I'm sure you're gonna try!" Alvarez said assertively.

"Of course."

Jericho picked up a rear-view photo and looked at it closely.

"From this head wound, it looks like he's been scalped," he said.

"That's correct," the ME responded.

"Strange. And... his lower spine has been cut out."

"Yes," Alvarez said. "Can you guess what section of his spine is missing?"

It took just a moment before it sunk in. "Jesus!" Jericho said. "C-3 to L-2?"

"Yep. The exact vertebrae we found on Turtle Beach."

"That means those bones didn't belong to Burt Cascadden."

Alvarez nodded in agreement.

Jericho pursed his lips, trying to figure this out. "Have you got the DNA results from the hair on Cascadden's hairbrush?"

"Not yet," Alvarez answered. "But I know that hair didn't belong to Cascadden either. You sent me his hair dye — Black 'Just for Men' Gel."

"Yes."

"Well, we did a lab analysis of the hair sample and it wasn't dyed."

"You're sure?"

"Yes. There was no ethanolamine, no erythorbic acid, nothing you'd find in hair coloring."

"So, Dr. Alvarez," Manos said, "you think that hair belongs to the Mexican guy?"

"Since the victim had his scalp removed, I'd say that's a pretty good bet."

"Okay...here's how it could've gone down," Manos said, thoughtfully. "This Mexican was in Cascadden's house — maybe robbing it — and he brushed his hair with Cascadden's hairbrush. Burglars do strange things — defecate, masturbate..."

He paused, trying to follow his own logic.

"But what about his murder?" Alvarez said. "And the excision of his spine and hair."

272

"Um, that could've been a separate incident", Manos replied. "Maybe some weird ritualistic killing."

"By whom?"

"I dunno. The Shinnecocks."

"Indians?"

"He was scalped."

Alvarez and Jericho were speechless.

"The Shinnecocks hate the Mexicans," Manos explained, "for stealing all the construction jobs they used to get."

"Interesting theory," Jericho said, trying not to look disdainful. "But my guess is — someone killed the Mexican man, scalped him to get his hair, placed his spine bones on the beach where he knew we'd find them, then sneaked into Cascadden's house and planted his hair in Cascadden's hairbrush."

"But why?"

"To make us think Cascadden was dead — that he went swimming and drowned."

Manos was working hard to follow all this. "You mean," he said, "the DNA on the spine and in the hair follicles would match, so we'd figure they belonged to Cascadden?"

"Right. The only mistake was — whoever did this forgot to dye the Mexican's hair."

"Man, that is some devious shit," Manos said. "But...how would someone know we'd need hair shafts with *follicles*, to get a DNA match?"

"You can probably thank television for that," said Alvarez. "Ever since the OJ trial, the airways have been flooded with shows about forensic pathology. Just look at *CSI*, *Forensic Files*, *Bones*, *Body of Evidence*... now everybody's an expert."

"You think this man was killed at Camp Hero?" Jericho asked the medical examiner. "Or was he killed somewhere else and moved there?

"Probably he was killed where we found him. It was dark when I arrived, but the Crimescope picked up some blood spatter on a nearby tree."

"Got a cause of death?" Jericho asked.

"Not officially, till I cut him up. But it's clear he was shot – execution style," Alvarez replied. "One bullet to the back of the head. Judging from the size of the hole, I'd say it was a big bullet, maybe 50 caliber."

"Glock?"

"Have to check ballistics, but that's a good guess."

"Mort!" Jericho said.

Alvarez and Manos looked at him questioningly.

"Mort used a Glock 50," Jericho explained. He thought for a moment, then went on. "Let's see, if the shooter was Mort... my guess is Cascadden came up with this whole scheme. He wanted us to think he was dead, so he hired Mort to do the killing. Mort delivered the spine and the scalp to Cascadden, who then planted the spine on the beach, and sneaked into his own house to put the hairs on his brush."

"But why would he want us to think he was dead?" Manos asked.

"Well, I know Cascadden was in serious financial trouble. It makes sense that he'd fake his own death, bail on the situation, and maybe get a new identity somewhere else, probably out of the country. His wife indicated he had major offshore money stashed somewhere."

"But doing that whole number so he could plant some fake DNA," Manos said. "He's gotta be intensely warped,"

"And fucking brilliant," Jericho added. "Except for messing up with the hair dye."

"Which was lucky for us," Alvarez said.

"I look at every crime assuming, or at least hoping, that the perpetrator has made a mistake," Jericho said. "That's what you've got to look for."

Alvarez got up. "Well, I've gotta get back up-island. Detective Jericho, I must say I'm very impressed with your analytical skills."

274

"Likewise," Jericho said. "But a lot of this is still conjecture."

"That's true," Alvarez said. "I mean, you've got two men who supposedly drowned, after leaving their clothes on the beach? And no body found in either case. They're awfully similar."

"So maybe they're related," Manos said.

"Could be," Alvarez said, stopping at the door. "And my biggest question would be this — why did Mort try to kill Cascadden's wife?"

After Alvarez left, Manos said, "Yeah, why?"

Jericho hesitated before he spoke. He didn't know the answer. And he was torn between investigating Susannah and protecting her.

"I...I've been trying to figure that out," Jericho said.

He got up to leave. "I've had a long day, Dominick. I'll talk to you tomorrow."

CHAPTER 52

At around eleven Susannah prepared herself for the night ahead. She'd cancelled the dinner with Gretchen and Arnold, and set the home alarm system to "activate". She checked twice to see that the green "on" button was lit.

When she got into bed, she tried to relax, but her nerves were still on edge. Although she knew her house was secure, it didn't stop her from imagining the worst. She kept going over and over the list of people who might be out to get her.

Gretchen and Arnold — not likely. That fantasy of them throwing me off the cliff was pretty far-fetched, so the idea of them breaking into this house to kill me is even more remote. Still...

Quinn Healey — by now, hopefully the lawyer's been informed about his business card on the hitman's body. So he shouldn't be a problem either. Still...

Jessie Russell — If he's alive, he's someone to be deathly afraid of. I would swear he was dead. Still...

Somebody Else — There's always the possibility that someone I haven't considered is part of some conspiracy to do me in. I can't think who. Still...

God, my imagination's running wild. Maybe it's guilt — I killed and now it's my turn. But I did what I had to — I defended myself. And I'll do it again if somebody comes through that door. I'll shoot to kill.

She reached into her nightstand, took out the gun and placed it under her pillow. After a moment, she pulled out the pistol again to check the safety. It was ON.

Alarm system ON, she thought. *Gun safety ON...maybe it should be OFF so I can use it quickly...don't be crazy, I could turn over in my sleep and shoot myself.*

Fatigue was starting to catch up with Susannah. It had been an exhausting and trying day.

The wind had died down and it was quiet — quiet enough to hear any strange noises. It had gotten cool and Susannah pulled the summer-weight quilt over her body. The flannel shirt she wore made her feel quite snuggly.

Her eyelids closed, opened, closed again. Her head kept dropping to her chest.

Eventually she nodded off.

A loud creak from the top step on the stairway jolted her half-awake, but she was too groggy to react. She drifted back into a state between wakefulness and dreaming.

"Susannah." A man's voice, guttural and menacing, breaks the silence.

"Susannah." Louder this time.

The disembodied head is floating in blackness, its features indiscernible. Susannah can make out his eyes — shiny green-black ovals that gleam like opals in the darkness. His hand reaches down toward her nose, the fingers pinching her nostrils closed.

She screams.

The creature laughs. The fingers pull away.

Susannah woke up as the bedside lamp flicked on. She stared in shock at the intruder — his body now joined to his head. He was holding a lit flashlight. He turned it off and put it on the nightstand. She saw his stocking-covered face wearing sunglasses.

"Hello, Sweetie," he said. His bee-stung lips moved in the stocking's hole.

"My God," Susannah said in a choked voice. "Burt."

"You should see the look on your face," Burt said. "I believe scared shitless would describe it best. It's even better than last night."

She looked at him in stunned confusion. "Last night?"

"Yes, last night I only caught a glimpse of you before I turned off my flashlight," Burt said. "Oh, my little Game might seem a bit over the top, but its purpose is revenge. And a big part of that is scaring the crap out of you."

The reality jolted Susannah into action. Her right hand snatched the gun from under her pillow as her left pushed off the safety.

"Get out of here," she said. "Or I'll blow your head off."

"Come on, Sweetie."

"I mean it Burt," she said, holding the gun in a two-handed grip. "I'll shoot."

He calmly stepped back. "I'm not here to hurt you. I just came to talk," he said.

"What do you want, Burt?"

"I told you — to talk," he said, inching closer. "But we can't have a civilized conversation with me staring down the barrel of your gun."

"Stop. Don't come any closer."

"Okay, okay."

"How...how did you get in here?"

"Easy. Remember you're my wife, so I know you quite well. The sign outside said you had an AHS wireless alarm. I went on their web site, and they actually described the option of controlling the alpha numeric keypad from the outside with a cell phone. Very informative of them. Anyway, I punched in your birthday on my cell, then Martha, then Graham, then Ethel, E-T-H-E-L. Bingo! *Alarm Disabled.*"

"But...you still needed a key to get in."

"Spare key under the geranium pot." He smiled smugly. "Now, Sweetie, put down the gun."

"Take one more step and I'll kill you."

"Don't be silly."

"I tried once before. Remember?"

"How could I forget? But why not let bygones be bygones. Put down the gun."

Burt reached for the weapon.

Susannah pulled the trigger. The only sound was a click.

She tried again. *Click.*

Burt laughed. "If you ain't got no ammo," he said, "gun won't go bammo." He reached into his pocket and pulled out a handful of cartridges.

Susannah pulled the trigger again and again.

Burt smirked as he stuck the ammunition back in his pocket. "I removed them yesterday afternoon."

He drew a large handgun from his holster. "This 50mm Glock, however," he said, "is fully loaded. It was recommended by our mutual friend, Mort — may he rest in peace. His only caveat was that 50mm bullets make messy entrance wounds."

He enjoyed her look — helpless, terrified.

"Burt," she said. "How did you...?"

"Survive?"

She nodded, mute with panic.

"I'm sure you're *dying* to know," he answered. "But first let me get this stocking off my head."

Burt removed his sunglasses. As he was pulling the stocking from his head, Susannah snatched the cordless phone from the nightstand, punched speed dial location 1, and hid the phone under the thin quilt.

She heard a faint ringing, and to cover the sound she spoke loudly to Burt.

"I'm warning you," she said. "there's a new man in my life. He's a cop and he's on his way over. You better get out of here. If he sees you with that gun, he'll kill you. You won't get a chance to explain."

280

He waved his gun at her, guffawing derisively. "Sure, Sweetie. Your boyfriend's a cop. I can just see that."

Burt's face looked leaner, and his hair was coming in gray under the dyed black.

Jericho, she thought. *Please be home. Please pick up!*

"I'm telling you," she shouted, praying Jericho could hear her, "he's a cop and he's coming over right now. Put down your gun and leave. It's your only hope."

Jericho was watching late night TV. He picked up the phone and heard Susannah's desperate voice.

"I'm warning you, Burt. Ditch the gun and get the hell out of here!"

Burt? Jericho thought. *Her husband!*

Their words were muffled but audible.

"You're getting hysterical, Sweetie. And shouting won't do any good."

"I'm telling you the truth, Burt."

"Oh, first you kill me, or *try*, and then you start dating a cop? You're not that stupid."

"Believe me. He'll be here any minute."

"Sweetie, it's one o'clock in the morning."

"He works late — night patrol. You better go."

Jericho was already mobilizing. Sticking the phone in his pocket, he buckled on his waist holster and service revolver. He rushed to the closet and strapped on his bulletproof vest, then threw on a sweat shirt. He heard talk on his cell phone but had no time to listen.

"Now, Sweetie, it's time for you to learn how I cheated death. It's quite an extraordinary story." Burt gave her a self-satisfied smile. He was in no hurry.

"You better get out of here," Susannah said.

Burt put his pistol to his wife's temple and twisted it into her skin.

"Cut the bullshit," he growled. "From now on, keep your trap shut or your brains'll be on the floor."

She nodded.

"I'm sorry, Sweetie," Burt said, resuming his witheringly gracious tone. "I don't mean to be impolite. It's just that I've been looking forward to sharing my secret with you, and I don't want this moment spoiled."

Susannah said nothing. Her mind was on Jericho, her only hope.

Burt took two pairs of handcuffs out of his pocket.

Jericho dashed to his car in the driveway. He started the engine, then stuck his cell phone into the car's adaptor. He wanted to call for back up but he didn't dare hang up the phone. He drove away, tires squealing. Burt's voice came over the speakerphone, sounding metallic and faraway.

"Assume the position."

"Please. Not that."

"You don't really have a choice, do you, Sweetie?"

What the hell's going on? Jericho wondered. He pushed down harder on the accelerator. With luck he could be there in ten minutes.

Burt handcuffed his wife's arms to the bedposts, fastening them in the grooves under the ball finials.

He pulled a rattan armchair close to the bed and sat down. He placed his gun on the nightstand.

"It's really quite simple," he said proudly. "You remember, of course, that in Benares I mastered yoga disciplines enabling me to concentrate my mind and control my bodily forces. As you attempted to drown me, I performed *Samadhi*, which is a form of self-hypnosis leading to a radical slowing of respiration, heartbeat, all life signs. The most difficult part is the *Kechari*, in which one must obstruct the

282

windpipe by doubling back the tongue — swallowing it, so to speak. Like so."

He pushed his tongue back into his throat with his fingertip. His face was again the Greek tragedy mask Susannah had seen when she dragged Burt's limp body onto the beach — eyes clamped shut, mouth frozen in a grimace.

Burt yanked his tongue out and regained his composure.

"Well, Sweetie?" he said. "Impressed?"

Susannah didn't respond.

Burt grinned.

"After I came ashore," he went on, "it would seem Lord Krishna, eighth avatar of Vishnu — the Protector himself, was watching over me. On the beach I found a Jeep with the keys in it, along with some clothing and even some cash. I drove to Montauk and took the train into the city. I moved into a cheap hotel and began to formulate my plan."

As Jericho swung his car onto the Montauk Highway, Burt was boasting about his Singaporean bank account; and how with that money he'd hired Mort to murder a Mexican illegal, planted his spine on the beach, and then pulled off the hairbrush DNA switcheroo, outfoxing Long Island's Finest.

Jericho floored the accelerator.

"Then, of course, Mort was to eliminate you," Burt said. "but after his unfortunate death, I was left to finish the task myself. It was my Purvakarma, my pre-ordained destiny. *I* had to be the one to cleanse my life of its poisonous negativity — you, my sweet, loving wife."

Jericho was struck by the coldness and egotism in Burt Cascadden's words. It was clear — Jericho faced a formidable foe, a brilliant, devious psychopath with a distorted moral system in which human life had no meaning. Susannah was in mortal danger.

He looked at his watch.

I'll be there in five minutes.

Burt stood up and whispered to Susannah, "Oh, one other thing — I'm sure you'd like to know what my plans are, I mean, after you've passed on to your next life."

Susannah panicked. "Help! Help!" she screamed, her hands clawing at the bed's finials. "Jericho, I'm in here. He's got a gun and —"

Burt backhanded her to the mouth. "That's enough," he said and pulled a roll of duct tape from his pocket. "From now on, silence is golden."

He stripped six inches from the roll and cut it with his teeth. He sealed Susannah's mouth and added a second layer for good measure. Her desperate breaths hissed through her nostrils.

"I've arrived at a new level of enlightenment these last few weeks," Burt said. "I've re-embraced the Hindu faith. Soon I'll be leaving for India, to study once more with my master Swami Nittiya Vivekanda, who's now in his 'eighties. The rest of my life will be devoted to striving to achieve Moksha, that purification and balance of Karma that will allow me to reach Swarga, the abode of the Divine Paramatma, and serve at His feet."

Again the painful question raced through her mind: *How could I have married this man? How could I have married this man?*

"I know what you're thinking," Burt said. "How will I live?"

He smiled. "Yes, I have some hidden money. But I've embraced poverty. I'm no longer interested in worldly possessions. In fact, what's left of my assets will go to the mendicants of Benares."

Jericho, she thought desperately. *Please. Where are you?*

Burt raised his right hand and touched the tip of his index finger and thumb together, like an "okay" sign.

"This is a *Mudra* — a Hindu hand position. I'm sure you've seen it on religious statuary. It's called the *Vitarka* Mudra, the gesture of Intellectual Debate. It's very powerful. Let me demonstrate."

He sat down on the edge of Susannah's bed and held his thumb and forefinger poised over her nostrils. Then, in a graceful gesture, he closed the two fingers. With her mouth taped shut, she could not breath.

284

She struggled in vain to wrench her face away from his fingers. She yanked on her cuffed hands. Her face began to flush, her eyes bulging.

"This game's getting exciting, isn't it?" Burt said.

With a flourish, he released his thumb and forefinger and lifted his hand. Susannah sucked air through her nose in desperate breaths.

"As I said," he whispered. "Very powerful *Mudra*."

He stood up.

"The Intellectual Debate is of course between two conflicting Hindu principles: nonviolence versus the purging of bad karma. That dichotomy has puzzled wise men for centuries."

Jericho turned onto East Dune Way.

A couple more minutes.

He heard Burt's threatening voice.

"All right, Sweetie, let's get those pants off. And don't try kicking me with those strong legs of yours, or the Vitarka Mudra will pinch off your life."

Silence.

"Ah, that's a good girl"

Jericho's tires made a gritty sound on the sandy asphalt road.

One more minute.

Burt's tone grew more sadistic.

"Susannah, the last time we played a Game together you were a big disappointment to me. I hope you will perform better tonight. Perhaps you've heard of erotic asphyxiation? They say when your lungs are deprived of air, you can achieve orgasm right on the cusp of death. Your body goes into spasm, your internal muscles clench, your nerve endings go haywire, and ineffable paroxysms of ecstasy suffuse your entire being. Sound nice? It is my sincerest wish that in your last

285

moments, you will experience this death rush. And that I am fortunate enough to share in it with you — vicariously, of course."

Jericho saw the house and cut his headlights.

CHAPTER 53

"Sick fuck," Jericho muttered to himself as he pulled up behind a Pontiac with rental plates. He cut the engine and ran back to his trunk. He grabbed a tire iron and headed for the beach house.

He saw the AHS sign on the lawn and the decal on the door. *I don't know how he got in,* he thought, *but I hope to hell he didn't re-set the alarm once he entered. But why would he? Well, I've got to take that chance.*

Jericho tried the front door. Locked. He inserted the crowbar between the door and the doorframe at the exact spot where the lock was. He threw all his weight against it and heard a crack as the lock sprung loose and the door flew open.

No alarm.

He drew his gun and entered the vestibule. The front door was far enough away from the upstairs bedroom that he figured his break-in couldn't be heard. *I better be right. I've got to catch him off guard.*

Jericho made his way across the darkened living room. When he reached the stairway he saw light coming from the bedroom.

He stopped, listened. There was the faint sound of Burt's laughter.

He began to climb the stairs. Midway he stopped again. No sound.

He resumed his climb. As his foot hit the top step there was a loud, echoing creak.

He held stock still for a few moments.

Then Burt's voice: "Come on. You need to do better than that, my girl."

Jericho eased himself onto the landing and waited.

"Oh, that's much better, darling," Burt said. "Yes, you're really getting into it now."

Jericho checked the straps and positioning of his Kevlar body armor. Then he edged along the hallway wall until he reached the bedroom door.

He gripped his revolver firmly in his hands.

Burt whispered, "Ah, Susannah, you excite me so."

Jericho took three deep breaths, then swung into the open doorway. He saw Susannah cuffed to the bedposts, hands clawing frantically at the finials. Her eyes were wide, beseeching, her taped mouth making muffled sounds.

But no Burt! Where was Burt? Why wasn't he on the bed with Susannah?

The answer came in four gunshots from the closet. The bullets tore into Jericho's vest. The impact felt like a pile driver punching into Jericho's torso. He was knocked backward and the gun flew out of his hand.

Burt ran toward Jericho, who lay on his back in the hallway, stunned.

When Jericho looked up, Burt was looming above him, pointing the Glock at Jericho's head.

"I've been bugging Susannah for months to fix that creaky stair," Burt said. "Fortunately, she didn't."

Jericho eyed his revolver nearby, but Burt kicked it out of reach.

"So she wasn't kidding about the cop boyfriend," Burt said. He leaned over and pulled up Jericho's sweatshirt. "Bulletproof vest and everything."

288

Jericho blinked. He was still disoriented from the fall.

"How'd you two meet?" Burt asked. "Did you stop her for speeding?"

Jericho said nothing. His head was clearing.

"No, wait," Burt said, "I bet you were investigating my disappearance. Oh, that's real ethical — humping a witness in a case."

"Killing a police officer is serious business," Jericho said. "They'll track you down no matter where you go."

"But I'm already dead, remember. I won't be very high on the list of suspects." Burt pointed the gun at Jericho's skull.

"No bulletproof *hat*, I see."

Jericho felt the gun barrel against his scalp. He tried to speak calmly.

"Don't be foolish," he said. "We know about your DNA switch. And we know you're going to India."

"You know all that?" Burt said with surprise. "Well, you're smarter than I thought. But there are two billion people in India, and I intend to get lost in the crowd."

"The police won't quit till they — "

"You know," Burt interrupted, "I believe in reincarnation. So to me, ending your life is just part of a cycle leading to rebirth. Do you believe in the hereafter?"

Jericho said nothing.

"Well, *hereafter*, quit fucking other men's wives." Burt said deadpan. "But seriously," he went on, "to comfort you, I will quote from the Bhagavad Gita as I slowly squeeze the trigger. This prayer expresses my profound belief that all things are eternal, thus there is no such thing as death. *Na jayate mriyate va ka kadacin nayam bhuta bhavita* — "

Burt's prayer was cut short by a searing pain in both his temples. He crumpled to the floor. Blood oozed from the sides of his head. His hands reached up, then dropped limply to his sides.

Susannah had crept up behind him, holding in her two hands the bed's wooden finials. With a motion like a cymbal crash, she had

289

brought the balls together with all her strength, crushing the sides of Burt's head.

Susannah saw the Glock on the floor and booted it away.

Jericho sat up. Burt wasn't moving.

"Jesus," Jericho said in amazement. "How did you get loose?"

"Something I remembered, thanks to Bloomingdale's".

"Huh?"

"When they delivered my bed, one of these finials was cracked, so they mailed me another one and I put it on myself. They just screw on and off."

"Wow." Jericho said and pulled himself to his feet. "Let's take a look at him."

He went over to Burt and knelt down. He felt Burt's carotid artery.

"No pulse. No chest movement. "

Jericho leaned over and placed his right ear on Burt's gaping mouth.

"Don't!", Susannah shouted.

"What?"

"He might still be alive. You could lose an ear."

Jericho smiled. "All right," he said. Jericho took out his pocket flashlight, peeled back Burt's eyelids, and shone the light into each eye.

"Pupils fixed and dilated."

He put his ear on Burt's chest and listened carefully. He looked up at Susannah.

"No heart beat, no respiration. The man is dead."

"I'm telling you, he knows how to fake it."

"But see that bruising around his eyes?" Jericho said. "That's the raccoon effect — indicates severe skull fracture. I've seen enough head injuries in my time to know this guy's brain is mush."

She sighed in relief. Jericho stood up.

290

"Thank you," he said. "You saved my life."

"Well, you saved mine. Tit for tat."

"Guess I'm the tat."

Susannah rolled her eyes, then embraced him. Jericho flinched and pulled back.

"What's wrong?"

"I'm kinda sore from taking those bullets in my body armor."

"Oh, sorry."

"Can you give me a rain check on the hug?"

"You got it."

"Listen," Jericho said, "you might, uh, want to button up. Some of my colleagues will be here shortly."

She looked down at her open flannel shirt and fastened the buttons. "I should put on a robe," she said.

"We need to get our stories straight before I call this in."

He retrieved his gun and picked up Burt's Glock.

Jericho sat down on the edge of the bed. Susannah put on a bathrobe and took a seat in the rattan chair.

She held up her handcuffed wrists and said, "Can they bring something to cut these things off?"

"Sure, but your husband probably has a key on him." Jericho said. "We'll take a look, but let's talk first."

"Okay."

Jericho leaned forward and looked in her eyes. "You'll probably be interviewed by Chief Manos. When he asks you about tonight, tell him the truth, in exact detail — how Burt broke in, what he did to you — even if it's embarrassing. Everything. Got it?"

"Yes," she replied. "What if he asks me why Burt did it?"

Jericho thought for a moment. "Tell him your husband was showing signs of unstable behavior in the months before he disappeared. Tonight he seemed to have gone off the deep end."

"Well, that's true."

"Now, I've got a pretty good idea of what happened the day your husband supposedly drowned. But I'm not about to tell anyone, and neither will you. Burt Cascadden was a violent madman; he was planning to have you killed, so you did what you had to do to protect yourself. It was self-defense. Do you understand?"

"Yes," she said.

"Burt didn't die anyway, so the homicide issue is moot. The police'll assume he faked his own death-by-drowning," he went on, "But if Chief Manos asks you why, you have no idea. Right?"

"Right."

"Okay. That's all they have to know."

Susannah nodded. She looked at Jericho intensely for a moment. "I...I want to tell you what happened with Jessie Russell."

"No need for that right now."

"No, no. I want you to know. He tried to rape me, and when I fought back, he cracked his head..."

"Madam," he said, interrupting. "You have the right to remain silent."

She shook her head. "I want you to know the truth."

"Okay, but tell me later." Jericho said. "The State Police are handling the case now and here's how they'll see it: Russell's a known rapist who once attacked a teenage girl on the Shinnecock reservation. They suspect Russell was killed by her family, who were seeking vengeance. But there's a code of silence within the tribe, so they'll never be able to make an arrest. Anyway, the way *I* see it, if you killed a rapist defending yourself, that's not a crime. Don't you agree?"

"I guess so," she said hesitantly. "But still, I've killed, I've taken a human life. And I'm not at peace with that."

"Of course. I understand."

"But it's different for you. I mean, you're a cop, so you're trained to use deadly force if you have to — in the line of duty."

"I do understand — believe me." Jericho said. "And I've gone through hell dealing with it. Susannah, I can help you get through this. And I promise — I will."

She nodded and embraced him.

"Where's your phone?" he asked. "I left mine in the car."

"Under the quilt."

"Very clever," Jericho said. The line was still engaged. He hung up, then dialed the precinct house.

Susannah looked down at the handcuffs. Her wrists had been rubbed raw in her struggles and were starting to hurt.

The key, she thought. Maybe in Burt's pocket.

She got up and went to Burt's motionless body. As she knelt down her heart began to race.

He better be dead.

Her hand trembled as it reached into one of Burt's windbreaker pockets.

No key.

She reached over to check the other pocket.

Suddenly Burt's fingers shot up and closed vice-like around her throat. His face grinned up at her, raccoon eyes open and glaring as he squeezed tighter and tighter.

The power of his grip seemed superhuman.

She tried to cry out, but his thumbs were crushing her larynx and trachea. Her vision began to dim, and inside her head she felt pressure building, a pressure only death could release.

She clawed out with her fingernails, trying to rip at his face. But it was futile. Her strength was failing, the blackness sweeping in, washing over her...

Jericho hung up the phone. He saw Susannah kneeling over Burt. Burt's hands were around her throat and Susannah's head was lolling to one side. Jericho drew his gun. Burt's head was blocked by his raised arms. Jericho's only clear shot was at Burt's ribcage.

He aimed carefully and fired once.

Susannah felt Burt's grip relax. His hands dropped and she could breathe again. Her vision cleared. She started to cough.

"Susannah," Jericho called out. "You okay?" He ran toward her. She was looking down at Burt's face. His eyelids fluttered as he croaked his dying words.

"Sweetie," he said, "YOU DID...A...BAD...THING."

Susannah knew instantly what he meant. Even with his last breath Burt was boasting, needing her to know that those e-mails were part of his final Game — the object of the Game was to make her life Hell.

She began to breathe more easily.

Jericho knelt down beside her. He felt around into Burt's pocket and found the handcuff keys.

Susannah extended her hands and Jericho gently unlocked the cuffs.

She rubbed her sore wrists, then reached over and touched the back of Jericho's hand.

He felt her warm palm, pressing gently. As he heard backup finally arriving outside, Jericho slowly turned his hand over, till their palms were touching. Once again they were skin to skin, hotness to hotness.

A SNEAK PEEK: "THE BATTLE OF JERICHO"

COMING SOON

CHAPTER 1

It was a foot — somebody's foot, bobbing up and down in the gentle, rolling surf. It was wearing a pink Nike running shoe, the Swoosh starting to peal off from the action of the seawater. There was a sock and part of an ankle. Nothing more.

An incoming wave caught the foot and for a moment it seemed to be surfing. As the wave crashed on the damp sand and receded, the foot was left on its side, a piece of slimy kelp tangled in its shoelaces.

It would've been a ghastly sight to any beach walker passing by. But to the golden retriever, it was just something to retrieve and carry back to his owner, where he could display it proudly and drop it at his master's feet.

Stunned, the dog owner stared down at the foot. He considered picking it up and examining it, but the idea made him queasy. Besides, he might be tampering with evidence. He took out his cell and called 911.

Detective Sergeant Neil Jericho peered at the eyes staring back at him in the bathroom mirror. They were early morning eyes; squinty, bleary, bloodshot. Were these the eyes of a brilliant detective? Eyes that could recognize minute blood spatter without *Luminol* spray, spot clues hidden in plain sight, pick up the revealing "tells" of a lying suspect?

He remembered reading once how Paul Newman, first thing upon arising, would plunge his whole head in a bucket of ice water. Impulsively Jericho turned on the cold tap, filled the basin, and ducked his head into it. After a few seconds he came up dripping, but definitely wide-awake and refreshed. Okay, he was no Paul Newman. Still...

As he finished shaving his phone rang. It was the Chief. "Jericho, I'm here with what looks like a drowning victim."

295

"Where?"

"Montauk. Gin Beach."

"Are you with the body?"

"There's no body. Just a foot."

"That's all?"

"Yes. Get your ass out here."

"I'm on my way."

As he took his keys from the hook near the door, Jericho saw Susannah's house key hanging there. He just couldn't put it away. For a year they'd tried to make it work, but they were a mismatch. She was a dancer, he was a cop. Susannah had inherited millions, Jericho earned a D3 base salary. She wanted to start a dance company in New York City, but Jericho, a former NYPD detective, knew the city wasn't for him.

The breakup still hurt.

But it was time to go to work. He ate his emergency breakfast — a mug of instant coffee mixed with hot tap water, and a handful of raisins.

Then he grabbed his camera and drove out to Gin Beach.

296

ABOUT THE AUTHOR

Walter Marks is a novelist, playwright, and songwriter. Besides his Broadway shows — "Bajour" and "Golden Rainbow", off-Broadway he wrote the score and book for the award winning "Langston in Harlem" (lyrics by Langston Hughes). His best known song is "I've Gotta be Me", recorded by Sammy Davis, Michael Jackson, Tony Bennett, Ella Fitzgerald, among others.

He also wrote the screenplay and songs for "The Wild Party" (Merchant-Ivory Films) directed by James Ivory. He is an Emmy winner for the PBS series "Getting On."

His current project is a musical incorporating the songs of lyricist/composer Johnny Mercer into a book show called "Accentuate the Positive." Mr. Marks has written the libretto.

His novels include "Dangerous Behavior", "Death Hampton" and "The Battle of Jericho."

He lives and works in both Manhattan and East Hampton.

ACKNOWLEDGEMENTS

My thanks to Marsha Brooks, Esq. and Larry Brooks for their support, Brisa Trinchero and Roberta Pereira for their know-how and guidance, Helen O'Reilly for being a driving force, and Henry Morrison for giving me my start.

Top Tier Lit
www.toptierlit.com
New York, NY
2014

298

21730970R00174

Made in the USA
Middletown, DE
09 July 2015